BAD
BEHAVIOR

BAD BEHAVIOR

KIKI SWINSON
NOIRE

Dafina
Books

KENSINGTON PUBLISHING CORP.

www.kensingtonbooks.com

DAFINA BOOKS are published by

Kensington Publishing Corp.
119 West 40th Street
New York, NY 10018

All Kensington titles, imprints, and distributed lines are available at special quantity discounts for bulk purchases for sales promotion, premiums, fund-raising, and educational or institutional use.

Special book excerpts or customized printings can also be created to fit specific needs. For details, write or phone the office of the Kensington Sales Manager: Kensington Publishing Corp., 119 West 40th Street, New York, NY 10018. Attn. Sales Department. Phone: 1-800-221-2647.

Dafina and the Dafina logo Reg. U.S. Pat. & TM Off.

ISBN-13: 978-1-61773-949-1
ISBN-10: 1-61773-949-9
First Kensington Trade Paperback Printing: January 2018

eISBN-13: 978-1-61773-950-7
eISBN-10: 1-61773-950-2
First Kensington Electronic Edition: January 2018

10 9 8 7 6 5 4 3 2 1

Printed in the United States of America

Nine Lives
Kiki Swinson
1

The Crushed Ice Clique
Noire
109

Nine Lives

Kiki Swinson

CHAPTER 1

THE END OF THE TUNNEL

Normally when niggas get released from jail they are all happy and shit. They walk around the prison making plans about what they're going to eat, who they're going to fuck, and what they're going to wear when they go to the nightclub. Not me. I'm kind of dreading going back into the streets. I don't have a woman. I don't have any kids. I don't have any money, so I'm pretty much fucked up. Realistically speaking, the only person I have waiting for me on the outside is my twin sister, Ava. She's been my rock since day one. I can count on her for anything. There has never been a time when I can say that she wasn't there for me. When I needed commissary money, money for the telephones, and visits, she was there every single time.

I'll be getting out of this hellhole in a matter of three days. Niggas been walking around the prison giving the handshakes, talking about, "Yeah, Aiden, you're about to get out of this joint! Nigga, I know you're happy." They say it with excitement. And I always come back and say, "Nigga, fuck the outside! I don't give a fuck about going home. This is my home. I've been in jail almost my whole life."

Most of the cats roaming around here talk behind my back

and say how crazy I am. And you know what? They're right. I'm fucked up in the head. I don't have any love for no one. The only person I can honestly say I love is my sister. So I vowed that if anything ever happens to her, or if a mother-fucker ever tries to take her from me, I'm coming killed them on site. End of story.

I was sitting on my bed minding my damn business when this cat named Winston Battle walked up to my cell door. I looked at this nigga like he was crazy because everybody in the jail knows not to bother me because I am not a friendly guy. "I heard you were about to hit the streets," he said.

"What do you want?" I asked him, straightforward. I wasn't feeling his company at all, and he knew it.

"I was told that if a person needed a job done, you were the person to do it," Winston continued.

"I'm listening," I said, giving him the same blank stare.

"A'ight, so here's a story. I need to get rid of this cracker who's standing in the way of my freedom. He told the cops that he witnessed me kill somebody. So I will pay you anything to end this motherfucker's life. He's got to go ASAP. You feel me?"

"How did you want that nigga eliminated?" I wanted to know.

"Execution style."

"Where does he live?"

"In some ritzy area of Virginia Beach."

"Is he a big guy? Little guy? What?"

"He's about the same size as me."

"How much are you paying?"

"You give me a number."

"Nah, dude, you give me a number," I instructed him, re-fusing to change my facial expression. I wanted him to stop wasting my time so we could get this conversation over with, because he was invading my space.

Winston hesitated for a second, and then he said, "I'll give you ten grand."

"When do I get my money?"

"My cousin will give you half up front and the rest after you do it."

"Done. Give me his name, address, and the names of anyone close to him before I get out of here," I instructed him.

"A'ight, cool!" he said, and then he walked away from my cell door.

After that nigga Winston walked away from my cell I thought about whether he was really serious or not. I also thought about if the ten thousand dollars he was paying me to execute that nigga was enough. I wasn't a contract killer, so I didn't know the going rates for bodies. I just hoped that if this was a legit hit, I would get the rest of my money after I completed my job. If not, then anyone connected to Winston was going to die.

CHAPTER 2

FREE MY BROTHER

My twin brother, Aiden, was getting out of prison today, and boy, was I happy. He's been in prison so much I've lost track of the time he's done. And as much as I tell him that I miss him while he's doing time, it seems to go in one ear and out the other. Aiden was definitely detached from everything dealing with people and feelings. I think he checked out a long time ago, when we both got in trouble for beating a kid up, ultimately killing him. After that, Aiden's view of life was: nothing really matters.

I often told him how much I loved him, but I never got an *I love you* back. I knew he loved me, but showing emotions and talking about them wasn't something that Aiden did. I've learned a long time ago that Aiden and I only had each other, so we made a pact that no one would ever come between us. And we've done that until this day.

I was front and center of the jail where Aiden was doing his time. I was sitting in a tan, four-door, late-model Cadillac SUV. The truck belonged to a guy I was fucking named Nashad Stone. He was a thirty-five-year-old merchant seaman. He was currently out to sea for a ninety-day trip, so he was scheduled to be back in Norfolk in two weeks or so. He and I had been seeing each other for close to six months now. I liked him, but sometimes I wasn't sure. Sometimes I thought I had feelings for him because my brother Aiden wasn't around. Now that Aiden's getting out of jail, I'd have to see if my feelings for Nashad would fade.

When I looked at the clock on the dashboard of the SUV, the time was 7:30 a.m. The Virginia Beach jail always let inmates that had been released from custody out by eight a.m. So I knew that at any moment my brother was going to be walking out of that iron door. While I sat in the truck and waited, I popped in one of Nashad's mix CDs that niggas be selling in front of the corner store. The CD had some of Lil Wayne's and Future's music. I started pumping the music loud as fuck, but when a Virginia Beach cop walked by the truck, he asked me to turn the music down before he wrote me a ticket. I almost flipped out on that rookie-ass cop, but when I saw movement on the left side, I looked in that direction and noticed that it was my brother walking my way. Ignoring the cop, I turned the music down, hopped out of the truck, and ran toward my brother. His smile was as bright as the sun. "Aiden, I missed you so much!" I yelled.

When I got within arm's distance of him, he dropped the brown paper bag he was carrying. I jumped right into his arms. "I'm so glad they let you out of that shit hole!" I said with excitement and kissed him on the cheek.

"You know me, I don't care if I'm in or not. All I care about is seeing you," Aiden said, his face showing no emotion. Ever since we were kids, Aiden has had this attitude that he didn't care about anything. I partly blamed my mother, because she never really gave a fuck about my brother and me. Okay, granted, we killed a little kid when we were in middle school, but what we did was only out of retaliation. That motherfucker kept bullying my brother, so we had to take a stand. My mother didn't care, though. She saw an opportunity and left my brother and me to rot in a juvenile detention center. So this man standing in front of me didn't trust or love anyone but me. He didn't even love himself. That's why I couldn't ever turn my back on him.

After he let me down on the ground, I grabbed his left hand and pulled him in the direction of the truck I was driving.

"What did that cop say to you?" Aiden wanted to know.

"He was just telling me to turn the music down."

"Fucking racist-ass cops! I fucking hate 'em!" Aiden huffed.

"Don't let them get you all worked up. It's not even worth it." I lifted his hand up to my mouth and kissed the back of it as we continued to walk toward the truck. When we got within arm's reach, Aiden asked, "Who does the truck belonged to?"

"This guy I know," I replied, trying to downplay my involvement with the owner of the truck.

After we got into the truck, Aiden looked around at the dashboard and then he peeped into the backseat. "This is really nice," he complimented.

"Yeah, it is. It drives nice, too."

"How long you been knowing him?"

"Knowing who?" I tried to play dumb.

"The nigga that owes this truck." He pressed the issue.

"Oh, not long. Maybe a month or so," I lied. I was getting uncomfortable answering Aiden's questions, because I knew where he was going to go with it.

"What's his name?"

"Melvin," I lied once again.

"Where is he now?"

"On a ship out to sea."

"How long he gon' be out there?"

"A couple of months," I lied. I was not going to divulge any information about this guy to Aiden. I knew my brother; he didn't like outsiders. So I was keeping all the information concerning Nashad under wraps.

"Well, when he comes back I want you to give him his truck back. I'm going to buy you a car as soon as I do a job for someone."

"What kind of job?" I wanted to know.

"When I get all the information I'll let you know," he told me.

"Whatcha want to eat?" I asked him while I started up the ignition. Everybody who got out of jail always wanted to get something to eat first. It was like we had to feed a craving that had built up while they were in jail. Unlike everyone else I knew, Aiden didn't want anything special.

"Stop by Popeye's Chicken and get me a two-piece with a biscuit," he said.

"Really? That's it? Popeye's Chicken?" I repeated as I pulled into the road.

"Yeah."

CHAPTER 3

MAKING MOVES

While I sat in the passenger seat of this truck my sister was driving, I stared at every car that we passed and wondered how those people's lives were. Were they happy or sad? Were they rich or poor? I even thought about whether they were good people or bad. In the world I came from, I was sad and poor. And I was bad. I was all those things because I had no other choice. Maybe if I had been raised in a different environment, I'd be a different person. But since that didn't happen, I was who I was.

Ava stopped by Popeye's Chicken like I asked her. After she ordered and paid for my food at the drive-thru, the cashier handed her a bag of food. After she handed me the bag of food and drove away from Popeye's, I asked, "Where are you taking me?"

"I was going to my apartment. Why? Do you need me to go somewhere else?" she replied.

"I need to get a throwaway cell phone."

"Does it matter where you get it from?"

"Come on, Ava, you know me. You know I don't give a shit about name brands. I just want the phone to work when I try to make a call."

"All right, well, I guess we can stop at the smoke shop on the next block. They sell throwaway cell phones for fifty dollars."

"Well, let's do it," I told her.

The smoke shop was less than a block away. As soon as Ava drove into a parking space directly in front of the store, I put my food on top of the dashboard.

"Do you want anything while I'm in there?" I asked her.

"You got money?" she wanted to know.

"Yeah, the jail gave me the money I had left in my commissary account."

"So, you got enough money for your phone?"

"Yeah, I got it."

"All right, well handle your business," she replied.

Without saying another word, I hopped out of the truck and headed into the store. "Can I get a cell phone?" I asked the Indian-looking cat standing behind a fiberglass partition.

"What kind do you want?" he asked me, motioning to the selection of phones on the wall behind him. I looked at the wall and decided to get the black Tech cell phone that cost forty dollars. "Does that phone come with minutes?"

"No. You gotta buy a phone card."

"How much?"

"I got twenty-five-dollar, forty-dollar, and fifty-dollar cards."

"All right, well, give me the twenty-five-dollar card."

After he rung up the cost of the cell phone and phone card, I paid him, grabbed them both from the counter, and walked back out of the store. The moment after I got back into the truck, Ava wanted to know had I gotten everything I needed, and when I told her that I had, she sped away from the curb and headed in the direction of her apartment. After I activated the phone, I pulled out the piece of paper Winston had given me with the information I needed on it and dialed the phone number. As I waited for someone to answer my call, I saw Ava look at me out of the corner of her eye. Instead of say-ing something to me, she waited.

Finally, after the phone rang three times, someone answered. "Hello," said a male's voice. I assumed it was Winston's cousin. "Hello, this is Aiden. I was told to call this number," I said.

"Yeah, I know," the guy said. "Can we meet up some-where?" the guy continued.

"Where?" I wanted to know.

"What about the car detailing spot on Princess Anne at the Longshoremen Hall?" he suggested.

"When?"

"What about within the hour?"

"All right, let's do it."

"See you there," he replied.

Immediately after I disconnected the call, Ava went into question mode. "Who was that?"

I shoved the phone into my front pants pocket and said, "A nigga that's gonna pay me to do a job."

"What kind of job?"

"I'm supposed to get rid of somebody."

"You mean kill 'em?"

"Yeah."

"Who does he want you to kill?"

I already had the information, but I told her, "I'll find out when I see him."

"Are you sure you wanna get involved with that shit? I'm not trying to lose you to another prison bid. I need you out here."

"Don't worry. I won't get caught. And if I do, I won't be taken alive," I told her.

Ava didn't say another word. She continued to drive in the direction of her apartment. After we reached our destination, she parked the truck and told me to follow her.

She lived in an apartment complex off Baker Road. I could instantly tell that the apartments were brand-new—well, at least to me, considering I hadn't been a free man in a few years. "Is this your spot?" I asked Ava while we walked toward the apartment building.

"It is while my friend is out to sea," she told me.

"You talking about that nigga that left you his truck?"

"Yep," she replied as she led the way up to the second floor.

The manner in which Ava answered my question about the guy who owned the truck and also owned the apartment sent up a red flag for me. I saw a spark in her eyes and she gave me a half smile. I didn't make mention of it, though. But I knew I needed to keep a close watch on her and this nigga she was involved with.

When she unlocked and opened the front door of the apartment, she let me go in first. I scanned the living room area and the kitchen area. I could tell that it was a bachelor's spot within seconds. There was nothing that told me Ava lived here. Normally when a man and a woman live together, you're gonna see some flowers on tables, nice feminine pictures on the wall, among other things. But not here, and it pleased me.

"When did you say this nigga was coming back home?" I asked her after I took a seat on the living room couch.

"A couple of months," she replied as she picked up the remote control for the television. "Wanna watch anything in particular?" she continued.

"Nah, I'm good. I just wanna relax a minute and eat my food before we head back out of here to see that nigga I called earlier."

"All right. Well, I'm gonna watch one of my favorite reality shows while you eat. And when it goes off, we can leave."

"Sounds good to me," I told her.

I watched Ava as she pressed play to watch the show she recorded, but then she walked away from the TV. I heard her go into what I assumed was the bedroom, and then I heard the door close. She stayed in the room for what seemed like halfway through the show. When she finally returned she looked a little disheveled. Her shirt was only halfway tucked into her pants, and her hair looked out of place. "What the fuck is up with you?" I asked her.

"Whatcha mean?"

"What's wrong with your hair and clothes? You look like you just came back from wrestling with somebody. You sure homeboy that owns this spot ain't back there?" I asked her, cracking a smile.

She burst into laughter. "No, boy, what are you talking about?" she asked me as she stood and looked into a framed glass mirror hanging on the wall behind her. At the sight of her disheveled reflection, she started fixing her hair and repositioning her shirt. "Damn, how did I do that?" she said. But only she could answer that question.

I didn't pursue any more information about how she got like that. I figured if she wanted to talk about it I wouldn't have to twist her arm to do it. So I changed the conversation altogether. "I'm gonna want to leave here in a few minutes and head to the spot to meet the guy," I told her.

"A'ight," she agreed.

CHAPTER 4

GOTTA BE MORE CAREFUL

Why hadn't I checked myself before exiting Nashad's bedroom? I needed to be more careful—I was slipping. Aiden was a very observant guy who would zero right in on anything he saw out of order. If he knew that I was hiding things, like intimate photos Nashad and I took together and a white gold Tiffany heart pendant that he had personalized to me, Aiden wouldn't understand, even if he knew how deeply Nashad was falling for me. I didn't want Aiden to think he had competition for my attention. I had to keep him in the dark about Nashad.

Fifteen minutes later, Aiden and I left the apartment. After we climbed back inside of the truck, I asked him to tell me exactly where we were going. "He told me to meet him in the side lot of the Longshoremen Hall off of Princess Anne Road. I think he's going there to get his car detailed."

"Are you sure this guy is legit? I mean, you could be going there to meet up with a cop," I pointed out.

"The nigga that gave me this guy's cell phone number said that this guy was his cousin. It had better be legit."

"I hope so," I commented. I knew I was casting a lot of doubt into the atmosphere, but I loved my brother, therefore it was my duty to make sure that he was all right. And if that meant I had to do something to protect him, then that's what I would do.

The drive to the Longshoremen Hall was only a twelve-minute ride. When we were two blocks from our destination, Aiden called the guy back to ask him what he was wearing and what kind of car he was in. After the guy answered both questions, Aiden disconnected the call. "He said he was wearing a gray hoodie and a pair of blue jeans. And he was standing outside of a white Ford Mustang."

Giving me the description of the guy's attire and the type of vehicle he was near gave me something to look out for. It only took Aiden and I a minute to lay eyes on the guy. "He's right there," Aiden said, pointing to a black guy standing next to the trunk of a white vehicle. As I drove toward him, I zoomed in on his facial expression. He looked nervous, to say the least. If I had to guess his age, I would say that he was in his early thirties, like Aiden and I were. I could see Aiden sizing him up as we got closer and closer to him. "This nigga look like a pretty boy," Aiden commented.

"Yeah, he does," I agreed. "So who is this guy again?" I wondered aloud. I needed Aiden to jog my memory about the role this guy was playing.

"He's supposed to be cousins with a nigga I was locked up with."

"Is the guy you were locked up with this guy's age?"

"Nah, the nigga I was locked up with was older."

The moment I stopped the truck and put the gear shift in park, Aiden got out and walked over toward the guy. I watched the guy's body movements as Aiden approached him. Once Aiden started talking to him, his nervousness seemed to ease and he became a little more relaxed. I couldn't hear what they were saying, but from Aiden's body language, I could tell that everything was going smoothly. Three minutes after the conversation started, they shook hands and then they went in opposite directions.

Aiden got in the truck with me, and the other guy got into his white Mustang and drove out of the parking lot and merged onto Princess Anne Road with the other traffic. Aiden and I watched the guy as he drove away while I made my exit, too. "So how did everything go?" I asked Aiden.

He opened his right hand, which lay on his lap. In his hand was a note, a photo of a white man, and a bunch of hundred-dollar bills folded neatly. "Yes, everything went fine."

I grabbed the photo of the white man and looked at it closely. "This is the guy they want you to kill?"

"Yeah, that's what he said."

"How much is that?" I asked Aiden while I placed the photo on his lap.

"Five grand."

"That's all?"

"No, this is only half of it. I'm supposed to get the other half after the job is done."

"When does he want it done?"

"Before the guy in jail goes to court."

"When is court?"

"Next Wednesday."

"You're kidding, right?"

"No."

"But that's only four days away," I noted. I was both shocked and worried at the same time. I mean, why would my brother get out of jail and take a job to kill someone soon thereafter? That's reckless!

"Look, Ava, you're worrying too much. I promise you that I've got everything under control," Aiden replied nonchalantly.

"What's your plan?"

"I'm working that out in my head as we speak."

"Have you thought about the possibility that the cops may have this guy under witness protection?"

"I was told that he wasn't. The nigga that just gave me the

money said that the guy was a utility worker that drives around in a company truck and that he goes to work every day."

"He sounds like a family man."

"Yeah, he is."

"Did he tell you where the guy lived?"

"Yep, I've got all that information on this little piece of paper."

"A'ight, well, let's do it."

"What do you mean 'let's do it'?"

"Do you think I'm gonna let you go out and do this alone?"

Aiden turned his head slightly around to look at me. "Now, that's the sister I know." He smiled.

CHAPTER 5

OUR FIRST HIT

My target was a rat by the name of Sam Carson. He was a white, middle-aged man who had witnessed a murder at the hands of Winston Battle in the parking lot of a local grocery store one late night. It was my job to track this dude down and figure out when and where it would be a good time to end this motherfucker's life.

Ava drove me by the house of the man who I was paid to murder. The address Winston's cousin had given me was in a middle-class neighborhood called Doves Grove, and it was only two minutes from highway 264. Seeing this was like music to my ears. If Ava and I had to make a quick getaway from this white man's house, jumping on the highway would be our best bet to escape.

In addition to that, I was told that Sam drove the company SUV alone, so I figured killing him in between jobs would be the perfect way to get the job done. "That's his house right there on the left," Ava said. She spoke in a whisper-like manner as if someone other than I could hear her.

The house she pointed to was a one-story, ranch style house. The yard was nicely cut and the small bushes around the front porch were manicured to perfection. "Somebody is coming out of the house," Ava announced, whispering again, and then she turned her head forward. Since I was sitting on the passenger side of the truck I knew I couldn't be seen, so I leaned my seat back a little and then I casually looked behind Ava's seat and in the direction of the front door. A white woman with red hair appeared. "That must be his wife," I told Ava.

"I wanna look so bad," she said, as she continued to drive by the house.

"You ain't missing nothing. She stepped out on the porch, picked something up, and now she's going back inside," I told Ava.

"Did you see that there was only one car in the driveway?" Ava asked me.

"Yeah, I saw that. So now we know that if her car is the only one parked in the driveway, then she's home by herself."

"I wonder if the kids were there."

"It's not even twelve o'clock yet, so you know that they can't be at home."

"I wonder what time he goes to work?" Ava's questions continued.

"Winston's cousin said that he leaves out of the house at six a.m. every morning."

"Well, I guess that's when our job starts, too," she said, and then she drove away from Sam's home.

Immediately after Ava merged back onto highway 264, I mentioned to her that I needed a gun. "Do you think I should call the cousin back and ask him to get one for me?" I asked her.

"Nah, don't call him until the job is done. I've got a gun you can use."

"Where is it?"

"It's back at the apartment."

"Ava, I ain't using that nigga's gun to kill that white man!" Aiden protested.

"It's not his gun, so chill out!"

"Then who does it belong to?"

"I stole it from a nigga that tried to take me out to eat on a dinner date a couple months ago."

I couldn't hold it in. I had to laugh after picturing Ava going out on a date with a nigga, and then, when the date is over, she robs him of his metal piece.

"Ava, you know you can't do shit like that when I'm not around. What if that nigga would've tried to kill you?"

"Let's not get into that. I'm alive and well. So let's keep this train going."

"Do you know what kind of gun it is?"

"Yes, it is a forty-five-caliber pistol. It came with a silencer, too."

"Stop fucking with me."

"I'm not."

"Where do you keep it?"

"Right now, I got it hidden in the closet of the bedroom."

"Well, I want you to pull it out of the closet as soon as we get back to the apartment."

"You got it," she assured me.

CHAPTER 6

TIME TO SAY GOOD-BYE

The following morning Aiden and I made our way back to Sam's house. We observed what time he left in the morning and what time he made it back home. After watching this rat for a couple days Aiden decided today would be the day to take him out.

Aiden and I were sitting in Nashad's truck and followed Sam as he drove away from the utility company he worked for. We knew he was on his way to his first appointment so we put enough distance between our car and his truck so he wouldn't get spooked and lead us to the cops.

We followed him to his first stop, which was a single-family home in a middle-class neighborhood in the downtown Ghent section of Norfolk. I parked the truck halfway down the block. Our position was close enough to see Sam's every move but it was far enough for him not to see us. It helped us that it was extremely foggy outside. The fog gave us a level of obscurity that worked in our favor, and I could see Aiden becoming intoxicated by the second because of it. I watched him as he locked and loaded his .45-caliber pistol, then screwed the silencer into the barrel. "I'm gonna go down there and get in position so when he walks back to the house, I can murk him before he even makes it back to his truck," Aiden announced.

"What do you want me to do?" I asked him. This was our first hit so I felt like I needed direction.

"Stay in the truck but keep the engine running and the door unlocked. When you see me coming toward you, be ready to drive off. But we're gonna turn around and drive back the same way we came. Got it?" he replied.

"Yeah, I got it," I assured him while I felt the rush of adrenaline pump through me.

I watched Aiden as he exited the truck. He put his hoodie over his head as he walked down the sidewalk toward the house where Sam was. One minute into the walk, Aiden disappeared behind a row of bushes a couple of yards away from the house. From that moment, I couldn't see what was to come.

I sat quietly in my truck while my heart rate sped up uncontrollably. I wanted to know what was going on. But I didn't dare leave the truck when I was told to stay still. Five minutes went by and nothing happened. I was becoming more nervous by the second. "Aiden, what are you doing?" I mumbled to myself while I glanced from the watch on my wrist to the bushes where Aiden had hidden himself.

I noticed another minute had passed when I looked back down at my watch, so when I looked back up I was startled to see Aiden running toward toward me. I immediately put my foot on the brake and put the gear in drive as he approached the truck. After he opened the door and hopped in the passenger seat, I took my foot off the brake and made a U-turn in the middle of the street. "Hurry up," he huffed.

"I'm trying," I snapped as I pressed down on the accelerator after I straightened the steering wheel. I was a nervous wreck.

"Make a left at the corner," he instructed me.

"Did you get 'em?" I questioned while I was making the left turn. Now it seemed like everything happened so fast.

"Yeah, I got 'em. But we might have to take a trip back over there," Aiden replied in a chilling manner. The hairs on my arms stood up.

"Why? Whatcha do?" I asked him. He was acting really weird.

"I think the lady of the house saw me. And if she did, then I've gotta go back there and kill her, too," he replied, and then he started unscrewing the silencer from the barrel of his pistol.

CHAPTER 7

TIME TO COLLECT

After I stuffed the gun and the silencer into the glove compartment, I took the throwaway phone out of my pocket and dialed Winston's cousin's cell phone number. He answered the phone on the second ring. "What's up?" he said.

"I just finished the job so I want to know when and where I can come and pick up the rest of my money."

"What guarantees do you have to let me know that the job has been completed?"

"Turn on the motherfucking news. And call me back within the hour with the location and time to meet," I instructed the guy and then I disconnected the call.

"What's up with him?" Ava asked me.

"I don't know what the fuck is up with him. But I know he better call me back and tell me where he's going to meet me so I can get my money."

"Do you think he's trying to renege on giving you the rest of the money?"

"He would be wise not to."

"So what exactly did he say?"

"When I asked for the money he said he needed proof that

the job was done. So I told him to turn on the news and call me back within the hour."

"Think he's going to do it?"

"At this point, Ava, I really don't care what he does. I can't control his actions. But I can control mine. So if he tries to play me for a fool, I'm gonna take his life, too."

"Well, I hope he does the right thing."

"I guess we'll find out soon enough," I said, and then I fell silent. I turned my attention toward the ongoing traffic in front of us. But I wasn't thinking about the traffic, I was thinking about the man I had just murdered. The thought of me sneaking up behind him, pointing the gun at the back of his head without him knowing that he was about to die gave me a sense of power. I felt like a god. And for the first time in my life I felt in control. I remembered back when I was younger, how I was always getting picked on. Kids older than me used to call me retard, dummy, old man, Beetlejuice, and a lot of other names. I also remember the kids running me home from the bus stop. They acted like they hated my guts. And it was for no reason, because I always stayed to myself. I never bothered anybody. All I ever wanted was for people to leave me alone. That's it. But no. Those kids wanted me to be their punching bag, so here I am.

It didn't take Ava long to get us back to the apartment. As soon as she drove into the lot and parked the truck, I hopped out of the passenger side. I couldn't wait to go inside so I could check the news and see what was being reported about the guy I had just murdered. "Come on, let's go," I yelled back at Ava. For some reason it seemed like she was walking in slow motion.

"I'm coming," she replied as she walked toward me.

About fifteen steps later, Ava finally reached the front door, unlocked it, and then she pushed it open. Immediately after I stepped across the threshold, I felt a sense of calmness come over me. I don't know why, but I felt safe. "Turn on the TV for me," I instructed Ava.

She picked the remote up from the coffee table and pressed the power button, and less than a second later the television came on. "Change the channel to ten," I instructed Ava once more.

I took a seat on the couch and waited to see what the news was going to report. I sat there for about two and a half hours, and nothing happened. By then I was losing patience. "What the fuck is going on? Why haven't the news reporters gotten their asses out there yet?" I roared. My blood was boiling on the inside. During that time, Ava cleaned herself up, washed a load of clothes, and fixed a pot of spaghetti. After she finished, she joined me in the living room with a plate of food for me and for herself.

"Nothing yet?" she asked me as she handed me a plate of food. I grabbed the dish and set it down on the coffee table in front of me.

"No," I told her, and then I buried my face in the palm of my hands. Anxiety was beginning to take over my entire body. My heart was beating erratically and my head started hurting at the same time. It felt like I was about to lose my mind. And then I figured, *What if the guy Sam isn't dead?* What if the paramedics got there and saved his life? I knew one thing, if that happened, then my job was botched and I knew that I would never have another chance to finish the job. The cops would be all over him. And I was more than sure they would put him in witness protection after this.

While my mind was spinning in circles, I heard a male voice coming from the television. I looked up at the television screen and zoomed in on a female reporter sitting behind a podium announcing that there was breaking news. "This just in," she started off saying.

"Ava, I think this is it," I yelled toward the kitchen.

Ava dropped what she was doing and raced back into the living room. She plopped back down on the couch and glued her eyes to the television.

"In breaking news this morning, Norfolk police are on the scene in the Ghent area investigating a murder. No word from the Norfolk police about how he was murdered but we spoke with a couple of the neighbors, who were not willing to go on camera, but they did say that they saw a black SUV fleeing the scene around the time the murder happened. They also said that a few of the other neighbors are saying that the utility truck parked near the crime scene belonged to the victim. I tried to get the homicide detectives to confirm it, but they declined to give a statement. They did, however, say that if anyone has any information concerning this unfortunate tragedy, to please call the tip line at 888-LOCKUUP."

"There it is," Ava said as she pointed toward the TV. "Call that nigga back and tell him that now he has fucking proof," she continued.

"If he doesn't call me in the next few minutes then I'm gonna call him," I replied. "But did you hear when the reporter said that she spoke to two neighbors that said they saw a black SUV leave the scene?"

"Yeah, I heard it. And so what?"

"Do you think they got the license plate numbers?"

"If they did, then the cops would've been here by now," Ava hissed. I figured she started whispering to prevent the neighbors from hearing our conversation through the walls.

I thought for a second, and then I nodded my head. "Yeah, you're right," I finally agreed with her.

Before Ava and I could utter another word, my throwaway phone started ringing. I answered the call on the second ring. "What's up?" I said.

"I saw what I needed to see, so meet me back at the same place in thirty minutes," he instructed me.

"A'ight, will do," I assured him, and then we both hung up.

"What did he say?" Ava wanted to know.

"He told me to meet him at the same spot we met up at the first time."

"Do you feel comfortable going back to that same place? Because personally I don't think that would be a good idea. I mean, what if the cops have a hunch that the guy Winston had someone to kill the guy? If that's the case, then whoever Winston talks to would be under surveillance, right?"

"That scenario definitely has some good points to it. So that's why it would be in my best interest to have the guy pay me now, before the cops start wiretapping his phone."

"I understand what you're saying, but I still don't think it's a good idea. I think we should meet him somewhere else."

"A'ight. Well, I guess I'm gonna call him back and tell him to meet me somewhere else."

Ava let out a long sigh. "Good. Thank you!" she told me.

Without saying another word, I called Winston's cousin back. "Hello," he said.

"Hey, let's meet somewhere else."

"Like where?"

"Tell him to meet us at the Feather and Fin chicken spot down the street from the Longshoremen Hall," Ava whispered to me.

"Meet me at the chicken spot, Feather and Fin, right up the block from the hall," I suggested.

"All right. I'm on my way there now," he replied.

"A'ight, I'll be there," I assured him.

The ride to the chicken spot Ava suggested didn't take long at all. When we pulled up and parked in the parking lot, Ave also suggested that we go inside and order some food; that way things wouldn't look suspicious. So I followed her inside. The eatery was small as hell. They only had limited seating for like ten people, but I counted at least twenty people in there waiting to order or waiting to get their food. In other words, the place and the people in it were ghetto as shit.

"Can I get three boneless breast sandwiches with cheese combos and three tea and lemonade drinks?" I heard one chick say. I could tell that she was very young. Maybe twenty-two years old, if that. She was loud and she looked unkempt, trotting around the place with a sleeping bonnet on her head and bedroom shoes on her feet. There was a housing project up the block, and I was sure she lived there.

After she placed her order, a couple other people asked for the same chicken sandwich combo. I immediately assumed that that combo was an urban favorite, so when it was my turn, I got Ava to order me the same thing while I sat down in a chair near the glass door so I could see everything coming my way.

Twenty minutes after we arrived there, Winston's cousin finally pulled up. He arrived in a different car this time, and it raised a red flag for me. In my mind, I started wondering why he'd do that. What was on his mind?

"Why do you think he drove a different car this time?" I asked Ava.

"He's probably paranoid just like us," Ava stated. "Shit, I would've done the same thing."

"Do you think he wants me to come outside to meet him?"

"I'm sure he does. Because he doesn't look like he's trying to come in here with all these fucking people. So go," she insisted as she nudged me in the back.

Listening to Ava, I stood and walked out of the chicken spot. I watched Winston's cousin closely as I approached him. I saw him look around at his surroundings the entire time he was sitting there. "Are you all right?" I asked him as soon as I got within arm's reach of him.

"Yeah, I'm a'ight. I just don't like this fucking area. Cops hang around this area a lot," he said.

I leaned in toward him. "Want me to get in the car or what?" I asked him.

"No. I'm gonna hand you the money right now," he told me, and then he lifted a wad of hundred-dollar bills from his lap and handed it to me.

"Is it all here?" I wanted to know. I wasn't in the mood to play games with my money.

"Yeah, everything is there."

"A'ight, well, I guess that's it," I said as I stood straight up.

"Good looking," the guy said, and then he sped out of the parking lot.

I shoved the money down into my pocket and headed back toward the door of the chicken spot, but as I approached it, Ava was walking out. "Everything good?" she asked me.

"Yep, we good," I told her.

"Ready to go and celebrate?" Ava continued as she smiled at me.

I smiled back at her and said, "Hell, no! I wanna go back to the apartment and wind down a bit."

"Well, back to the apartment we go," she replied.

A few minutes into the drive, I rolled down the passenger side window and tossed the throwaway phone onto the street. I heard it crack that instant, so I knew it had broken, which was what I wanted.

CHAPTER 8

MAKING MORE MOVES

It had been a week since Aiden had done the job and got paid for it. The shocking thing about it was that when he got the money from that hit, he gave all of it to me and told me to get my own car because no sister of his would ever depend on a man. I thought the gesture was sweet and accepted the money. I hadn't used it yet, but I started looking for a new car. So while he and I were sitting in the living room watching TV, I searched the Internet for a really nice used car. I ran across a handful of Hondas and Acuras, but they were just a little over my spending budget. "Can you believe this shit?!" I cursed while I thumbed my way through the car section of Auto Trader online.

"What's the matter?" Aiden asked me. But before I could answer him, the front doorbell rang. That shit startled the hell out of Aiden and me both. I mean, who in the hell could it be? What, the cops? I swear, I wasn't trying to go back to jail. Not right now. I've got too much shit to lose. Hell, I had just got into a relationship with a guy I finally liked. So whoever was on that side of the door wasn't going to come in here. No way. I refused to let anyone turn my life upside down.

Aiden looked at me with a spooked look. This was the first

time I had seen my brother looked scared since we were kids. "Who do you think that could be?" he whispered.

I hunched my shoulders because I didn't know. No one has ever knocked on that door. Even when Nashad is in town, no one comes here. So answering my brother's question wasn't going to happen.

We sat there in silence and heard the doorbell ring a total of eight times. Then, when the ringing stopped, the person started knocking on the fucking door. This shit started off a panic alarm in my head. "Why the fuck are they still ringing the doorbell and knocking? If no one hasn't answered the door by now, then that means that no one is fucking home," I continued to whisper.

"Wait, I'm gonna look through the peephole to see who it is," Aiden volunteered as he stood up.

"No, don't do it. They may hear you walking toward the door," I warned him.

Aiden waved his hand at me. I knew that meant to be quiet and let him do him.

I watched Aiden as he tiptoed toward the front door. It felt like my heart was about to jump out of my fucking chest. I swear, this whole scene was becoming unbearable, to say the least. "Please be careful," I whispered. Aiden looked back at me and waved his hand at me again. I knew then he really wanted me to shut the fuck up.

Finally, he made it to the door without making a sound, so I was relieved at that point, but as he leaned forward and put his right eye near the peephole, my body started doing all kinds of weird things. First it felt like my heart was going to jump out of my chest, then it felt like I was about to hyperventilate. And then it felt like a headache was about to come on. I couldn't tell you if I was coming or going.

When Aiden pulled his head back from the peephole, he looked at me and said, "It's Winston's cousin."

"What?" I replied. I was puzzled but relieved all at the same time.

After Aiden opened the front door, I got a chance to see that it was really the guy who had paid Aiden for the hit. "What the fuck is you doing here?" Aiden asked him. Aiden was extremely irritated.

"Can I come in?" he asked Aiden.

"Fuck, no! For what? My business with you is over," Aiden spat.

"I've got another job for you," the guy said in a volume that no one would hear but us.

"Whatcha trying to set me up?" Aiden reached out and grabbed the guy around the throat.

I jumped up from the sofa. "No, Aiden, don't do that," I pleaded as I raced over to the front door.

The guy was trying desperately to get Aiden's hands from around his neck. "Please let him go," I pleaded with Aiden once more.

Finally, after grabbing hold of Aiden's hand, I got him to release the guy. So when that was done, I grabbed the guy by the arm and led him into the apartment.

"I don't think you should be letting him in the house," Aiden said.

"I'm just trying to help him get his self together. I mean, you did almost choke him to death."

"What if that nigga is wired?"

"I'm not wired," the guy said as he began to massage his neck.

"Well, tell us, how the fuck did you find us?"

"Winston wanted me to make sure you wasn't working with the police, so he had me follow y'all from the day you were released from prison."

"Yo, the next time you talk to that nigga, tell him to fuck himself. I'm not no fucking rat! The rat was the cracker I eliminated a week ago."

"Well, now that you know my brother isn't working with the cops, then tell us why you're here?" I asked him.

"I tried to tell him that I had another job for him."

"What kind of job?" I wanted to know.

"Check that nigga to see if he's wired before he says another word," Aiden instructed me.

Before I could frisk the guy, he took it upon himself to lift up his shirt and pull down the jeans he was wearing. All that was left covering him were his boxer shorts. "See, I told you I'm not wired," he said.

"Take your fucking shorts off, too, nigga!" Aiden roared as he stood only a few feet away from the guy and me.

"See, I'm not wearing a wire," he insisted while he removed his boxer shorts.

I can't lie, after the guy took off his boxer shorts my eyes froze at the sight of how big his fucking dick was. It was unbelievable. "All right. You can put your clothes back on," I told him.

While he was putting his clothes back on, Aiden said, "Where the fuck is Winston?"

"He's home," the guy answered.

"So, the judge dropped the charges?" Aiden wanted to know.

"Yeah, his charges were dropped the next day when he went to court," the guy explained.

"So, tell me what do you want now," Aiden pressed him.

"Well, I figured since you did the last job without any hiccups, I thought that you would do me a good service by eliminating some more people."

"How many people are you talking about?" Aiden asked.

"It's a total of nine lives."

"Nine fucking people? What the fuck do you got going on that you need me to off nine more fucking people?" Aiden challenged him.

"Yeah, what kind of shit you got going on?" I interjected,

because my brother had a point. Who orders a hit of nine people at one time? My brother and I needed more answers.

"Look, it's like this," he started off. "Winston and I run downtown. We got the best heroin money can buy. But while Winston was locked up, shit got a little crazy. Niggas started trying to take over our territories. I have a little bit of muscle on my team, but it's not enough. And plus, we've already lost two of our people. Remember that nigga Winston shot?"

"Yeah," Aiden acknowledged.

"Well, he was one of the top enforcers in that group. So, after Winston did him in, they retaliated by killing two of my niggas, and then they tried to take over a few of our spots."

"Who are these cats?" Aiden asked. I could tell that he was getting more interested by the minute.

"Niggas around town call 'em the Hot Boys. They sell heroin, too. But their shit is straight garbage. So what they do is try to intimidate our customers into buying their shit. And if they don't buy it, then they get beat up really bad," the guy pointed out.

"Damn, so these niggas are crazy, huh?" I spoke.

"They ain't as crazy as I am," Aiden said.

The guy looked at Aiden as if he was hoping he would say that he was going to take the job. But Aiden turned his attention toward me. "Whatcha think?" he asked me.

Aiden always valued my opinion, so I knew that if I said yes, then he'd do it. So I thought for a moment, and then I looked at the guy and said, "How much are you paying?"

"I'll pay ten thousand dollars per head," he said as his face lit up.

"Whatcha think about that price?" I asked Aiden. Aiden looked at the guy and said, "If you give me fifteen grand per head, then you got yourself a deal."

The guy thought for a second and then he said, "You got it."

"So when does he get paid?" I interjected.

"Later on tonight."

"So, you're gonna give him sixty-seven thousand five hundred dollars later on tonight when you see us?"

"Yes, I am. But I'm gonna need another phone number from you, because I tried to call that other phone, but it doesn't work anymore.

"That's because I threw it away."

"Don't worry. I'm going to take him out right now so he can get another one. But you still have the same number, right?" I asked the guy.

"No. I got a new phone, too."

"Well, give me your number, and I'll put it in my cell phone. And when he gets the phone, he will call you from it," I instructed.

"A'ight, sounds good," he said, and then he gave me his new phone number. After I stored it in my cell phone, Aiden and he shook hands, and then Aiden let him out of the apartment.

Once he was gone, Aiden looked at me and said, "What do you think about that nigga?"

"What do you mean?" I wondered aloud.

"Something just ain't right about him. Every time he's around us, he starts shaking and shit!"

"Wouldn't you be if you had to stand around someone like you? Aiden, you're intimidating. I mean, look at how you grabbed the poor man by his neck and started fucking choking him. I thought you were going to clean him," I joked.

"Well, thank God you were here, because I didn't." Aiden smiled. "Let's go."

"Okay," I replied as I gathered my handbag and the keys to the truck.

CHAPTER 9

NINE MORE LIVES

It seemed like everything was happening so fast. Ava took me by another corner store so I could get another throwaway phone. And right after I got it, I activated it, and then I called Winston's cousin so he could have the number when he was ready to give me the money and the list of names.

While Ava and I waited for him to call we decided to stop by the Jamaican Restaurant off Military Highway in Norfolk. She and I ordered our food and waited for the waitress to bring it back to us. As the time passed, Ava and I noticed how packed the restaurant was getting. I started getting paranoid and made her aware of it. "Doesn't it seem like as soon as we got here, now everybody is trying to come in here?"

Ava took a look around. "Yeah, I guess it kind of does," she replied with a shrug.

"Well, have you noticed how everyone that comes through that door stares right at us?"

"That's because we're sitting near the door."

"Well, then tell me why that nigga standing in line to order his food with the blue polo shirt keep looking over here at us?" I pressed the issue.

Ava turned her attention toward the guy I pointed out to

her. When she finally got a chance to see who I was talking about, the guy had turned his head. She still got a good look at him. "Wait, that guy looks like the guy that stays in the apartment next to the one we're in," she said.

"Well, you're probably right, because I caught him looking at you a few times. And I wanted to say something to him, but I didn't want to cause a scene, so I kept my mouth closed."

Ava continued to stare at the guy, hoping she could get a better look at him. While she tried to make that happen, the waitress brought our food to the table. "Here you guys go," she said as she placed both plates of food in front of us. "Enjoy!" she continued.

"Thank you. We will," Ava told the lady after she took her eyes off the guy in the blue polo shirt.

"This looks so good," I mentioned.

"Yeah, it does," she agreed as she periodically looked over to where the guy was standing.

"Why the fuck do you keep looking at him? Fuck that nigga and enjoy your food!" I told her.

"But what if that is the guy that lives in the same building? I don't want him going back to Nashad and tell him he saw me and you together. For all I know, that guy could be thinking that you and I are boyfriend and girlfriend."

"So what? Let him think it. It ain't like you're gonna marry the dude anyway. Don't ever let another nigga dictate how you supposed to live your life. I'm the only nigga you need to worry about. I'm your blood, so I ain't gonna let any man upset you or come between that bond we have. You understand?" I spat. I was getting tired of her acting all paranoid like she can't walk around and do what the fuck she wants to do. That shit ain't going down while I'm around. Fuck that!

When Ava finally got a chance at a better look at the guy in the blue polo shirt, she saw that it wasn't the person she thought he was. But that didn't matter to me either way. I say fuck everybody and the boat they came in on.

CHAPTER 10

MORE MONEY—MORE MONEY

Aiden made it perfectly clear that he didn't give a fuck whether that guy was Nashad's neighbor or not. But I cared, because I liked Nashad. Nashad was good to me. He let me in his home when I had nowhere to go. So it was hard for me not to care if someone saw me and reported back to him that they saw me with another man. Was I wrong for feeling this way? And was I wrong for not taking that stance with my brother? That's an argument I refused to have with my brother so I was going to leave well enough alone.

After sitting in that restaurant for an hour, Winston's cousin finally called Aiden back. "So where we gonna meet?" I heard Aiden ask him.

I couldn't hear what the other guy said, but after Aiden hung up with the guy he looked at me and said, "He's gonna meet us here in the next thirty minutes."

"Cool," I said. While Aiden and I waited for this guy to show up, we started chatting about the possibility of him dating an attractive young lady, but he shot it down as soon as I opened my mouth. "I can't think about hooking up with a chick right now. Family is the most important thing to me right now. You're my priority. And I won't let a chick come between us."

After he shot down the idea of him dating a woman, we started talking about things he had to go through while he was in prison this last time. He gave me the brutal details of him beating up guys that either stole from him or disrespected him. As much as I wanted to know what happened to Aiden, I was relieved when Winston's cousin called back and told us he was outside the restaurant.

I turned around and looked at the glass door of the restaurant. "Are you gonna go outside and talk to him?" I asked Aiden when I turned back around to face him.

"Yeah," Aiden continued as he stood up from the chair.

"Want me to go with you?" I asked him.

"Yeah, come on. Because as soon as he gives me the money we gon' hop in the truck and leave."

"A'ight," I said and stood up. Before I walked away from the table I threw forty dollars near my plate of food.

"Think that's gonna be enough?" he asked me.

"Yeah, that's more than enough," I told him and walked away from the table. He followed suit.

When we got outside we noticed that the sun had set. It wasn't that dark out and the moon was definitely peeping through the clouds. "Did he say where he was parked?" I asked him while I scanned the entire parking lot.

"Nah, just look for either one of his cars."

Moments later, a set of headlights blinked on and off. Aiden and I both looked in that direction. "There he is," I said as I pointed at a row of cars about fifty yards away from us. "Do you think he wants us to walk over there to him?"

"I don't know, but come on," Aiden instructed.

Aiden stepped off the curb and headed in the direction the guy was parked. I followed right in his footsteps. While we proceeded in that direction, I scanned the parking lot again just to make sure that no one was sitting off to the sidelines. Now I may be wrong, but there was something about this guy that just didn't sit well with me. Every time Aiden and I got around with him, he started getting all jumpy and shit. I didn't like him. I decided to let Aiden know that after he did this job for him, that's it. No more.

Aiden reached the car before I did. When he approached him, he went straight into talk mode. This time Winston instructed Aiden to get in the car with him. "Why does he have to get in the car now? He didn't have to do it before," I blurted out.

"Calm down, baby girl, this job is different. We need to have a more in-depth conversation," Aiden said.

"Yeah, it's okay. And it ain't gonna take nothing but a couple of minutes," the guy said.

I looked at this nigga with a side-eye. "Don't try no funny shit!" I warned him.

Immediately after Aiden got into the car with that guy, I walked over to the truck and hopped inside of it. I figured by me getting into the truck and starting up the ignition, Aiden and I would have a better chance of getting away if something wrong went down. I refused to let my brother get bamboozled by the crooked-ass niggas out here in these streets. Not on my watch!

It took Aiden exactly five minutes to iron out the details with that guy. I was happy to see him get out of the car. To prevent him from having to walk across the parking lot, I put the truck into drive and met him halfway. "Is everything good?"

He smiled at me while he closed the passenger-side door. "Yes, it is," he told me and dropped a manila envelope on my lap. I swear it looked like a freaking brick.

I picked up the stack of money from my lap and looked at it while I steered the SUV out of the parking lot. "So, this is sixty-seven thousand five hundred dollars?" I asked him, while

I tried wrapping my mind around the fact that I was holding that much money in my hands at one time.

"Yes, it is. And it's all yours," Aiden said.

I threw my foot on the brake. The truck stopped suddenly, rocking back and forth.

"Girl, what the hell is wrong with you?" Aiden shouted. I knew I'd scared him because it was written all over his face.

"Big brother, you're giving me all of this money?" I needed clarity.

"Fuck, yeah! I mean, what am I going to do with it?"

"You could do a lot with it. You could buy yourself a car and get a place to stay."

"Nah, I'm good. I'll let you handle all of that. Now, can we go?" he asked.

While he explained to me how I could do more with the money than he could, I looked in his eyes and saw a man who really loved me. It might seem weird to someone else, but Aiden had treated me more like a wife than a sister—minus the intimacy part. I mean, what else could I say?

After going over everything in my head, I finally pressed my foot back on the accelerator and headed back to the apartment. Aiden and I needed to go over a solid plan to get rid of those nine lives that Winston's cousin had ordered. I was almost sure that our lives would be in jeopardy if we fucked it up; especially with the kind of money we were being paid to do these hits.

"Aiden, we're in the big leagues now!" I said with excitement as I cruised down the boulevard that led back to the apartment.

CHAPTER 11

LAYING OUT THE PLAN

"Okay, check it out. Here are the pictures of the niggas I gotta put on their back," I started off saying, while I showed Ava two group pictures that were posted on Facebook of all nine guys.

"Looks like these niggas took these pictures at VA Live nightclub," Ava commented as she studied both photos. "Wait, I know these niggas," she continued.

Hearing her say that she knew these niggas was like music to my ears. This was a great thing, because I could use that factor to my advantage. "You know all of them?" I asked her.

"Yeah, I know every last one of them," she assured me. "This is Nu-Nu," she said, pointing to the guy wearing a brown Gucci jacket. "This is Monty," she said, pointing to the guy wearing all black. "This is Eric," she said, pointing to the guy wearing a red polo shirt and blue jeans. Ava went through everyone in the picture and named them. She even gave me some history about these niggas, too. According to her, seven out of the nine guys were related by way of brother or cousins. The other two guys were best friends to the guys. Ava also said that those niggas were always together so it would be virtually impossible to murder them one by one. She said they hustled on the blocks together, they hung out in the trap houses together, and they went out to nightclubs and strip clubs together. But she did give me something to work with when she told me that she and the guy Nu-Nu had dated for a couple of months. That meant she knew where that nigga laid his head, where his favorite spots were, how often he carried a pistol, and his vulnerabilities.

"This job they gave us isn't going to be as easy as it was to kill that white man. It's not going to be hard, either. But keep in mind that we may run into a few bumps in the road. And when that happens, we're gonna need a plan B," she said.

Out of the blue her cell phone rang. I'd been with her since I got out of jail and I'd never heard her cell phone ring, so to hear it now shocked me. I watched her give me a blank stare.

"Give me a second," she said and stood up from the table. Her cell phone was stuffed down in her front pants pocket so when she pulled it out, she looked at the caller ID and then she walked out of the kitchen. Now I can't lie, I was pretty pissed off that she'd walk out of the kitchen to answer her cell phone. Shit! She and I were family. Who and what is she trying to hide from me?

I sat at the kitchen table and waited for her return. But while I waited, I sat there quietly hoping to hear her conversation with whomever she was talking to. But that didn't work, because after I heard her close a door down the hall, I knew she went into the bedroom. I can't front. That shit made me mad! I mean, what the fuck she could be talking about that she doesn't want me to hear? I am the only person in the world who would lay their life down for hers, so to have this bullshit happen was like a slap in the face.

After sitting there for a little over one minute, I figured that she could only be talking to that nigga that was letting her stay in this house. And the reason why she left the kitchen was because she didn't want the guy to know that I was in his house.

"Oh, but he's going to know today," I huffed and shot up from my chair. I stormed out of the kitchen and stormed down the hallway.

When I reached the bedroom door, I grabbed the doorknob and pushed it open. The power behind my strength forced the door to hit the wall behind it. *BOOM!*

"What the fuck you do that for? You scared the shit out of me!" she yelled after she turned around, stumbling.

"What the fuck were you doing?"

"I was looking at myself in the mirror," she replied as she turned back around to face the mirror that was attached to the dresser.

"Not that. Who called you on your cell phone?" I pressed the issue.

"It wasn't nobody special."

"Ava, don't play games with me. I know you were talking to that nigga that lives in this apartment."

Ava stopped rearranging her hair in the mirror and turned back around to face me. "Aiden, does it really matter who I was talking to?" she asked me.

"You damn right it matters, because I don't want no lame-ass nigga getting all in your ears telling you shit that you wanna hear and then that shit comes between me and you. You know all these niggas out here ain't shit. All they wanna do is fuck you and leave you. And the ones that decide to keep you around longer will use and cheat on you."

"You don't think I know that?" she came back at me. "I've been out here on these streets by myself while you were in jail. I've run through niggas and used them like they do to other chicks. I'm hipped to the game, Aiden, so don't come at me like I don't know what I'm doing."

"Tell me why you had to leave the kitchen and come all the way back here in the bedroom to talk to him? Are you trying to hide something from me?" I wanted to know.

Ava stood there for a moment without saying another

word. She acted as if she was trying to think of something to say, and that pissed me off. I stormed toward her and got in her face. "Answer my question Ava," I screamed at her.

She looked up at me and said, "Why do you have to get in my face?"

"Just answer my question," I roared.

At that point, she pushed me back. "What the fuck is wrong with you?" she spat, then she stormed out of the bedroom.

I stomped behind her and grabbed her by the arm midway down the hallway. I twirled her around to face me. She tried to break loose.

"Get off me, Aiden," she said.

But my grip was tight. "Tell me the fucking truth and then I'll let you go."

"What do you want me to say?" She resisted a little more.

"I want the truth," I told her. I wasn't backing down.

Once again she stood there like she was trying to debate what she wanted to tell me, and again this made me even more angry. "What the fuck is wrong with you? Just fucking tell me already," I yelled as I shook her a few times.

"Stop, Aiden, you hurting me." She resisted more, trying to pry my hands away from her. But my strength was too much for her.

"Just tell me and I'll let you go."

"Okay, fuck it! I have a lot of feelings for this guy. And I left the kitchen because I didn't want you to hear the way I talk to him, and I didn't want him to know that you were here. Now are you satisfied?" she yelled back, and then she finally broke free of my hands. I watched her as she walked away from me; it happened in slow motion. In my mind and heart it felt as if she was literally walking out of my life.

I stood there in complete silence as I mulled over every word she had just uttered, and with every word it felt like she was stabbing me in my heart. I swear I couldn't believe that she told me that she had feelings for this new nigga that was in her life. This had never happened before. Ava never loved anyone else but me. And now, to know that I had to share her heart with another nigga killed me inside. I mean, what if he fucked around and won her over and took all of her heart? How would I ever be able to cope knowing that I might lose her indefinitely? I couldn't let that shit happen to me. No way.

After running all the possibilities through my mind I headed into the kitchen, because that was where Ava went. When I turned the corner and stepped on the kitchen tile I saw her pouring herself a drink. Her back was turned to me, so I approached her from behind, but I kept about three feet in distance between us. "As soon as we're done doing this job, we're leaving this place, and I don't want you talking to that nigga anymore. I want you to cut all communication with him."

Ava turned around with the glass in her hand and said, "Okay. That's fine." And then she raised the glass of lemonade and took a sip of it.

I stood there for a moment and looked into her eyes to see if she really meant what she'd just said. After looking at her for a couple of seconds, I was assured that she was. "Come on, let's finish mapping out the plan to get these niggas we've been paid to murder," I said, and then I took a seat at the kitchen table.

CHAPTER 12

MY BROTHER IS REALLY FUCKING CRAZY

After Aiden took a seat at the kitchen table, I followed. But while I was sitting there, watching him talk about what he was going to need to make these hits, I couldn't help but think about how he ran up on me in the bedroom. He literally burst into the bedroom like he was my fucking man. And the way he questioned me like I was a kid or his woman threw me for a loop. Aiden has never yelled at me, or even put his hands on me, for that matter. Then again, he never knew me to love anyone else but him. But did that give him the right to rough me up like that? And then to tell me that after we completed the job, we were going to leave this apartment and I couldn't talk to Nashad anymore. Was he fucking crazy? I mean, I knew he might feel threatened because of my feelings for Nashad, but that didn't mean I was going to erase Nashad from my life altogether. We weren't kids anymore. It wasn't a situation where Aiden and I were against the world. I was a grown woman and I had needs. I couldn't walk away from Nashad just like that, even though I had told Aiden that I would. That would be impossible on so many levels. I didn't know how I was going to handle this situation with my brother and Nashad. But I was going to have to figure it out sooner rather than later, because when I had talked to Nashad a few minutes ago, he had told me that he was coming home in three days. This was Tuesday, and he was going to be here by Friday night. So I had to come up with something fast.

"You said you know where they hang out, right?"

"Yeah."

"Well, we're gonna have to take a ride so we can come up with a precise plan. I need to find out how they operate. When they get up, how many of them leave out the house at the same time, where they go eat, but most importantly, what are their weak spots. In the world of hustling, niggas think they stay ahead of the cops and niggas that wanna rob them, but there's always a weak spot in their routine. And we're going to find out what it is," Aiden said.

But by this point, everything he was saying was going over my head. I saw his mouth moving, but I wouldn't be able to repeat anything he said. My ears were closed shut. My body had been completely engulfed with anxiety, and I had no idea how to control it. Maybe if I just took a deep breath and drank the rest of this lemonade I'd be fine. I guess I wouldn't know it unless I tried.

"What time do you want to leave?" Aiden said, breaking my train of thought.

I didn't know what to say to him, because I hadn't heard the question. I mean, I saw his mouth moving and I heard him say something, but once again, I wouldn't be able to repeat it. "Did you hear me?" he said.

"I'm sorry, what did you say?" I replied.

"Were you even listening to me?" he asked me, and he seemed irritated, too.

"Yes, I was listening to you, but I drifted off for a minute," I lied. And he knew I was lying, too. Thank God he didn't press the issue, though.

"I said when do you wanna leave so we can go and check these niggas out?"

"Oh, I guess we can go out tonight."

"I'm ready to go out now. The quicker we can get the intel, the quicker we can get this job done," he said matter-of-factly.

"All right, we can leave now. But let me use the bathroom first," I told him. I really didn't have to use the bathroom. I just needed to get away from him for a few minutes to regroup. I figured going into the bathroom and washing my face would snap me out of this funk I was presently in. And as much as I wanted to get over what had happened back in the bedroom, I couldn't. So hopefully, after I went off by myself, I'd be able to move forward with this job with a clear head. Leaving out of here with a bunch of shit clogging up my mind wouldn't be a wise thing to do. Whether I wanted to or not, I knew I gotta get my shit together. After all the years of shying away from having women as best friends, now I wished I had one, because I couldn't go to Nashad to get advice about my situation with Aiden and I couldn't go to Aiden and ask for advice about dealing with the situation with Nashad. What was a girl to do?

"I'll be back in five minutes," I told him, and then I walked off.

CHAPTER 13

BOYS IN THE HOOD

Ava suggested that we roll out to the Norview area of Norfolk because that's where her ex-nigga Nu-Nu had a trap house. The trap house was near five points on Alexander Street. It was good that it was dark outside. Getting intel on street niggas is best done at night. Driving around in different hoods in the daytime is for amateurs. Plus, you'd mess around and get shot, too, staring at niggas while you're driving by them. Real hustlers don't play that shit. And considering what Ava said about these niggas, it was not gonna be an easy job to get them. So I knew that I had to be on my A game when I went in for the kill.

"Nu-Nu's trap house is on the right," she said as she slowed her speed down.

"Which house?" I wanted to know.

"It's that brick duplex," she replied as she pointed in the direction.

I looked into the direction she was pointing and saw the brick house. I also saw a group of niggas standing outside of that spot. It couldn't tell who was who, so I asked Ava to take a look. "Do you see any of the niggas that was in those pictures?" I asked her.

"Yeah, I see four of them. The other guys standing out there with them I don't know."

"Which are the ones you recognize?"

"The guy with the blue fitted cap on is Eric. The guy standing next to him in the green jacket is Monty. Calvin and Big Mel are the guys slap boxing each other."

"Is that what those dumb niggas are doing?"

"Yeah, they do it all the time."

"I see the lights on in the apartment. Do you think Nu-Nu is in there?" I asked Ava.

"No, he's not there. I don't see his car."

"What kind of car does he have?"

"A black Porsche Panamera with tinted numbers."

"So do you know who's driving that Lexus with the rims?"

"I think that's Monty's car."

"Are you sure?" I wanted to know.

"Yes, I'm sure," Ava continued as she cruised by everyone on the block. Unfortunately for us, only four of the guys were outside when Ava and I rode by. I wished I could've seen the rest of them. But it was okay. Tonight was still young.

"Since Nu-Nu wasn't out here, where do you think he could be right now?" I asked Ava, who by this time had made a left turn from the block onto the next street.

"He's either at his crib or at this bitch's house I heard he's fucking with right now."

"Well, let's go and see," I insisted.

"I'm on it," she told me and sped up the street.

CHAPTER 14

TWO DOWN, SEVEN TO GO

The drive to Nu-Nu's side bitch's apartment was a hop, skip, and a jump from the trap house on Alexander Street. It was a five-minute drive, so Aiden and I got there in no time. Just as fate would have it, Nu-Nu's Porsche was parked outside of his side bitch's house. Her name was Tiffany, and she lived in one of the Oak Mount North apartments off of Chesapeake Boulevard. Oak Mount North was a low-income-housing neighborhood so she wasn't living in anything fancy. It was one step up from the projects.

Tiffany was a twenty-seven-year-old stripper chick Nu-Nu had been fucking on and off for a year now. She was an average looking ho. She, along with some of her other stripper friends, paid top dollar to get breast enhancements and booty shots to look more appealing while they were on stage. Tiffany couldn't hold a candle to me, so I've always wondered why that nigga chose her over me. Anyway, it didn't matter now. He was going to be dead in less than forty-eight hours, so he did me a favor by leaving. Good riddance.

I drove into the complex slowly. The buildings were built in a horseshoe configuration so when you drove into the neighborhood you had to drive in a circle. Halfway around, I finally came to the apartment where Tiffany lived. "There's the house right there," I told Aiden as I pointed at a bottom-floor apartment. Nu-Nu's car was indeed parked outside, and Tiffany's beat-up Honda Civic was parked next to it. I was surprised to see that she wasn't at work yet. But when I looked at my watch, it dawned on me that she always worked the eleven p.m. to eight a.m. shift.

"I wonder how many people are in there?" Aiden asked aloud.

"Tiffany got two kids. So it's probably him, her, and her kids."

"So you don't think none of his niggas are in there with them?"

"If they were, more cars would be out here," I explained to him while I slowed the truck down. I didn't come to a straight stop because I didn't want to bring any attention to us. It was important for us to stay under the radar this entire time.

"Does Nu-Nu be here all the time?" Aiden asked me.

"Yes, he is. But if he's not here then he's chilling at his stash spot," I replied as I continued to drive around the horseshoe.

"How far is the stash house?"

"It's about ten minutes from here."

"Well, let's hit it, then," Aiden instructed me. "We gotta get this shit popping so we can get the rest of our dough so we can bounce from this whack-ass city," he continued as he turned his focus toward the cars in front of us.

While I was driving to Nu-Nu's stash house, I couldn't help but think about Nashad. The fact that he was going to be back in town in three days made my heart dance with joy. The flip side to that was trying to figure out how I was going to see him after I move Aiden out of the apartment. It was going to be really hard especially with Aiden sniffing up my ass like he was doing. I knew Aiden was going to try to do everything within his power to keep tabs on me. I also knew that if he had the slightest idea that I was sneaking around to see and be with

Nashad, shit was going to hit the fan. So how was I going to make this shit work? Ugh!

Finally we made it to the stash house located down in the Ocean View section of Norfolk off Pretty Lake Avenue and Fourth Bay. The lighting situation on Pretty Lake Avenue was pretty much nonexistent; I thought Aiden and I could use this in our favor. "You see this?" I pointed to a dimly lit streetlight at the corner of the block while I cruised by it.

"You talking about the light?"

"Yeah."

"What about it?"

"Do you see any more?" I asked him after the truck passed it.

"No."

"Exactly. Now take a look at the brown vinyl siding house on the left of us."

"Okay, I see it."

"Can you see anything else over there?"

"It's dark as fuck over there. I can see a car, though. Can't tell you what kind it is."

"My point exactly," I said and quickly made a U-turn in the middle of the street, but I made sure I was about thirty feet away from the stash house before I did it.

"I don't get it," Aiden said.

After I turned the truck around, I slowly drove back past the house and said, "This will be a good spot to get rid of everybody coming out of that house, because it's so dark over there. No one is going to see us do it."

"Fuck, yeah, sis! Good job," Aiden replied and gave me a high-five. "So when are we doing it?" he continued.

"We're gonna do it tonight. If my memory serves me, Nu-Nu only has two to three guys at each house at a time: one to collect the money when the drug addicts come knocking; the other one passes the drugs to the buyer, and the last guy watches everyone's back," I explained as I drove back in the direction I had come from.

"So if there's gonna be three guys in there, how do you think we should run up on them?" Aiden wanted to know.

I pulled the truck over to the curb on the next block. Then I turned the ignition and the headlights off. I didn't want to bring any attention to us. I wanted the truck to look like no one was inside. "I've got the advantage because they know me, so if I go up to the door and lure their dumb asses outside, they aren't gonna be suspicious."

"What are you going to say to them?"

"I haven't figured that part out yet."

"Well, figure it out, because we can't sit here all night. If somebody drives by and see this truck and then they later hear that somebody got killed, they're gonna tell the cops that they saw this truck. And who knows, they may get the license plate numbers, and then we'd really be fucked because you know if they get in touch with the nigga that owns this, he's gonna sing like a canary and tell the police everything about you. And after that happens, you're gonna appear on *America's Most Wanted*."

"Aiden, the Norfolk city cops ain't gonna put me on *America's Most Wanted*. They don't give a shit about drug dealers. If anything, we're doing their asses a favor by getting rid of the motherfuckers. Killing those niggas gives the cops less paperwork to do."

"Yeah, you got a point there." Aiden chuckled after I made my speech. "Okay, so are you going to get all of them to come out of the house at the same time?"

"Do you think I should?"

Aiden thought for a moment, and then he said, "First things first, knock on the door and find out who's in there and if there's two or three niggas in there. If you find out that all those niggas are in there, then invite one of them to come outside. Say you're in the neighborhood, and you came by to see if Nu-Nu is there. And when they say he's not, then tell the same nigga that you got a home girl in the car that you want to introduce him to. If he bites the bait, then I'll be there to take his ass out. Got it?"

"Okay, so I get everything you're saying. But where are you gonna be by the time I lure the first guy out the house?" I wanted to know. I needed to be clear on everything Aiden was saying. We couldn't afford any fucking mishaps.

"I noticed there's a big-ass tree near the front porch. I think that would be a good spot to hide."

"All right. Well, there you go. Let's get this job done," I said.

"Why don't you get out of the truck first so I can make sure no one is watching us?" Aiden suggested.

"It's completely pitch dark out here. No one is going to see us," I assured him.

"Just go up to the house before they leave and then we're fucking screwed," he replied sarcastically.

I opened the driver's-side door. "Yeah, yeah, yeah…" I said, and then I slid out of the seat and closed the door.

The moment I took the first step toward the stash house my heart rate picked up, and before I could blink my eyes fear engulfed me. So many things started running through my mind while I headed toward Nu-Nu's stash house. My first thought was: What if there were more than three guys there? Then I started thinking about what if nobody wants to come outside? What if they're on to me and know that I'm trying to set them up? Where would that leave me? As crazy and insane as those niggas were, they would kill me on the spot. And I wasn't trying to die. I've got a life to live so I was crossing my fingers that this plan worked.

I looked back at the truck at least five times before I got within fifty feet of the stash house. One part of me wanted to turn back and walk back to the truck, but the other part of me convinced me to do it because of the amount of money that was involved. Aiden and I had never had that much money at one time. Shit, the most we've ever seen was probably two thousand dollars. And now that I thought about it, it may not have been that much. Nevertheless, Aiden and I took on the job so we must go through with it.

Now before I made the left turn to walk up the driveway, I looked back at the truck for the last and final time, and that was when I saw Aiden walking my way. Boy, did I feel a load of pressure lift off me. Now it didn't feel like I was alone on this mission.

Immediately after I walked up the driveway I took a deep breath and exhaled while my heartbeat raced at an uncontrollable speed. "Just calm down and relax, Ava, you can do it, girl," I said, giving myself a pep talk.

I took the first step on the stairs and then I took another step. There were a total of five steps all together, so after I hiked all of them, I came face-to-face with the front door. I could see the light on in the front of the house, so I knew that was where those niggas were. I forced myself to knock on the door lightly. I refused to alarm those niggas like I was the cops or something.

"Who is it?" I heard a male's voice ask.

My heart started beating even faster. It felt like I was about to have an anxiety attack. But I knew I couldn't. Showing signs of fear would derail my entire plan.

"It's me—Ava," I finally said after taking another deep breath and exhaling. I even rubbed my hands across my chest, hoping this would calm my nerves down.

"Ava who?" the same guy yelled through the door.

"It's me—Ava. Nu-Nu's ex-girlfriend," I yelled back.

I took it the guy on the other side of the door must've heard my voice because he opened the door immediately after I yelled back through the door. I stood there still as I looked up at the guy standing before me. I recognized him as Trey. Trey was Nu-Nu's younger brother. I hoped like hell he remembered who I was.

"Hey what's up, stranger?" I said, forcing myself to smile.

"Where I know you from?" he asked me.

"Who is that out there?" I heard another guy yell.

"It's me, Ava. I used to mess with your brother Nu-Nu," I explained.

"Oh, hey, what's up?" Trey replied.

"Who she say she was?" the other guy asked, and then he appeared over Trey's shoulder.

When he showed his face I immediately recognized him, too. His name was Al. He was Nu-Nu and Trey's cousin. Trey and Al were both in their early twenties. They were Nu-Nu's muscle. If Nu-Nu told these idiots to gun somebody down, they'd do it in a heartbeat. That's how recklessly they lived their lives. I just hoped that the plan Aiden and I had set tonight worked.

"It's Nu-Nu's old girl, Ava," Trey said.

Al smiled. "So you used to fuck with my cousin, huh?"

I smiled back at him. "If you wanna call it that," I said, feeling a little relieved that he had lightened the mood.

"Whatcha doing out here?" Trey wanted to know.

I thought for a second, trying to remember what I was supposed to say. But I completely lost my train of thought. You should have seen how Trey and Al were looking at me. Once again, anxiety consumed me.

"You a'ight?" Trey asked me.

I chuckled, trying to remain calm. "I'm sorry. When you said something I completely lost my train of thought," I told Trey.

"Oh, shit! My bad. So, what's up anyway?" His questions continued.

"Well, I was in the neighborhood and thought about Nu-Nu and was hoping I could catch him over here," I lied. I swear, this was not what I was supposed to say. I was supposed to convince them to come outside, not tell 'em I was looking for Nu-Nu. Damn! I fucked up! Ugh!

"Nah, he ain't here," Al spoke up.

"Yeah, he don't come out here like that no more. He supposed to be at the other spot in Norview. Do you have his new number?" Trey said.

"Nope," I said, standing there trying to figure out what else to say. I needed to get these guys outside so Aiden could make his move.

"Trey, call your brother for Ava," Al suggested.

"Nah, you ain't gotta do that," I interjected as I watched Trey pull his cell phone from his pocket.

"Why you don't want him calling Nu-Nu? Didn't you come over here to see him?" Al said. He gave me this look of suspicion. I didn't know what else to say. So, without thinking about it, I snatched the cell phone from his hands and ran off the porch with it.

"What the fuck!" I heard Trey say as I heard his footsteps coming from behind me. I heard Al's footsteps, too.

"Get that bitch, Trey!" I heard Al say.

The moment I got to the driveway, I made the sharp left turn to run by the bush where Aiden said he was going to be. But right after I made that turn Trey caught up with me and hit me in the back of my head. I couldn't tell you what he hit me with, but I do know that it hurt really bad, because I hit the ground hard. *BOOM!*

"Give me my cell phone, you stupid bitch!" I heard Trey say, while tugging on the back of my shirt. Before I could react I saw feet coming from behind the bush, and then I heard a whip-cracking sound fly through the air, and when Trey flopped down on my back I screamed out of fear. "Aggghh."

"What the fuck?!" Al roared, and then he turned around to make a run for it. But Aiden sprinted behind him.

By the time I moved Trey's lifeless body off me, Aiden was walking back in my direction. After I stood up, I reached down to the ground and grabbed Trey's cell phone. My fingerprints were all over it, so I wasn't about to let the cops get their hands on it. They wouldn't pull my DNA off of it. No way!

"Come on, let's get out of here," Aiden said as he grabbed my arm. While he escorted me away from Trey's body I caught a glimpse of Al's body not too far away. Aiden had shot him in his back so he was lying facedown near the porch.

"Don't you think we should go in the house and take their shit to make it look like a robbery?" I suggested.

"No. Let's get out of here before the cops get here."

"All right," I said and walked side by side with him as we headed back toward the truck.

Thankfully, no cars drove by while Aiden and I were making our escape. But most important, I was thankful that Aiden's and my plan succeeded, and now we could move on to our next victims. *Two down, seven to go.*

CHAPTER 15

NO MORE SLIP-UPS

The plan that Ava and I had laid out didn't go so well back at the stash house. I couldn't believe that she almost fucked the whole incident up. While I was unscrewing the silencer I had to pick Ava's brain to find out what happened. "You all right?" I started off.

"Yeah, I'm good," she said as she made her way out of the Ocean View area of Norfolk.

"What fuck happened back there? You completely forgot what you were supposed to do."

"Aiden, I don't know what happened. I mean, I was rehearsing what I was going to say over and over while I was walking to the house, but as soon as Nu-Nu's brother opened the door my mind went blank. I tried thinking really hard but that shit wouldn't come to my mind at all."

"Is that why you took his damn cell phone?"

"No. I took his fucking cell phone because he was getting ready to call his brother Nu-Nu. I couldn't let that happen. If Trey would've been able to make that call to Nu-Nu, we would've been fucked!"

"Yeah, we would've. That's why I was about two seconds from running up on the porch," I replied.

"I'm glad I reacted the way I did because who knows what would've happened if you ran on the porch and shot Trey but Al got away? It also could've been another guy in the house, too."

"Yeah, I thought about that, too," I told her. This murder-for-hire gig Ava and I did tonight was going to have to run smoother than this the next time. I mean, she could've gotten hurt or, worse, shot. I wouldn't be able to live with myself if something had happened to her on my watch. Like I said, the next time we went out and made our rounds, we were going to have to be on point.

When Ava got us back to the apartment I retreated to the couch and turned on the television to see if the news media had gotten wind of what happened. I mean, it was highly likely that they wouldn't, considering I had just smoked those niggas. But in the world of social media, half the time you just don't know.

Ava went into the bedroom and closed the door. My first thought was that she was going to try to get that nigga Nashad on the phone. So I got up and walked to the bedroom door to see if I could hear anything. But when I heard the shower water running I felt relieved, and that's when I walked away from the bedroom door.

I returned to the living room and sat down on the couch. I sat there for at least thirty minutes, and nothing came on television. No breaking news. Nothing. But then I heard a cell phone ringing. I jumped to my feet and raced down the hallway. I tried to open the bedroom door, but it was locked. That bothered me. It actually infuriated me. So I started knocking on the door. "What is it?" Ava yelled through the door.

"Open the door," I demanded.

"For what? I just got out of the shower," she replied.

"I heard your cell phone ringing," I roared.

"That wasn't my phone Aiden. It's the cell phone I took from Nu-Nu's brother, Trey," she said.

"Open the door," I instructed her once again, because I didn't believe what she was telling me.

"Give me a second," she said, and then I didn't hear anything. All the movement in the bedroom went silent. I started knocking on the door.

"Why is it taking you so long to open the door?" I questioned her.

After waiting for what seemed like forever, Ava finally unlocked the bedroom door. When she opened it, it was just slightly ajar. "Here, see it for yourself," she told me and handed me the cell phone she had taken from that guy. Immediately after I took the phone from her she closed the bedroom door.

I turned around and headed back into the living room. I sat back on the couch for the third time and threw all of my focus to the cell phone in my hand. I looked at the call log and realized that Ava hadn't been lying. The ringing I had heard did come from this phone. When I looked closely, I noticed the call had come from Nu-Nu. I wanted to call back and tell that weak-ass nigga that his brother was dead, but I knew it wouldn't be a good idea to do so. I was being paid a hefty amount of money to get rid of the whole crew; I'd be a fool to fuck that up. So, instead of calling that nigga back, I looked through the entire call list and saw phone numbers for all the niggas I was supposed to kill. Ava's picking this up was the best thing she could've ever done. If I planned the rest of these jobs just right, I'd be able to kill every one of these niggas and do it quickly.

As I continued to look through this phone I read a lot of the text messages he had sent and received from different chicks. This guy was definitely a lady's man. Lucky for them, none of them were at the stash house when he got murked, because I would've had to put a bullet in their asses, too. Since they dodged my bullet, I wondered how many of them were going to show up at his funeral. Judging from the number of chicks in his DM, they were going to come in droves.

CHAPTER 16

REALITY CHECK

Aiden was about to run me fucking crazy! The fact that he tried to come in the bedroom when he heard the cell phone ringing blew my fucking mind. And then when I told him to give me a second to cover myself up, he acted like I was lying to him. That shit pissed me off. It irritated me to no end too. I mean, he knew he could count on me. Was he becoming obsessed with me or what? He was starting to act more like a stalker than a brother, so I was going to have do something about that before it really got out of hand.

Once I slipped into a pair of shorts and a t-shirt, I joined Aiden in the living room. As soon as I entered the room I noticed that Trey's cell phone really had him focused. "Whatcha doing?" I asked him as I took a seat on the sofa across from him.

"I just got done reading the text messages that he got from a lot of chicks he was fucking," Aiden replied like he was amused.

"Did you find out whether that call you heard came from that cell phone?" I wanted to know.

Aiden looked up at me and gave me a half smile. "Yeah, I saw it," he admitted.

"Now tell me how you felt after you saw it."

"I felt relieved."

"Okay, well, what if you would've found out that I was lying?"

"I would've been really angry," he said as he continued to look through Trey's cell phone.

"Listen," I started off saying, but was abruptly cut off when Trey's cell phone started ringing once again. I watched Aiden look down at the caller ID while I moved to the edge of the sofa and held my breath. "It's Nu-Nu," Aiden told me.

I finally exhaled when I realized I couldn't hold my breath anymore. "What should I do?" he asked me.

"Don't answer it," I replied sarcastically. I mean what kind of freaking question is that? Does he want me to tell him to answer it and tell Nu-Nu that his brother and cousin are both dead? I knew one thing, Aiden needed to get his shit together, because whether he knew it or not, he was acting like he's falling apart.

Finally the cell phone stopped ringing, and that's when our eyes locked. And right when I was about to speak, Trey's cell phone started ringing again. Aiden and I looked at the cell phone and then we looked at each other. "That's Nu-Nu again, huh?" I asked him.

Aiden nodded.

"Turn the cell phone off," I instructed him.

"Why?" Aiden questioned me.

"I know Nu-Nu. He's calling Trey because he knows something is wrong. And besides, I know they use their cell phones for GPS too. So turn it off because one of those niggas might activate the phone locator app and find out that we have his brother's phone. Believe me, shit would get real ugly if he ever caught us with the cell phone," I warned Aiden. But Aiden wasn't trying to hear that shit. I've always known my brother would never back down from anybody, especially some niggas way younger than he was.

"And he's going to find out exactly what it is too," Aiden commented as he powered off the cell phone. The moment he turned it off, he placed it on the coffee table in front of him.

"I wonder if the cops are at the stash house yet."

"You see how fucking dark it was out there. There's no way the cops know about those niggas that quick," Aiden said, then stood.

"Where you going?" He was about to walk off in the middle of our conversation.

"Into the kitchen to get some water."

"Have you thought about when we're gonna do our next hit?" I wanted to know. Nashad would be home in a couple of days, so this assassin shit needed to be over and done with in less than forty-eight hours.

"I was thinking about going out tomorrow night. Hitting them in the dark is the best way to get rid of them."

"Yeah, I think you're right," I agreed.

"So have you thought about how we're going to do it?" I wanted more answers. I didn't want to fuck up like I did the last time.

Aiden stopped in the middle of the floor and turned to face me. "You know what?" he started off saying. "You said that Nu-Nu can track his brother's cell phone with the GPS system, right?"

"Yeah, why?"

"Well, we're gonna use the GPS to locate those niggas too."

"How?"

"Tomorrow night when we leave, you can run everyone's number in Trey's cell phone and track all the niggas on Nu-Nu's payroll. The GPS will also tell us how many of them will be around each other at the same locations. So if we run it to-morrow morning it may say that each of those niggas are by themselves, and if that's the case, then it would be real easy to take. Do you follow me?"

"Yeah, loud and clear."

"Are you going to be on your A game tomorrow?"

"Of course I am," I assured him.

"Yeah, we'll see," he commented, and then he went into the kitchen.

CHAPTER 17

WHAT'S REALLY GOING ON?

Today was the day that Ava and I would go out to meet up with our next victim. Before we left the apartment I grabbed the two photos that Winston's cousin had given me and crossed off Trey's and Al's faces with a black marker while Ava was in the kitchen fixing herself a bowl of cereal. After she poured the milk in the bowl and put the carton of milk back into the refrigerator, she joined me in the living room.

After she sat down on the couch across from me, I said, "I'm going to need more bullets."

"Don't worry about that. Nashad has a box full of them."

"Good. So I was thinking that we do what we talked about last night. You know, running a GPS on the other cell phones so we can find out where everybody else is at."

"Hold up a minute. Let's turn on the TV. I want to see if the cops found their bodies," Ava suggested between chews of her food.

I picked up the remote control and powered on the television. I turned to every news channel we could get, and no one was talking about the two murders we did last night. This shocked me. "Go on the Internet with your cell phone and find out if any of these news stations around here know about the murders," I instructed her.

I watched Ava as she took another mouthful of cereal, and then she set the bowl down on the coffee table. Then she took her cell phone from her pocket and powered it on. "Did you just turn your phone back on?" I asked her.

She gave me this blank stare. "Yeah, why?" she asked me.

"Why would you turn it off?"

"Aiden, I turned my cell phone off last night before we went to the stash house and never turned it back on," she explained.

"But you're still not telling me why you turned it off?" I pressed the issue. Once again she was making me feel like I couldn't trust her. This began to anger me all over again.

"Haven't you seen *Dateline* and *The First 48* TV shows? Where the cops tell suspects that they knew they were near a crime scene because their cell phones pinged from a nearby cell tower?"

"Yeah."

"Well, that's what I did," she said.

I sat there and gave her a look of uncertainty. But I will say that the longer I sat there, the more her explanation made sense. "Okay, I can believe that," I finally said, and then I smiled at her. But I don't think she was in the mood to smile back at me.

"Why are you constantly putting me in situations where I have to explain everything to you? I mean, you act like I'm your wife or something."

"I don't act like that."

"Then tell me what you call it? Because you're running me insane behind it."

"I'm just trying to keep you on point because I know how niggas are. They start talking that sweet shit to you so they can get your ass in bed, and then after they fuck you that's when they start treating you like shit."

"So that's what you think Nashad is going to do to me?"

"All niggas do that shit to chicks. You should've heard the shit niggas was talking about while I was locked up. They don't respect y'all. All they want from women is sex and a home-cooked meal. That's it. So do you think I'm going to sit around and let the nigga that live here mistreat you? Fuck that! I'll kill that nigga first."

"Aiden, not everybody is like those guys you were locked up with." Ava tried to reason, but I wasn't listening to her. I knew what the hell I'm talking about, so I would not change my mind about it.

"Look, Ava, I said what I had to say about it. None of these niggas out here is good enough for you. And that's just how it's gonna be."

"So that's it. I have no say on how I wanna live my life, huh?"

"That about sizes it up."

"All right," she said, and then she proceeded to access the Internet on her cell phone. I watched her while she sifted through one of the news station's websites. "I don't see anything on here," she said.

"Which station was that?" I asked her.

She hesitated like she didn't want to open her mouth. But after a few seconds passed, she said. "It was WAVY TV ten."

"I know you're mad with me, but know that I'm only doing it because I love you and don't want you to get hurt," I expressed.

She let out a long sigh and said, "I don't wanna continue to talk about that."

"All right, I'm good with that," I assured her. "Are you on the other news station's site?" I changed the subject.

"Yeah."

"Which one?"

"Thirteen News Now."

"Do you see anything up there?" I asked her.

"Wait, I'm trying to see now," she answered, and then she

fell silent. So I sat there and waited patiently for her to give me an answer. After three minutes had passed, I asked her the same question again. "Do you see anything yet?"

"Can you wait a minute? I'm pulling down all of the website's menu bars to see if they'd have it listed underneath there. But so far I don't see anything," she finally responded.

"Well, go to WTKR three."

"I'm already on it," she replied, swiping her phone's screen.

Once again, I had to wait for her to give me the news about whether or not the murders had been reported by this station. And after waiting for a few minutes, she finally said no.

"No," I repeated.

"Yeah, no. I don't see shit up here about Nu-Nu's brother Trey or Al," she assured me.

"What's really going on?"

"That's a good question."

"What if they're not dead? What if some other niggas came right after we left and took them to a hospital?" I asked Ava. I needed some fucking answers, and right now I was not getting them.

"Calm down, Aiden, they were dead when we left them lying on the ground. Now I can't tell you why they are not in the fucking news, but I am certain that they aren't alive."

"So where the fuck are their bodies at?"

"I don't know."

"Well, before we make our moves on anybody else, we gotta find out where those niggas are. All right?"

"Yeah, all right."

CHAPTER 18

SURVEILLANCE TIME

My brother was acting like a fucking weirdo! He had literally become this delusional guy from outer space. He either had mental issues or was just plain ol' fucking weird to think that I won't be with another man. The way this thing was going, I might have to get missing in action with this guy. I'm talking about taking half of the money he'd already given me and leaving this fucking town for good. I couldn't see any other way to do it because he'd made it perfectly clear that I would never have a life with a man while he was around. Ugh! He was so freaking nerve-wracking. I knew he meant well, but needed to take his paranoia elsewhere, because I refused to be torn between two men. I wouldn't ever tell him not to be with a chick. I would welcome it with open arms, especially if she wasn't a ho. So I figured he should do the same thing for me.

Immediately after I couldn't find anything on the Internet related to Trey and Al's murders, I suggested we take a ride back to Ocean View and roll by the stash house to see if any activity had happened since we left last night. Aiden stressed that we bring Trey's cell phone with us, but leave it turned off until we needed to track the other niggas down.

As Aiden stepped to the front door, I said, "Here, take these bullets," and handed him a box of bullets I had gotten from Nashad's stash.

Aiden stuffed the ammo down into his pants pocket and headed out the front door. I followed him.

After we got into the truck, I felt an uneasy chill come upon me. It felt like someone was watching me. When I looked around my immediate area, I didn't see anything out of the ordinary, and that bothered me because I'm pretty good when it comes to spotting stuff out of place. But instead of wracking my brain, I started up the truck and headed back into the streets.

"When we get close to Ocean View, I'm gonna power on Trey's phone to see if we can find out where the rest of the crew is," I mentioned.

"Yeah, let's do that," he replied.

"Are you nervous because the news media isn't broadcasting the murders?"

"My main focus is you. Before I shot those niggas, they saw you. They were in your face. And then you stole their phone. So you know I've gotta feel some type of way because I don't want them niggas walking around saying that you set them up. Other than that, I don't give a fuck what happened to them," Aiden explained. And I had to agree that he was right. I would be dog shit if those niggas didn't die and were able to tell Nu-Nu that I set them up. Knowing how vengeful Nu-Nu was, he'd hunt me down until he found me. But of course I wouldn't be fazed by him, because Aiden was a psycho-ass nigga. And Aiden wasn't about to ever let a nigga like Nu-Nu get that close to me. No way! It wouldn't happen.

The moment I entered the Ocean View neighborhood, I felt another chill run down my spine. The hairs on my arms even stood up. Aiden noticed it. "You a'ight?" he asked me.

"I got a little nervous all of a sudden," I told him.

"Well, calm your ass down. You know I ain't gonna let nothing happen to you."

"I know that. It's just that I don't like surprises. And I feel like as soon as we ride by the stash house, there's going to be a surprise waiting for us."

"Well, if you feel like that, then don't do it. Just pull the truck over on the side of the road when you come within a half of mile to the spot, and I'll walk the rest."

"No, you don't have to do that. I'm gonna take you all the way."

"Are you sure, Ava? Because walking to the spot don't mean shit to me."

"No, it's okay. I'll take you," I insisted and continued to drive in the direction of the stash house. I sat up in the truck and I looked straight ahead mulling over in my mind how I was going to act the second I rode by the stash house. Then I thought about what if I rode by the house and saw the cops out there? Or what if I rode by it and Nu-Nu or some of the other guys were there? How would I react then? I knew I couldn't do the same shit I did last night, because if that happened, I might not get the same result as last time. Long story short, I needed to be on my toes.

As I approached Pretty Lake Avenue, my heart started beating erratically. The palms of my hands started sweating profusely, even though it was sixty-five degrees outside. How could this be? My mind was telling me I could handle this mission, while my heart sung a different tune. To be perfectly honest, I just wanted all of this bullshit to be over. I wished I could snap my fingers and everyone else in the crew would be dead and Aiden and I could collect the rest of the money. He'd take his part. I'd take my part, and everything would be done.

"I don't see any cop cars," I mentioned as I cruised toward the stash house. Aiden leaned forward in the passenger seat so he could get a better look. We couldn't see the stash house yet because the house next to it blocked it, but we could see part of the driveway. But as we drove closer, the front of the stash house became more visible.

Aiden and I locked eyes on the front porch and noticed that the front door was closed. "Somebody has been there," I uttered. And then Aiden and I looked down at the ground around the front of the house. We scanned that immediate area with our eyes while I cruised by the house. "Do you see anything?" I asked Aiden.

"Nope. I don't see shit!" he replied.

"What the fuck is going on? Where are those niggas bodies?" I huffed. And as bad as I wanted to stop the truck, I knew it wouldn't be a good idea to do that. I've had myself enough of run-ins with the cops to know that there was a huge possibility that they could be staked out in this area watching this stash house and all the movement around it. Cops think they are slick as hell, but I've always found myself a couple of steps ahead of them at all times.

"I don't know. So let's get out of here before somebody sees us," Aiden said.

I followed his instructions and cruised back out of the neighborhood. "Where do you think we should go now?" I wanted to know. I needed some directions because I had started having mixed feelings about everything that was going on.

"Let's ride by the girlfriend's house in Oak Mount North," he replied. "No, better yet, turn on the cell phone so we can track and see where the rest of the niggas are," Aiden continued.

About two miles out of the Ocean View area, I pulled the truck to the side of the road and powered on Trey's cell phone. After the phone powered up and I saw that it didn't have a security lock, I went into the settings and clicked on the tracking app.

"How long is that going to take?" Aiden wanted to know.

"Not long."

"I met this white girl in the lobby of the parole office who told me about all the fraud shit she used to do, and hacking cell phones was one of them. She told me that you could do all sorts of things with people's phones. But the one thing that stuck out with me was when she told me how to use some-one's phone to track another one. Using the cell phone num-bers from Trey's call log, we can find his crew on a GPS map," I explained as I showed Aiden the phone. I watched as his eyes lit up.

"Yo, Ava, you fucking did it!" He got excited. "But whose phone is that?" he asked, pointing at the image on the screen.

I smiled and turned the phone back toward me. "I'm not sure, but I think it's Nu-Nu's. Wait, let me check," I told him and then I closed the window of the GPS and opened up the text window to see if I could find correspondence from the number I assumed to be Nu-Nu's new cell phone number. After sifting through the text messages, I finally found the number that matched with the number on the call log. I read the first message: "*Bae where r u? I been calling u all nite. Hit me back.*" The second message read, "*Trey u coming by my crib 2nite?*" And the third message read, "*Will u call me back please. U bet not be wit a bitch!*" After I read the last message, it was very clear that this cell phone number belonged to a woman. Aiden knew it too.

"Sounds like she wanted to get fucked last night!" Aiden chuckled.

"You got that too, huh?" I agreed, and then I scrolled down to another cell phone number in the text message section. "Hey, wait, I found something," I told Aiden. I showed him the text while I read it out loud. "*Yo lil bruh, wen u done holla at me. Dis time we got a missile.*" Immediately after I read the text I looked at Aiden. "That's Nu-Nu," he said and smiled.

I smiled back. "Yep, it sure is," I said, and then I pro-grammed Nu-Nu's cell phone number to my memory. After I came out of the text message screen I pulled the GPS tracker up and typed in Nu-Nu's cell phone. And just like that, I got a hit. The red dot started illuminating that instant. I zoomed in on the location of the map. "He's not in Oak Mount North at

Tiffany's house. He's in Norview, at the trap house," I told Aiden.

Right when Aiden was about to speak, Trey's cell phone started ringing. It scared the shit out of me. I looked at Aiden, and he looked back at me. "Is it Nu-Nu?" Aiden asked me.

"No. It's coming from another number. Should I answer it?"

"Fuck, no!" Aiden said and snatched the cell phone from my hand. "I'm turning this shit off!"

I sat there motionless. I didn't know what to say or do at this point after Aiden snatched Trey's cell phone from my hands.

"Come on, let's go," he said, and then he threw the cell phone into the glove compartment.

"Where are we going?" I asked him.

"To the trap house," he replied.

Without saying another word, I put the gear in drive and sped off in the direction of Norview.

CHAPTER 19

MISSION ACCOMPLISHED

The whole time Ava was driving I was trying to figure out how I was going to bust all these caps in those niggas' asses. I wanted to plan something out, but that shit didn't work out the last time. I refused to allow her or myself to slip up this time around.

While I was thinking about the options I had, I couldn't get my mind off the fact that none of the news stations in this area had reported the murders. That just seemed so odd to me. Not only that, the front door of the stash house was closed and none of the bodies were still lying on the ground. What happened there? Where were the bodies?

"We're about two blocks away from Alexander Street," Ava announced. She looked nervous as hell.

"Are you okay?" I asked her.

"I will be when all of this is over," she replied.

"Don't worry, it's gonna be over very soon. And then we can collect the rest of the money and leave this shit-hole town," I told her.

"Have you figured out what you're gonna do? I mean, am I just supposed to ride by there or what?"

"I'll let you know as soon as I see what's going on outside the spot."

Ava let out a long sigh. "Okay," she said.

Ava finally made the turn onto Alexander Street. From the beginning of the block I noticed that the front of the duplex was empty this time. No one was standing outside like they were last night. There was only one vehicle parked along the side of the street. It was an old model, white four-door Acura. The back of it was facing us. "That's Monty's car right there," Ava blurted out as she pointed to the vehicle.

"Are you sure?" I asked her.

"Oh, shit! It's moving. What should I do?"

"Follow 'em," I instructed her, and then I pulled the pistol with the silencer from the inside of my jacket and placed it on my lap.

"Follow them and what?"

"Just follow the car until I say otherwise," I told her while I watched the car and everything around it. "I don't want the driver to know we're following him so don't follow them too close."

She sucked her teeth. "I'm not."

"Can you see how many niggas in there?" I asked her.

"It looked like it's four of them."

"A'ight," I said and studied the positions that everyone was sitting in.

"We're coming up to a light, and it looks like Monty is going to drive right through it," Ava warned me.

"Well, drive a little bit faster, but do it so they won't notice," I advised her. I really needed to get her to drive at the precise speed so we didn't blow our cover. I knew we had the GPS tracker for these niggas, but finding out firsthand where these niggas hung out at was crucial.

Just like Ava had mentioned, that nigga Monty did run the light, and thankfully Ava was on their asses. But what made it better on our part was that two cars on the left side of us ran the light as well. That shit couldn't have happened at a better time.

"They look like they're going into this Church's Chicken parking lot," Ava said as we both watched the white car slow down with the right turn light flickering on and off. "See, I told you," she continued as the car turned in the parking lot.

"Think they're gonna go inside or what?" I wanted to know.

"No, they're going in the drive thru," Ava said.

"Follow them."

"And do what?"

"Just pull the truck up behind them like we're gonna order some chicken too," I instructed her.

Ava gave me a puzzled expression like she didn't understand what I had just told her to do. "What's wrong?" I asked her.

"I'm just trying to figure out what you're about to do," she said to me.

"Keep driving until you get directly behind them," I replied while I screwed the silencer into the barrel of the gun.

"You're gonna shoot them in broad daylight?" she asked me, her voice sounding weary.

"After I get out of the truck I want you to back this mother-fucker up, turn it around and drive away."

"Where do you want me to drive to?"

"Drive it to the neighborhood across the street from Feather and Fin, and I'll meet you there."

"That's far. How are you going to get there?"

"Don't worry about me. Just do like the fuck I said!" I told her, and then I hopped out of the truck.

Immediately after I slammed the door shut, Ava put the truck in reverse and turned it around. Without stepping on the brakes completely, she sped off. The niggas that were in the white Acura didn't see me coming because they were too preoccupied by the way Ava drove out of the parking lot. So by the time I walked up on them they weren't ready. I opened fire on the driver first so he wouldn't be able to drive off. I shot him in the chest and face. After the niggas realized that I had shot the driver up they scrambled to pull out their guns.

"Oh, shit!" I heard one guy yell.

The other ones yelled, "He just killed Monty!"

Another one said, "Get that nigga!"

But it was too late; while they were looking for their pistols I was filling their asses up with metal. I shot the guy in the front seat in the chest, and he died instantly. The two in the back got it the worst. I offloaded three bullets each into their faces. They wouldn't be able to have an open-casket funeral. After I emptied my clip off on these niggas, I sprinted across the Church's Chicken parking lot and ended up crossing the parking lot of McDonald's too. I heard screaming in the distance but I didn't let that concern me. I had to get out of there before the cops came or someone was able to get a positive ID on me.

CHAPTER 20

DEAD MAN WALKING

I can't believe how fast my heart was beating. At one point I thought that my heart was going to burst through my ribs. Aiden hadn't told me exactly where to fucking go so I parked the truck on the side street where the nightclub Casablanca used to be. This street also was directly across from the Feather & Fin fast food spot too. There was some heavy traffic there so I knew that I wouldn't stick out.

So while I awaited my brother's arrival, all I could think about was why the hell had he jumped out of the truck and blasted those niggas in broad daylight? I swear Aiden is beginning to show me a whole other side to him. I think this last prison bid he did kind of fucked his head up. He never had a problem with beating niggas up. But the way he does it now is reckless. I mean, he acts like he doesn't care who sees him. I just hoped that he was all right and no one would be able to ID the truck. If they did, then I would be fucked because they'd be able to track it right back to me.

I sat in the truck for what seemed like forever. I kept looking down at my wristwatch, and it seemed like the time wouldn't move. One part of me wanted to go and look for my brother. But the other part of me told me to sit tight and that

Aiden would be here in a matter of minutes. So as I sat there I monitored the foot traffic that went in and out of Feather & Fin. I have to admit that Feather & Fin is a favorite fast food restaurant of mine, but as I could see, it was also popular among other black folks. Feather & Fin was also a hangout for dope boys, too. In the short time that I'd been parked here, I noticed two drug deals. I even saw a black, medium-build guy hustling CDs out of the restaurant. Any way a black man could make some money, he did right out of Feather & Fin.

I looked down at my wristwatch again. This time I noticed that ten minutes had gone by. But, unfortunately, Aiden hadn't shown up yet. So I called him. His phone rang three times. "Hello," he answered. I swear I was so happy to hear his voice.

"Where are you?" I wanted to know.

"I'm walking up Princess Anne Road."

"Where at on Princess?"

"I'm walking by the corner store off Cromwell Road."

"Okay, keep walking. I'm less than a block away on the left side. And I'm directly across the street from Feather & Fin. I can literally see everything that's going on over there," I let him know.

"A'ight, well, I'll be there in a second," he told me and disconnected his call.

I was relieved to hear my brother's voice and to know that he was all right. I was about to have a damn fit if I found out that something happened to him. As the truck engine idled, I prepped the questions I was going to ask Aiden once we finally met back up. First I wanted to know if he killed everyone. Then I wanted to know if he was all right. I was talking about mentally and physically. Killing people like he did had to affect you in some way. You just couldn't go and kill someone and not feel something after it was done. I wasn't sure what my brother felt, but I did know that he was a fucking psycho and I was going to need to figure some shit out so I could make my escape when all of this was over.

Two more minutes went by and still no Aiden. "Where the hell are you?" I mumbled underneath my breath. Had he gotten picked up by the cops right after he got off the cell phone with me? I couldn't see it happening that way, so where the fuck was he? Then my cell phone started ringing. I looked at the caller ID and noticed that the number calling said UN-KNOWN. I started not to answer but I did anyway. "Hello," I said.

"Hey, baby," I heard Nashad say.

"Hey to you too," I replied.

"Are you ready to see me tomorrow?" he wanted to know.

"Come on, Nashad, what kind of question is that? You know I miss you like crazy," I told him.

"So you're gonna be ready to give me that pussy when you see me?" Nashad asked me.

I chuckled. "You know I am."

"Okay, well meet me at the gate of pier two at ten p.m. tomorrow night."

"I can't wait," I told him, smiling from ear to ear. Hearing Nashad's sexy voice always put a grin on my face. It was intoxicating, so while I was relishing the moment, I took my eye off the task at hand. While I was melting away, I didn't realize that Aiden had come to stand outside the truck. When I finally turned around and looked at the passenger side door, I saw Aiden glaring at me with the most evil expression I'd ever seen on his face.

My heart instantly dropped to the pit of my stomach while my hands became sweaty all over again. I knew why he was looking at me that way, so I went into damage control mode. "Hey, baby, can you call me back?" I asked Nashad with a sense of urgency.

"What's wrong?" he wanted to know.

But I didn't have time to answer him. Aiden had just pulled the car door open so I disconnected the call. After I pressed the end button, I placed my cell phone on my lap and waited for Aiden to speak first.

"Who was that you were talking to?" he didn't hesitate to ask.

I didn't know whether to lie to this guy or tell him the truth.

"Tell me who you were talking to?" He repeated the question as he slid into the passenger seat and closed the door.

Anxiety engulfed me. But this time my head started spinning in circles like a hamster on a spinning wheel. So while I was trying to figure out what would be the most appropriate answer, Aiden reached over and snatched my cell phone from my lap. I wanted to take the phone from him, but I was frozen solid. Completely paralyzed. I couldn't move one inch. "Let me see what the fuck is going on here," Aiden said as he navigated his way into my call log.

I sat there and watched him. "So, that nigga Nashad just called you, huh?" he asked me, like he had just taken a wild guess. The phone number that Nashad called from was blocked so even if I'd lied to Aiden about the caller being Nashad, something on the inside whispered to me that somehow he would find out later that it was.

"Yeah, but he was only calling me to say that I need to change all the air filters in his apartment," I lied. I swear I don't know where that lie came from, but it came right on time.

"You better not be fucking lying to me!" Aiden hissed. "Now let's get out of here," he continued and then he tossed my cell phone back onto my lap.

"Where are we going?"

"Back to the apartment. We gotta regroup," he told me, and then he turned his attention toward the road in front of us.

There were at least a couple minutes of awkward silence in the truck for the first two minutes of my drive back to the apartment until Aiden finally spoke. "I betcha those murders be on the news," he finally said.

"Did you get everyone?"

"Yep, I got all those niggas. I saw them fall one by one and they didn't even see me coming. They were so busy watching how you barreled out of the parking lot that they didn't realize I was standing there until I killed the driver, Monty," he explained.

"Did you leave any witnesses?" I asked while I maneuvered in and out of traffic. If there was someone following us on our way back to Nashad's apartment, I'd be able to pick it up.

"There were a couple of people that saw me when I let off the first few shots at the driver but after that, they ran."

"Okay, so we can scratch off four more bodies, huh?"

"Yep, we sure can. Now all we got is three left," he said proudly, and then he fell silent all over again.

I didn't say another word. I was more focused on how he kept scaring me when he started questioning me about my personal life. Now that I knew what time to meet Nashad tomorrow night, I had to think of an exit plan: now or never.

CHAPTER 21

THREE SOULS LEFT

I was very proud of myself after taking all those niggas' lives at the same time. That shit was gangster as fuck! And to do it in broad daylight put another notch on my belt. Damn, I wished I could see Nu-Nu's face when he found out that I just ended the lives of four more of this gang. I knew it would be priceless.

"I wanna get the rest of those niggas by tomorrow night," I told Ava.

"Why not tonight?" she asked me.

"Because I know that Nu-Nu and the rest of his gang will be on high alert. There's no way they're going to hang out in the open again. With six of his boys dead, I bet you any amount of money that those cats are gonna go in hiding for at least a few days."

"So if you know they're gonna go into hiding, why don't we find the rest of them now and finish the job?"

"Because it's not gonna be safe."

"I think it will," she kept protesting.

"Okay, I'll tell you what. I'll agree to going out tonight. But if I don't see an easy way to take the rest of the niggas out of their misery, then I'm gonna wait. Got it?"

"Yeah, I got it," she replied while she kept her eyes on the flowing traffic in front of us.

The drive back to the apartment didn't take long at all. Ava got us back there in a matter of eight minutes. Upon entering the apartment, plans about how I should kill the rest of those niggas started coming together in my mind. I just needed to make sure this plan wouldn't get me killed or sent back to prison. So after crossing the threshold of the front door, I took a seat on the couch and laid the pistol and the silencer on the coffee table.

Ava glanced at the gun as she passed it and went into the kitchen. "What's on your mind?" she asked me.

"I'm trying to figure out how I'm going to get the rest of those niggas. I'm ready to finish what I started so we can get the rest of the money and blow this joint," I told her.

"Where do you wanna go when all of this is over?" she asked while she grabbed a bottle of water from the refrigerator.

I changed the subject. "Bring me the black permanent marker and the two Facebook pictures of those niggas. I think I left it on the kitchen counter."

"Could you answer my question please?" Ava said while I watched her pick the pictures up from the kitchen countertop.

"I think we should go to Cali," I finally answered.

"Aiden, Cali is too far away. What if something happens to Mama? We won't be able to come back here and check on her."

"Fuck that bitch! She let those people lock us up. So why should I care about something happening to her. She didn't care about us. Do you know how long it's been since we last saw her?"

"I don't know," Ava replied with uncertainty.

"Well, the last time she saw me was when she let those crackers lock us up because we stole her car. She didn't come visit me one time. So do you think that I'm gonna make her a priority in my life? Hell, no! She's an evil bitch! And I wish she was dead! But since she's not, don't ever bring her name up to me again."

"Okay, I won't," she replied as she stood there before me. Without saying another word, she tossed the two photos of the guys and the black marker onto the coffee table before me and walked away.

I picked up the marker and put an X across the faces of the four guys I had just shot. From the looks of it, I had just murdered Monty, Calvin, Vince, and Big Mel. The last three niggas I had to kill was Keith, Eric, and Nu-Nu. So I wondered to myself when and how that was going to happen.

Ava made it perfectly clear that she wanted it to happen tonight. While I understood her wanting to get these hits over with, she had to also understand that our execution techniques would have to be flawless.

While I was in the living room, and Ava was in the back of the apartment somewhere, I decided to turn on the TV. There was no doubt in my mind that there were news reporters on the scene of the Church's Chicken restaurant in Norfolk because there were witnesses. So immediately after I powered on the television I turned the channel to WAVY TV 10 and what do you know, there was a breaking news live broadcast about the shooting. I became so excited that I jumped to my feet and yelled out Ava's name.

"What happened? What's going on?" she asked me after she rushed into the room where I was.

I pointed toward the television. "Look, they're talking about the murders at the Church's Chicken," I told her.

Ava stood there and watched the news reporter while she delivered the news live. I sat there and watched, too.

"In breaking news, Norfolk police and three coroner's vehicles are on the scene at the Church's Chicken restaurant on Princess Anne Road, where three men were shot and killed while parked in a drive-thru."

"I thought you said you killed all four?" Ava looked at me.

I looked back at the TV as the reporter said, "The fourth victim was carried away from the scene in a paramedic transport. No word how serious his injuries are. There are several investigating officers on the scene as well as a couple of forensic technicians. The entire area of the parking lot of the restaurant is blocked off with yellow homicide tape, so they aren't letting anyone in. I spoke with two witnesses who said they saw a tall, black male open fire on the white Acura parked right there in the drive-thru of the restaurant, and then he fled away on foot. No one can give a good description of the shooter, but they did say that right before the killer opened fire on those men, a black SUV sped out of the parking lot. No word on whether the driver of that SUV and the shooter are related in any way, but one homicide detective confirmed that they would be following up on that lead. He also said that if anyone has any information concerning this unfortunate tragedy, to please call the tip line at 888-LOCKUUP."

"I am going to shit bricks if one of those niggas is still alive!" I spat. I was mad as fuck. I mean, how did I fuck that up? I aimed at all those niggas with precision when I shot them. So why the fuck was one of them still alive? This just didn't make sense to me.

"This is not good," Ava said as she started pacing the living room floor back and forth.

"Fuck!" I roared.

CHAPTER 22

THIS CAN'T BE REAL

I could not believe that one of those guys was still alive. And then to know that a witness saw me leaving the parking lot in a black SUV got me unraveling at the seams. What was I going to do now? What if the witness saw the license plate? And what if the cops were running the tags now? I was going to be up shit's creek without a paddle.

"What are we going to do now?" I questioned Aiden, who was by this time pacing the floor in the kitchen. I stood at the entryway of the kitchen and waited for him to respond.

"I don't know. You are going to have to give me a minute to sort this shit out in my head."

"Do you realize that we may not be able to drive that truck again?"

"You are overreacting. They only said that they saw a black truck leaving the parking lot at the time of shooting. They did not say they had a license plate number. So calm down," he snapped.

"You can say what you want. But I heard what she said," I snapped right back at him.

"Just shut up, will you!?" he barked.

"Yeah, I'll shut up for now. But don't come back to me

later today talking about you need me to take you around town because I am going to tell you no," I threatened, and then I walked away from the entryway of the kitchen.

I thought Aiden was going to walk out behind me, since he does it all the time. I guess he was on some new and improved shit. It's all good, though. After this gig was over I was leaving and never coming back because I wanted a normal life. I was tired of stealing, committing fraud, and fucking men for a place to stay and food to fill up my tummy. I wanted to get married, I wanted a man who was going to love me. I wanted a great sex life, I wanted money, and I wanted to be able to have kids someday. But if I continued to spend most of my time with my brother, none of that shit would happen.

I went back into the bedroom and sat on the edge of the bed. I buried my face in the palm of my hands while I began to feel sorry for myself. Here I was in yet another fucked situation that could land me in jail. In the beginning, I couldn't care less. It was my brother and me against the world. But now I wanted to live a different life. I liked the way I felt when I was with Nashad. So I didn't want to give that up. What Nashad and I had was special and I intended to hold on to it.

A few minutes later, Aiden showed up at the bedroom door. "Listen, I got it. I know what we can do," he started off.

I lifted my face up from my hands and gave him my undivided attention. "What's up?"

"I figured out how we can kill the rest of the guys," he replied. He seemed very excited.

"I'm listening," I said nonchalantly.

"First, we need to go to the hospital and find out which room that guy is in. After we do that, I'm gonna kill him. Then, after that we're gonna use the GPS tracking to take us to the other niggas, and then after we get the locations for them, we go and get those niggas too."

"I see what you are saying, but what if the homicide cops

decide to watch the rest of them because they have a hunch that the whole gang is being targeted?"

"Don't you worry about that. I've got that all under control."

"Apparently you don't. Because if you did, you wouldn't have run up on Monty and the other guys like you did. That was pretty freaking careless. And to know that someone saw the color of the truck I was driving makes me sick to my stomach. Remember, we are driving someone else's vehicle. So do you think it's fair that he gets in trouble because of us?"

"I don't give a fuck about that nigga! And you shouldn't be, either. I told you to leave that situation alone."

"I have," I lied. I refused to let on that I had feelings for Nashad and that I intended to run away with him. And as long as I kept my plans to myself, everything would work out perfectly.

"Look, just get ready because we're going back out tonight," Aiden instructed me, and then he turned around and left.

CHAPTER 23

FALSE ALARM

I knew Ava was pissed off with me but I had got a job to do. And this job didn't come with a fucking manual. She'd better be glad that I wasn't going to kill that nigga that owned this spot.

A few hours passed by and the tension between Ava and me was still thick. She acted like she didn't want to say a word to me until another breaking news story hit the airwaves. This time the TV was changed to channel three, and what the news reporter said made me sit up and take notice.

"In breaking news this afternoon, the African American gunshot victim who was transported to Leigh Memorial Hospital earlier today has been pronounced dead. He was immediately taken into surgery for several gunshot wounds to his face, chest, and head, but there was nothing the ER doctors could do for him. I spoke with one of the relatives of the deceased man, whose name the police have not yet released, who said that these acts of violence need to stop. Once again, if you any information concerning this unfortunate tragedy, please call the tip line at 888-LOCKUUP."

"Yes, that nigga is dead!" I jumped to my feet. "Now, do you feel better?" I asked Ava.

She didn't give me a complete smile, but it was good enough.

"You ready?" I continued.

"Ready for what?" she asked me. She gave me this blank facial expression.

"Ready to go back out. We gotta finish this job."

"Aiden, tonight won't be a good night to leave. I know Nu-Nu. Trust me, he's waiting for us to run up on him. Do you wanna walk into an ambush? Because that's what will happen if we go looking for him."

"Where's your heart?"

"Right here," she replied as she pointed toward her chest.

"Look, you ain't gotta go with me. I'll go by myself," I told her.

"Please don't go by yourself. Let's just wait. Give it one more day," she pleaded with me.

But I wasn't trying to hear her. I had already made up my mind that I was finishing the job tonight. "Look, like I said, if you don't wanna come with me tonight then I'll do the shit alone."

"And how are you going to get there?" she questioned me.

"I'm taking the truck."

"You ain't taking that man's truck. He trusted me with it. And besides, it's too hot right now to be rolling up on niggas."

I wasn't liking the tone of my sister's voice, so I walked over to where she was standing and got in her face. "If you don't drive me where I need to go then I'm taking that nigga's truck," I said, my hands curling into fists. I had to let my sister know who was in charge.

"You know what, Aiden, you're being a dick right now! Ever since you been home, you've been fucking bullying me and I don't like it," she spat.

"You call that shit bullying?"

"You freaking right."

"Well, get over it. Because what I am doing is trying to

protect you. I can't let you go off on your own or stay in this place by yourself. No way. Because if something ever happened to you, I wouldn't be able to live with myself."

"Aiden, I am a grown-ass woman. And what do you think I was doing out here on my own while you were locked up all the time?"

"Barely fucking making it!"

"That's bullshit and you know it."

"Look, Ava, I'm done talking about this shit! You're taking me out to look for these last three cats and that's the end of it," I told her and then I walked away from her.

CHAPTER 24

WHY ME?

Aiden made me so mad that I wanted to choke him to death and leave him lying dead on the floor. I mean, he was like a fucking virus that wouldn't go away. Who acted like this toward their freaking sibling? I almost wanted to ask him if he wanted to fuck me. Because he sure acted like we were more than just family. I needed some fucking help and I needed it now.

Instead of hanging around with him in the living room, I went back into the bedroom and started packing my Puma duffel bag with a few clothes I had collected while I was staying here. I didn't have much, but it was enough for a couple of days. I even stashed fifty thousand dollars of the money Aiden gave me. I didn't want to take the whole sixty-seven thousand. I figured since he and I were going in different directions, he was going to need a little more than me. I mean, after he got paid the other half of sixty-seven thousand, he was going to end up with a total of eighty-four thousand dollars. That's a nice sum of cash to live off of.

So, after I was done packing, I slid the duffel bag underneath the bed so Aiden wouldn't find it. Who knew what he would say if he found it and opened it and saw that I only packed fifty thousand dollars of the money he gave me. Trust me, he'd have questions for me for days. Especially since he gave all the money to me and told me it was mine. So if he found out that I left the rest for him, things would get really ugly. And with his state of mind, he could have done anything at the drop of a dime. And to him, it would have made sense.

After I slid my bag underneath the bed, I climbed on top of the covers and powered on the television. I was tired of watching the news about the fucking murders so I changed to VH1 and started watching a repeat episode of *Basketball Wives*. I needed some entertainment in my life, and this life here with my brother wasn't cutting it.

Twelve minutes into the episode, Aiden knocked on the bedroom door. "You ready?" he yelled from the other side.

"Do you know what time it is?" I asked him after I looked at the cable box. It read 8:11 p.m.

"Yeah, it's a little bit after eight o'clock," he replied.

"So you're trying to leave now?"

"Yes. I wanna hurry up and be done wit' this shit so that nigga can pay me the rest of my money," he explained.

I let out a long sigh, dreading to say yes, but I said it anyway, "All right, give me ten minutes so I can put something on," I told him.

It took so much energy to drag myself out of bed, but I did it. I also said a quiet prayer to God, asking Him to help me get out of this situation with Aiden. I didn't know that guy who was standing on the other side of the door anymore. I kept thinking that something must have happened to him while he was locked up. Maybe he was raped or beat up really bad. Or maybe he was thrown in the hole for more time than he deserved, but whatever it was, it didn't do him any justice. It only made him worse.

Before I ended my prayer, I also asked God to remove my brother from me after all of this was over. I sensed that he would hurt me if I gave him a reason, and I didn't want that. I had a lot of life left in me so I asked God to please honor this prayer.

I opened the bedroom door and was startled by Aiden's presence. He was literally standing at the bedroom door the whole time, while I thought he had walked away. "Ugghh! Aiden, you scared the shit out of me," I spat.

"Who were you talking to?"

"When?"

"Just a few minutes ago," he asked as he continued to stand there before me.

"I was talking to God. I was praying for us. Asking God to help us get through this night," I told him.

"God ain't gon' help us. We about to sin!" Aiden said, and then he smiled. It wasn't a handsome smile. It was a demonic looking smirk. It scared me even more. I did my best to maintain my composure, because this guy had spooked me for the last time. I wouldn't be able to take this mess anymore after tonight.

"Come on, let's get out of here," I said, and then I stepped to the side so I could pass him.

He followed me down the hallway and stood in the middle of the floor while I took a seat on the sofa. "So what's the plan?" I asked him.

"We're gonna turn the phone on and track them on the GPS, and then I want you to take me where they are. I'll handle the rest."

"That's it. That's how you're gonna run up on them?"

"Yep," he replied nonchalantly.

"What if they see you coming and think you're the tall black guy that killed their other homeboys? Don't you think they're gonna put two and two together and start busting rounds at you?"

"They ain't gonna see me coming."

"Aiden, you're gambling with your life, big brother."

"I know what I'm doing," he told me, and then he started walking toward the front door. By him walking to the front door, I knew that meant that he was ready to go. So I stood up and followed him outside. After I locked the front door, I followed him to the truck.

I really didn't want to leave the apartment for fear that someone was going to recognize the truck and call the cops. But I figured that since it was dark outside, maybe we could slide underneath the radar.

CHAPTER 25

WHO'S NEXT ON THE LIST?

Once again I was on the prowl looking for the rest of these niggas so I could get my money from Winston's cousin. I knew my sister thought that this shit was a bad idea, but I wasn't trying to hear her. I knew what the hell I was doing. I knew how to put this pistol up to a nigga's head and take it off. Okay now, what if I fucked up? All right, then I accept the responsibility and take what's coming to me. Tomorrow wasn't promised, which was why I wanted to handle my business tonight. If I got shot while I was trying to end those niggas' lives, then so be it. I wasn't afraid to die. Fear was for suckers! I was a champion, and champions didn't lose.

"Where's that nigga's cell phone?" I asked Ava. I was ready to put the phone numbers inside the GPS tracker so I could get down to business.

"It's in the glove compartment," she replied. I opened the glove compartment, and when I looked inside of it, I didn't see the phone.

"Ava, it's not in here," I told her while I moved shit around inside of the glove compartment.

"I don't know why. It was in there earlier."

"Well, it's not in there now."

"Maybe I took it into the apartment. Want me to turn around?"

"No! Fuck it! Just keep going," I instructed her. I didn't want to waste any more time looking for that cell phone.

"Are you sure, because we've only been on the road for five minutes, so I don't mind turning around," she insisted.

"No. Just keep going," I told her. I was getting aggravated just thinking about how the fucking cell phone got in the apartment anyway. Was Ava fucking with my head? Was she trying to derail me going out to find these niggas tonight? I hoped not, because I would make her ass pay for it if I ever found it out.

"So, where am I taking you?" she wanted to know.

"Let's go by Nu-Nu's girlfriend's spot first. And if Nu-Nu's car ain't there, then drive by the trap house."

"I don't think driving by the trap house is a good idea. Remember a witness said that they saw a black SUV leaving the parking lot of Church's Chicken around the time Monty and them got shot."

"A'ight, well, go by the girlfriend's house, and if his car ain't there then I'm gonna get out of the truck at the corner of Alexander Street and walk the rest of the way."

"I don't think that'll be safe, either."

"What am I supposed to do? You took the fucking cell phone from the damn glove compartment!"

"Don't get all worked up, Aiden. I'm just looking out for your best interests."

"Man, fuck that! Just swing me by Tiffany's house and then drop me off at the corner where the trap house is."

"All right," she replied, and then proceeded to drive.

The drive to Oak Mount North was only a hop, skip, and a jump. Ava had us out there quicker than I had expected. But what I did expect was to find Nu-Nu's car there, but it wasn't. The house looked dark like no one was there. Maybe Nu-Nu told Tiffany to hang out somewhere else until he found out who was killing his boys off one by one. Too bad for her: after tonight, she wouldn't see that nigga again.

"Take me over to Alexander now," I instructed Ava.

"All right," she said, and then she headed to the other destination. But surprisingly, the block was lit up. It was more niggas out there than a Chris Brown concert. It looked like those clowns were having a block party. But who has a block party when niggas from your clique got murdered earlier in the day? That shit didn't make sense to me, so I let it go over my head.

"Are you sure you want me to put you off right here?" she asked me.

"Yeah, I'ma be all right. Go park on the next street, and keep the engine running," I said, and then I eased out of the passenger seat.

I started walking toward the center of the block where the party was being held. I saw t-shirts with "RIP" and the faces of the niggas I had gunned down yesterday and today. And that's when it clicked. Nu-Nu and the rest of his family knew about Trey and Al's murder. But why the news people didn't report it was beyond belief for me.

Anyway, I continued to make my way toward the trap house, because I needed to get these last three niggas. As I got closer, I started to see niggas looking at me. This made me feel real fucked up. Why were they starting to look at me? I couldn't figure it out, so I put some pep in my step so I could get to where I was supposed to be.

The music was loud outside. It sounded like somebody was DJing and had all the latest hip-hop songs playing these days. "Hey, cutie," I heard a chick say as I walked by her. I pretended not to hear her so she wouldn't stop me. Finally, I made it to the trap house. I was standing in the driveway when out of the corner of my eye I saw Eric and Keith standing a few feet away from me. They were smoking blunts filled with exotic weed. And that shit smelled good, too. I felt myself getting caught up in the aroma of that shit and the trap music they were playing, but I quickly got out of it when someone tapped my shoulder. I turned around in a flash, and who did I see? The same fucking chick who tried to talk to me when I walked by her. Now here she was again.

"You're so cute. Who you here with?" she yelled so I could hear her over the music.

"I'm looking for my girlfriend right now," I yelled back, and then I turned my back to her. And when I looked back, Eric and Keith had started walking toward the trap house. So I followed them.

By the time I caught up with them, they had just made it to the front door of the trap house. And when I looked over their shoulders, I saw the HNIC standing in the front room of the duplex, grinding on some ghetto-ass bitch with a champagne bottle in one hand and a blunt in the other one. This scene was so perfect. I couldn't have asked for a better ending. I pulled my pistol from the waist of my pants and opened fire on Eric and Keith, and then I hit Nu-Nu with four bullets. No one knew I had just opened fired on these niggas because the music outside was up so loud. They only realized what had happened after they saw all three of those niggas fall down dead.

To make shit look good and not to bring any attention toward myself, I pushed the pistol back inside my pants and then I walked off like nothing had happened. The music kept playing, and the people on the block kept dancing and getting high.

I can honestly say that it felt good to complete the mission. If I would've listened to Ava, I wouldn't have gotten this chance. Walking up on these niggas tonight when they had their block party was perfect. I mean, who would've thought? Now I could collect the rest of my money and get the hell out of town. Ava and I were going to live the life that we always deserved.

CHAPTER 26

I'M SORRY!

I saw Aiden walking toward me with his head held high. He seemed proud. And right then I knew that he had killed someone else. I didn't know who it could've been or how. All I knew is that he had taken another man's soul.

As he drew near the truck, I started backing away from him. And that's when he threw his hands in the air, as if to say, *hey, what are you doing? Where are you going?* But I ignored his gestures and began to turn the truck completely around in the opposite direction. This made him walk a little faster. And then his walk turned into running. But by this time, I had turned around and started driving away slowly. And within the blink of an eye I saw red-and-blue lights flash like we were about to see a circus act.

I looked back at Aiden through the rearview mirror and saw how the cops had surrounded him. He was definitely caught red-handed. And when he pulled his pistol out and started shooting at the cops that surrounded him, I saw the cops returning fire. Two seconds later, I saw my brother fall down to the ground. And that's when I knew he was dead.

I knew if I ever told anyone this story, they'd say that I was a rat and a snitch and that I needed to be dead, too. But that wasn't the case. My brother had turned into someone else. He had turned into a monster, and that monster inside of him was going to control me to the point of death. And I couldn't have that. So I had called the cops on him and told them everything. I told them about the guy Winston, who'd just had his case dismissed because he'd put a hit out on the utility worker witness for the prosecutor. I also told them that Winston put the hits out on Nu-Nu and his whole crew because of the drug territory in Norfolk, and that he got my brother Aiden to commit all the murders.

Now that all of this is over, I could now move on with my life and be happy for once. Aiden was now resting in peace. If he wasn't, then so be it.

The Crushed Ice Clique

Noire

Some cuties need rubies, and some girls need pearls,
But crush my ice and watch me rock this world!

CHAPTER 1

Honore Morales and her cousin Cucci Momma Jones were two beautiful but thirsty tricksters from the hustle hard blocks of Hollis, Queens. Get-money bitches who were all about that life, Cucci and Honore had grown up together in the wicked and wily projects where they learned the art of scheming and skullduggery from some of the best street legends in the game.

While Cucci Momma was a ghetto princess extraordinaire who rocked the latest fashions, slung the silkiest Brazilian, and sported the type of smooth cocoa-colored body that was displayed on the cover of *Big Booty* magazine, her BFF Honore was softer in tone and easier on the eyes, although no less tricky or deadly about her business. Honore had a classic type of beauty about her, and she was known to stop traffic and weaken the coldest of ballers and mesmerize them with her hazel eyes, honey-colored skin, rudely bodacious ass, shapely legs, and long, wavy hair.

On the real, Honore's package was put together way too perfectly for her to be so damn broke, and right now her brain was deep in scheme mode as she played with a sticky ball of gum in her mouth and gazed at the ceiling with a bored look on her mug. The sounds of smacking and slurping rose in the air as an OG named Chimp Charlie crammed his face deeper between her soft thighs and slurped up her sweet juice like his long, pink tongue was a twisty-turny crazy straw.

Charlie gasped in delight as he came up for air then dove right back in headfirst again, but Honore's mind was on a million other things as she got her pussy ate from one end to the other. The musty motel room they were in was chilly and the television was blaring on channel seven. Honore sucked her teeth, wishing this shit was over with already and pissed as hell that she was even laying there with her legs cocked open in the first damn place.

"This shit feel good, don't it, baby?" Chimp Charlie bragged as he lifted his peasy gray head up from outta her wet box. "I know you like what ol' Charlie be puttin' on you 'cause this pussy is wet as fuck."

"Nigga shut up," Honore ordered as she looked down and rolled her eyes at the ancient baller in disgust. "More eating and less talking. I ain't got all day to be messing with you. I gotta go to work tonight. Time is money, yo."

Honore pushed his face back into position and Charlie went back at it.

Stupid-ass nigga! she thought as his tongue swirled around her clit and he spread her thick ass-cheeks wide so he could toss her salad and add extra dressing.

As old and ugly as Chimp Charlie was, and as much as he made her skin crawl, Honore knew she was lucky to have a simp like him to yank back and forth on a string. It wasn't every day that you could find a limp-dick old-head who was willing to drop big dollars just to eat your coochie out like it was buttery grits and eggs. And even though her pussy was dead to Charlie's mouth mauling right now, Honore gapped her legs open even wider and let him have at it because business was bad in the hood and she needed to put some cash in her pockets real quick.

Honore prided herself on her ability to turn a dollar, but

the street hustle she had going with her cousin Cucci was getting harder and harder to maintain these days. Out of desperation the two of them had started managing a small stable of strippers and renting them out as dancers and escorts, but lately them bitches were getting thirstier and thirstier by the hour. Every time Honore turned around one of them thots had their hand out demanding more and more of the cut. For some reason them bitches had it in their heads that they were doing all the work and Cucci and Honore were collecting all the profit. They didn't understand that advertising sex parties on P.O.F. and other Internet sites wasn't as easy as it sounded. All those types of places were on the government radar these days, and undercover vice-types were lurking around mad corners left and right looking to make a bust. Them ungrateful pole freaks didn't realize how risky it was for Cucci and Honore to search for the right tricks who had heavy pockets, set up the parties, pick out just the right spot, and provide the proper security so the girls didn't get licked and picked every time they opened their legs.

But with her and Cucci holding tight to the purse strings, some of the girls had already started branching off on their own, and Honore was getting more and more frustrated and desperate for cash every day. On the real, a bitch like her had expensive tastes. Plus, she owed niggas money for this and that, and now her aunt was hollering about making her pay rent too. If things kept going like this then her ends wasn't never gonna fuckin' meet, and since right now she needed to get her nails done, her brows waxed, and some fresh new gear to drape on her phat sexy ass, giving up the trim to Chimp Charlie was her best fall-back hustle of the day.

Honore rolled her hazel eyes and glared up at the ceiling as Charlie's false teeth clicked together and raked over her clit. Everything had been going real smoovy and groovy for them up until just a few months ago when outta nowhere they got shit on by the game. Her and Cucci had been working as prime money mules for a hood legend named Sly McFly, and under his street guidance and cut-throat protection they had been bringing home the bacon, the spare ribs, and the pork chops too.

Sly happened to be Honore's godfather *and* Cucci's step-daddy, so he stayed looking out for both of them. He was a real OG from back in the day who had already earned his stripes living the thug life, and now in his older age he was all about stacking chips and living the high life.

Sly moved product, collected payments, and ran businesses all over Hollis, Queens, and with his type of trade constantly flourishing he kept all his workers laced nice and lovely. Not only did he keep Cucci and Honore looking like two bright shiny dimes, he footed the bills and taught them the business of the streets while they partied their asses off and lived like project princesses.

But all that good shit was a wash now. Sly's old ass had got caught up in a trick bag a few months earlier, and now the pigs had him locked up out on the Rock with no bail. His high-priced lawyers had promised that he was gonna beat the case when it went to court, but in the meantime, while they waited for that to happen, Honore and Cucci were left out there on their own to fend for themselves and keep their pockets up the best way they knew how.

Honore gazed down between her legs and frowned at the sight of the peasy gray head that was rotating around in big slow circles and lapping at her clit. Chimp Charlie was Sly McFly's personal driver and one of his very best friends. He was also a fat stankin' slob-ass nigga with a lotta money who didn't mind tricking it off. Cucci Momma had been fucking with Chimp Charlie ever since she was a teenager, and recently Honore had secretly slid right in on her cousin's game so she could get some of that bank too.

On the low-low and dipping way behind Cucci's back, Honore had started letting Charlie get a lil sniff and a taste here and there in exchange for a few dollars, and like a hope-less dope fiend, he had gotten addicted to her prime body. Honore felt kinda shitty for cutting in on Cucci's dough, and she couldn't stand Chimp Charlie's wrinkled, ashy ass not even a little bit, but she kept up her "lease and lick" game because the fat OG paid it like he weighed it. Besides, whenever her other little side hustles slowed down Honore could always fall back on chimp-ass, trick-ass Charlie, and just like a trained puppy, he would come running.

Honore lay back on the raggedy lint-balled bedspread and stared at the ceiling again. She tried to relax as Charlie lapped at her pussy with his extra-long, abnormal tongue. That shit slithered like a garden snake, and he stiffened it and probed up inside her tunnel deep enough to touch her damn cervix.

The effect of Charlie's head game was starting to kick in, and despite her reluctance Honore began to hump against his face. Her clit throbbed like crazy as Charlie swirled his tongue around and around until it grew long and stiff. Dipping his tongue deeply inside her pussy hole, he gathered a glob of warm sticky cream and rubbed it all over her clit. Honore started humping harder, mad that her body was responding even though her mind didn't want it to. Charlie slid his big rough hands under her thick booty cheeks and lifted her up slightly. He looked like he was eating a gourmet meal, and Honore was practically helpless as she gapped her legs open wider and surrendered to him. Her fingers were all in that peasy hair of his as she fucked the shit outta his face. He sucked and swirled and massaged her soft ass until her whole body was on fire. Warm juices ran outta Honore's pussy slit like a river, and all that liquid sugar trickled down and dripped right into her ass crack. Charlie went after that juice like it was liquid gold. He probed his tongue around her asshole and licked that juice right on up.

Soon a feeling of irritation mixed with pleasure overtook Honore and she couldn't hold her nut back no more. She reached up her body and squeezed her firm, melon-sized breasts and fingered her stiff nipples until tiny sparks shot off in her clit. Moaning loudly, she humped real hard a few times until her clit started quivering and jerking, and then she whimpered with pleasure and released a hot shot of sweet cum all over Charlie's big lips and scraggly mustache.

"Okay, okay, now get up," Honore barked as soon as she caught her breath. She had busted her a big one and now she wanted that nigga offa her. She pushed his sticky face from between her legs and frowned. "Good job nigga, it was better than the last time."

"I bet it was," Charlie said as he wiped her wetness from around his mouth and chuckled. "This shit been getting better and better, ain't that right? I'ma have yo ass turned all the way out soon, girl."

"Nigga please," Honore scoffed as she got up and walked naked toward the bathroom. She could feel Charlie's eyes glued to her bold round ass the entire way. "I'm a paper-chaser, dummy. How the fuck you gonna turn me out? Plus, your tongue is short and kinda rough. I've had better."

"Shut ya broke ass up." Charlie laughed as he laid back on the bed and wagged his snake tongue out at her. "You know my shit is damn near as long as my dick."

Speaking of dick, Charlie reached down between his legs and grabbed his. After all that pussy he had eaten his shit was still limp and soft. Unfortunately, he had just fucked another young chick right before Honore called him, and that's why he wasn't able to get his shit up for her. One erection a week was about all he could muster up at his age, although his mind still wanted pussy every day.

Charlie could have easily fronted Honore off when she called begging for money like he was broke or he wasn't interested in seeing her, but he liked the girl. He didn't mind coming up off the few dollars he had in his stash, but he had wanted to eat Honore's pretty pussy a lil bit first, that's all.

"You ain't chasing shit!" Charlie called out to her in a de-layed reaction. "You still running around here with them lil bum-ass looking-for-a-come-up niggas who barely got pocket change, baby! What you need to do is bag you a baller, Honore! I know you waiting on Sly to get out, but I'm telling you I can put you on to some real ends with the type of shot you got."

"Miss me with that shit, Charlie," Honore yelled back at him. "Sly McFly ain't raise me to be out there on the streets selling my ass, nigga! I get other silly bitches to do that shit for me. I only hit you off with some pussy every now and then be-cause it's quick and easy. Besides, I'm beautiful and I got a good brain. My time is coming, ya heard? A smart bitch like me is only gonna stay down for so long. Trust and believe, Sly or no Sly, I'ma be on my feet in a minute, son."

"That's what all the hoes say." Charlie grinned as he flipped through the channels on the small television. "I been running game for years out here, and one thing I know is this city is too big not to be getting some real paper, especially with a face and a body like yours. You, Cucci Momma, and all them lil chickenhead broads y'all be trickin off in that escort service just ain't the move, baby girl. Y'all need to put some real heavy action down and get out there and grind."

"Don't you worry yourself about our bizz, fat boy," Honore said as she cut on the water and wet a rag so she could clean her-self up. "Me and Cucci know how to handle our handle."

Honore was steady popping shit, but Charlie was abso-lutely right though. The escort business wasn't what it needed to be. Bitches in their line of work were fickle these days. They were all about getting that cash any way they could, but they didn't really wanna work hard for it. If they wasn't showing up at the parties late, then they were showing up high, or some-times not even showing up at all. Them lazy bitches were straight up trifling, too. After Cucci and Honore busted their brains to get everything all set up, the strippers would walk in looking tired and worn out and putting on some lil weak-type performances and half-ass dancing so bad their customer's dicks wouldn't even get hard. Yeah, Charlie was 100 percent correct. This escort game was almost played. It was time to for her and Cucci to put their heads together and rack the fuck up.

And the motivation was right there too.

Honore was a natural-born stunna and she wanted everything. She wanted to live the high life and claim her spot in the glamorous world of drugs and money. She loved stepping out fly and rocking the latest purses and shoes. She knew she had a sweet face and a killer body, and she knew she was smart enough to touch some real cake too. All she had to do was find a solid hustle and then work the right angle to pull it off. And once Honore got her foot in the right door she would kick that bad boy all the way open!

The ambition was deeply embedded inside her and she would do whatever it took to get what she wanted. No matter who she had to let eat her pussy from time to time, or who she had to double-cross and scheme on, Honore Morales was determined to find her a new hustle and get her life!

CHAPTER 2

Waaaa-aaaaa! Waaaaa-aaaaaa! Waaaaa-aaaaaaaa!

It was Honore's third day working her night job and the two-month-old infant she was babysitting was working her nerves. While her cousin Cucci stunted hard at a receptionist job in the corporate town of money-makin' Manhattan every day, hair on fleek and flossing lovely in all the flyest fabrics, Honore was dressed in a pair of linty sweats and a raggedy t-shirt that had baby vomit on the shoulder.

Waaaa-aaaaa! Waaaaa-aaaaaa! Waaaaa-aaaaaaaa!

Honore rolled her eyes as the nagging wails of the fussy baby demanded her attention. It had been a minute since she'd last tricked off Chimp Charlie, and once again her pockets were empty and her mind was in scheme mode. Cucci was out there hosting a sex party and tricking off some strippers, while Honore was stuck in a mansion on Long Island changing Pampers and dodging spit-up like a damn loser.

Waaaa-aaaaa! Waaaaa-aaaaaa! Waaaaa-aaaaaaaa!

"Why can't this baby take his tired butt to sleep!" Honore bitched under her breath. She reached out to rock the expensive ivory bassinet with one manicured hand so she could keep on responding to the nigga who was blowing up her Instagram timeline with the other one. She had just posted some real sexy ass-shots to her timeline that highlighted her thick curves and creamy goodies, and the nigga she was talking to was tryna run her some game about a possible modeling opportunity.

"C'mon, now, take your tired butt to sleep lil man," Honore cooed at the baby as her fingers flew across her phone. It was two o'clock in the damn morning, and other than the screeching cries from the tired baby who was fighting his sleep, the beautiful three-story house where she worked was silent.

Ignoring the wails of the cranky baby, Honore stared down at her phone absorbed in a mind-space all her own. She was desperate to keep the convo going with dude because he mighta been the type to offer big ends, and she wasn't about to miss out. She knew the possibility that she was dealing with an Instagram imposter was high, but what the fuck. Wasn't nothing else popping for her right now, and besides, jerking these pussy-fiends around on social media all night made the time pass faster. Besides, she stayed hopeful whenever there was an opportunity to make that quick dough, so if dude was actually being legit about a modeling job then she was all for it.

And why not? Honore glanced down at the crying baby and frowned. She was getting paid some pretty shitty ends for all the crying and boogers and pee-pee Pampers she put up with while working as a nanny for Slimy Sal Silberman and his flat-assed, stringy-haired wife, Leah. If it wasn't for that shoplifting charge she had caught and the court ordering her to keep a full-time job, Honore woulda been somewhere out in the street with her cousin Cucci right now, lining niggas up and getting her hustle on.

Slimy Sal had rescued her right on time, though, which was proof that them Jews ran every damn thing in New York. They gave each other the hook-up and had their fingers in every pie. Sal Silberman was an executive at the New York Diamond and Jewelry Exchange and he worked with Cucci's boss, Joel Samuelson. When Honore got busted and the judge threatened to throw her under the jail if she didn't come up with a full-time job within forty-eight hours, Cucci had begged Joel to put in a good word and ask Slimy Sal to hire Honore as his nighttime babysitter.

Honore didn't even like babies, but working for the Silberman family on the night shift was better than having to roll her ass outta bed at the crack of dawn and work a regular minimum wage fast-food job just so she could stay outta jail. At least chillin' in the nursery at the top floor of the mansion there wasn't no greasy-ass burgers to flip or no soggy fries to burn. Wasn't nobody looking over her shoulder or telling her what to do in the nursery all night long, neither. Just as long as she showed up on time and kept the baby quiet so his mama and daddy could slobber on their pillows and get their precious z's, they were all the way cool with her.

Slimy Sal was wheeling and dealing and climbing the corporate ladder at the New York Diamond and Jewelry Exchange, and his wife, Leah, was a high-powered banker. Between the two of them they were caked up lovely and rolling in dough. They both worked long hours down in the diamond district of New York City, so having somebody at the mansion who they trusted to take care of their baby at all times was a must. They had two elderly nannies who cooked and cleaned and took care of the infant during the day, and they had hired Honore practically just to sit there and watch the lil tyke sleep at night.

"You better hush that noise up, you lil red-faced tink-tink," she muttered at the baby. At two months old he was baldheaded with dimpled cheeks and scrawny legs, and he had been hollering his head off for over an hour straight now.

"C'mere," Honore sighed as she reluctantly slid her phone into her back pocket so she could reach into the bassinet and lift the baby out. She had been pacing the floor back and forth with him off and on all night, and like males of all ages he definitely liked snuggling up under her big juicy titties.

"You just had a bottle not too long ago and you still hungry, right?" Honore cooed again as his little lips puckered in the air. She kissed the top of his head and pressed him to her chest as she held him close and jiggled him up and down. "See there! I told your ol' silly-behind momma you needed some damn grits in ya bottle boo!"

The cute baby boy was their only child, and his rich Jewish parents had spared no expense on him. His nursery was done up in the best of the best with all types of pricey accessories. In addition to the expensive satin-lined bassinette, there was a gold-trimmed oak crib that was large enough to hold five toddlers, plus two fully stocked changing tables, a hand-carved rocking chair, and a small kitchenette off to the side of the room with a fridge, a sink, and a microwave.

Rocking the crying baby, Honore walked over to the kitchen area and plopped down at the table. She took the plate of chicken and mashed potatoes she'd been eating earlier and dipped her index finger down into the soft potatoes and then stuck it in the baby's mouth.

"Here," she said as he opened his tiny lips and sucked down the pat of potatoes greedily. She wasn't surprised when his lil pink tongue darted outta his mouth and his lips puckered and started searching for more.

Honore waited to see what would happen next, and moments later the baby's face turned red again as he let out a loud, angry screech that let her know he had liked them damn potatoes and was ready to go in hard again.

Honore raised up and slid her cell phone outta her back pocket, then she adjusted the baby in her arms so she could feed him with one finger and still have access to social media. Over and over she dipped her finger into the mound of potatoes and fed the baby while responding to the chaser who was still complimenting her ass-poses on Instagram.

"Damn sexy, ya pics are lit as hell."

"Thanks."

"I saw the link in your bio. So what type of prices do you charge for your booking sessions, Ma?"

Honore grinned. This was her favorite part. The money part.

"Ten grand," she lied.

"Damn you must be real good to be charging all that. So what type of stuff do you perform for ten grand?"

"It ain't just me. It's my girls. We have an all-night party going on tonight. Drinks, drugs, and the best pussy poppers in the city, ya dig?"

"Well my pockets run deep but I ain't no sucka neither. Am I the only one who gotta pay ten grand?"

"Hell naw, this party is for big boys only," Honore typed with her thumb, already planning on how she could use this simp to get jacked. "We got some white boys on deck tonight, and everybody gotta pay ten stacks. If you scroll down my timeline you'll see the chicks I fuck with. We some get-money bitches. We clean, we fine, we got condoms, and we provide a stress free environment. Time is money nigga, w'sup? Are you in or you out? You wanna video chat so you can see I'm for real? I got other niggas that I could be entertaining, you know."

Honore knew if this nigga was running a fake page then he would never video chat. That was a sure way to find out if a nigga was playing with your time.

"I'm definitely down," he typed. "I can see from ya pictures you got some bad bitches on ya team. Me and my homey tryna see what them cheeks is hittin for. Ten grand ain't nothing. We blow that in a regular strip joint ere' other night. We'll swing by and party wit'cha. So w'sup with the info?"

"I'm about to send you the address and the room number to the suite," Honore typed back with a smile. She was already counting that extra bread in her head. This was going to be a nice lil come up. "Send me your name and phone number and call me when you're downstairs."

"My name is Rasul," he responded back. "I'ma see you real soon sexy."

Honore was hyped as shit. She had just bagged another customer for Cucci and the girls to snatch up. If the girls put that pussy on 'em right they would be returning with more bread and more friends. Shit was all the way lit. Honore thought about telling Cucci about the new arrivals but she decided not to. She wanted to wait and see if her cousin would hold out on that extra bread, or come legit from the gate. Hell, Honore shrugged as she rocked the bald-headed baby. Every fuckin' body was running game these days and looking to score something for nothing. Including her!

CHAPTER 3

Rayven "Cucci Momma" Jones was in the cut with a bottle of EFFEN Vodka sipping it to the face. She was working a criminal side-hustle tonight and a whole lotta greenbacks was on the line. Cucci also had a legit job as a lowly clerk at the New York Diamond and Jewelry Exchange, but that shit paid peanuts compared to the stacks she could make pitching out on the streets. Besides, with her step-daddy locked up in jail and his regular hood connections drying up, Cucci was now carrying the whole load for both her mother, Frita, and her cousin, Honore.

It was late night and the private hotel party she was hosting was lit, and the high-roller white boys who were funding it were having a blast. While Honore was busy babysitting for her new Jewish boss, Cucci was smoking some black weed and holding shit down. Her primary role was to supervise their five female escorts and make sure shit ran smooth at their party tonight. The white boy who had hired them was named Aubrey, and he was paying top dollar for an all-night fuck-fest for him and his corny frat boys. There was plenty of blow, weed, and liquor damn near flowing outta the faucet, and right now the sloshed dudes were dancing with the girls, sniffing coke, and running around naked in the spacious hotel suite.

"Jeez, you're sexy as fuck," an ass-naked college dude said as he stumbled over to the couch where Cucci was staring down at her cell phone. He stood in front of her swaying in a wide-legged stance. "What you doing sitting over here all by yourself? You should come over here and sit that black ass on my big dick."

"Back up off me, white boy," Cucci snapped, gripping her vodka and smirking at his stiff piece of pink meat as she shot him a mean ice grill. "There's plenty of pussy around here for you to play in. I'm not a part of the party so step off."

"Oh, you got a smart mouth," the guy said with a cocky sneer on his face. "But I'm sure there's a price on your chocolate twat just like there is on the rest of these hoes. I tell you what. I'll pay you two hundred dollars extra on top of what my friend is already giving your gorgeous ghetto ass. Now be a good little bitch and come put that black pussy on this dick."

"Okay, I got you baby," Cucci said calmly. She slid her cell phone deep down between the sofa cushions, then leaned forward and reached for his pale woody and gently took it in her fist. Suddenly in one motion she squeezed it real tight and yanked that shit and twisted it so hard she almost broke his dick bone. The white boy yelped and fell to his knees. Cucci dropped her bottle and jumped up. She pulled a razor from her bra as she stood over him ready to amputate his lil three-inch knob right down to the root.

"How about you sit on this blade mothafucka," Cucci spit. "I told you to fall back, but your stupid ass still had to try it, huh? Don't make me carve yo pink ass up in this bitch."

The partying had stopped and all eyes were on the situation that was beginning to turn ugly. The escort girls were amped to make some moves straight for the door. These sweet Polly Purebreds talked a mean fight game, but they were cold-footed frauds on the low, and they were ready to take the money and run if any shit popped off.

"Hey Dustin, I see you've met our lovely host, Cucci," Aubrey said calmly as he walked over and tried to smooth things over. "Let me see if I can figure this out. You probably said something enormously stupid to her and she put you in check. Is that about right?"

Dustin shook his head yes as he wiggled around on the ground gripping his dick as it changed all kinds of colors from pink to purple.

"Sorry about him, Cucci," Aubrey said with a grin. "He's an idiot, but he's a good guy too. I don't wanna ruin the mood or our business relationship. Can we move past this and keep the party twerking?"

"Of course. As long as he finds some chill it's all cool, Aubrey," Cucci said, smiling with dollar signs in her eyes. She wasn't tryna fuck up the money neither so she raised her hand in the air and signaled for the girls to keep working. "Just make sure the rest of your boys stay in they damn lane too."

Cucci had just turned her head to say something slick to the doofus-looking white boy who was still laying on the floor, when suddenly the hotel room door opened up wide. Three masked gunmen walked calmly inside and closed the door behind them.

"Hey! What the hell is going on?" Aubrey said as the blood drained from his face. He held up his trembling hands as one of the dudes advanced on him. "Ay, I don't want any trouble guys, really."

Instead of responding, the masked gunmen sent a quick unspoken message that told everybody in the room to shut the fuck up and pay attention.

POP!

Dustin, the naked guy on the floor, caught a hot slug to the face. The back of his head exploded and one of the strippers screamed real loud before she could catch herself.

"*Shhh,*" the shorter gunman of the group warned. "Scream again bitch and I promise you it'll be the last sound you ever make. I ain't here to fuck around," he said coldly, "so I'm only gonna ask you muthafuckas one time. Where the fuck is the bread at? If I gotta ask again I'ma splash every last one of y'all pussies in here and then look for that ten grand myself."

Without hesitation Aubrey walked nervously over to the closet to retrieve his black briefcase. Dustin was already dead and his other friends were being manhandled and shoved face-down to the floor and getting their pockets ran through by one hitta, while the other one pointed a high-caliber weapon at their domes.

Cucci stood there frozen and watched as the ski-masked hitta moved quickly and efficiently, ripping wallets, car keys, Rolexes, and expensive rings off the terrified white boys as fast as he could.

"Here," Aubrey said, thrusting out the briefcase. "This is it. This is everything that I brought with me to pay for the girls tonight. It's ten grand in cash. Please take it because I don't wanna die. Look at us; we're obeying your commands and we're not fighting back. Please, we're young and we're drunk. Take the money." He practically flung the damn briefcase at the dude. "Take every damn thing you want, just let me and the rest of my friends live."

"That's *my* fucking money, yo!" Cucci hollered. The words flew out of her mouth before she could even check herself. She glared at the stone-cold hittas with nothing but getting them dollas on her mind. "Y'all niggas know this shit ain't right! I worked for that bank! Me and my girl tryna come up just like y'all are!"

"Bitch, *what*," the short guy in the mask said as he stepped over Dustin's dead body to get to Cucci. "You got a smart-ass fuckin' mouth, don't you bitch!"

SLAP!

Dude smashed Cucci with the .45-caliber gun that was

gripped in his hand and she dropped like a rock, falling backward on the couch halfway unconscious. She was so dazed she
could barely hear all the yelling and crying and screaming that
was coming from her strippers and the white boys alike. The
side of her face throbbed like an elephant had kicked it in, and
the last thing she felt was somebody tugging at the waist of her
skin-tight leggings, and then she went completely into dream-
land.

When Cucci Momma's eyes fluttered open she couldn't
tell how much time had elapsed. She was laying on the couch,
flat on her back. The whole right side of her face was swollen
and numb, and her thong and leggings were dangling from
one of her ankles. Two used condoms were on the floor and
the empty wrappers had been tossed down there too. She
swallowed hard and tried to sit up. Her whole body ached like
crazy and the last thing she remembered was getting smacked
in the face with a gun.

She stuck her tongue out to lick her swollen lip, then
winced in pain and looked around. The Beats by Dre radio
was still playing loudly over the speakers, but the only people
in the room were her and the dead white boy that Aubrey had
called Dustin. Everybody else had broke the fuck out and left
them behind.

Cucci stared at the blood and red goo spread on the floor
by Dustin's blown melon and it all came rushing back to her.

Their lil shit had gotten stuck the fuck up! *Licked!*

A sudden wave of pain flooded her body and she looked
down and saw a bunch of large red welts covering her arms
and legs. Her right knee was swollen so bad it looked like an
orange was sitting up under her skin. One of her shoes was
missing from her feet, and her rings, necklace, and diamond
earrings were all gone. Cucci sucked in a deep breath then
winced as she tried to bend her knee. That shit was tender and
stiff, and as the reality of her situation came raining down on

her she realized her knee was the last damn thing she needed to be worrying about because her real problem wasn't pretty at all.

They had gotten run down on. Somebody had scoped out their lil hustle and moved in for the kill. Not only had the masked hittas stolen her stash of money, they had kicked her ass while she was knocked out, and judging from the wetness and the throbbing pain she was now feeling between her legs, she had gotten fucked raw real good too.

Cucci's heart banged and her gut clenched. Her body had been brutally violated but there was also ten thousand fuckin' dollars gone! Just like that!

No! she screamed out in her mind. Her fuckin' cousin Honore was gonna kill her! She was supposed to have set this shit up nice and tight so they could pocket some dough, but instead there was a dead white boy on the floor and they were ten grand short!

The sight of Dustin's dead body had Cucci happy as hell to be alive, but she was still furious as fuck. There was mad throbbing going on between her legs and that meant that more than one of them gun-boys had stuck his dick in her! She was on the pill, but she didn't know what kinda diseases them nasty scrubs was carrying around!

Cucci reached down in the sofa cushion and retrieved her cell phone. She was dizzy as fuck when she stood up, and everything in her stomach felt like it was gonna explode outta her throat. Holding onto a chair, Cucci bent down and stuck her foot back in her thong and leggings and yanked them up on her damp ass. Despite the intense pain that was roaring through her body from head to toe, all she could think about was getting her ass outta that hotel room before the pigs showed up. Even beaten up and fucked, Cucci didn't trust a blue boy under no goddamn circumstances. With that white college boy stretched out on the floor dead, she was sure to be taken down to the station for questioning. Instead of seeing her as a victim them savage cops woulda probably slapped the metal bracelets on her and charged her with a crime.

Barely able to see outta her punched eye, Cucci staggered into the small bedroom wearing one high heel and went searching for her purse at the top of the closet. Of course that shit was gone, just like the bag of money that she was supposed to collect.

Cucci felt like fuckin' crying as she crossed back into the living room and stepped over the white boy's naked body. She busted outta the door hoping like hell that none of those hittas were laying in the cut waiting to jump on her again.

"Bitch come and get me!" Cucci shrieked into her cell phone as she busted through the stairwell door and hobbled down the steps as fast as she could. Wincing in pain, fear and panic were bubbling all up in her throat and all she could do was pray to God that none of them hittas were still lurking around the hotel waiting to skim her weave and wet up her scalp the way they had wet up her drawers.

"What's wrong? Where you at?"

"I'm on the staircase at the Hussy Hole Hotel!"

"What you mean come and get you?" Honore said, sounding real confused on the other end of the line. "Girl you know I'm at work watching this damn baby all night! I can't just walk out and leave him!"

"Girl, we got set up! Stuck the fuck up too! Some ski-masked niggas had a key to the room and they slid in whipping out burners everywhere! They blasted one of the white boys and took all the cash, and I think some of them niggas fucked me too!"

"*What?*" Honore shrieked into the phone as she keyed in on the most important detail. "They took our *cash?*" She hollered that shit so loud that immediately the baby stirred and started crying again.

"Yeah! And they shot a white boy and dug my shit out too!"

"Shit!" Honore muttered as she flipped the baby onto his

stomach and started patting on his back real rapidly. "Hold up." She peered suspiciously at the phone. "Cucci Momma, you been smoking that black weed again? You know that shit be having you fucked up, girl. It was supposed to be an orgy, dammit. What the hell you talking about you got fucked, some dude got blasted, and all the money is gone? I know damn well you ain't telling me no extra-ass shit like that!"

Cucci was breathing so hard it felt like she was gonna pass out. A wave of dizziness and nausea washed over her, and cradling the phone between her cheek and her shoulder, she sank down on the steps and put her head between her knees.

"Bitch come and get me!" she barked at Honore again as soon as she caught her breath. "I don't know how them niggas knew we was in there partying, or how they knew ten grand was gonna be stashed in the room, but they knew! Them niggas took my purse and I lost one of my shoes! I'm sitting on the fourth floor staircase and for all I know they might be in the lobby waiting to kill me!"

Honore's hand was steady patting. "But who's gonna watch the baby?"

"Wake his goddamn mama up!" Cucci snapped. "And tell her to come watch him her damn self! I don't care *what* you gotta do, just come and get me and hurry the hell up!"

Honore hung up the phone and immediately called the number to that Rasul nigga that she had sent to the room. She was fearful that not only was she not gonna make any extra bread tonight, but that she had fucked around and set her own squad up to get booked.

"Yo who dis?"

"Pussy nigga, you know who the fuck it is!" Honore barked. "Did you really just do that shit to my party?"

"Ha-ha, w'sup sexy," Rasul said with a sick laugh. "I didn't see you up in the spot, sugar. It was jumping though. Me and my homies had a great night. Y'all stupid bitches really know how to show a nigga a good time. I hope you invite me back again."

"Oh, yo bitch ass got jokes right?" Honore spit with utter disgust and venom. "Ya name is Rasul, right? I promise you I'ma find out who you are and get yo ass turned into maggot food. I can promise you that nigga! You did some real hoe-nigga shit tonight and you gonna pay with your fucking life!"

"Bitch you stupid," he responded calmly. "You think I would really give a chaser like you my real name? It's all a part of the game, baby girl. You gotta take it on the chin. Y'all got caught slippin, that's all. Stop crying and making them dry-ass threats. Now if you'll excuse me, I got some money I need to go spend. Ten grand, to be exact. Like I said, tonight was a good night. Thanks again. *Click!*"

Less than an hour later Honore was grasping a pissed-off Cucci up under her arm as she struggled to get her and the bulky car seat she was carrying into the backseat of an Uber. The hotel lobby was clear when she walked in, and she pretended like she could barely believe the wild story her cousin had told her.

"Ow!" Cucci moaned and grabbed her knee as she tried to skooch her way deeper into the ride and make room for her fellow passengers. "This shit is completely crazy, yo!" She stared at her cousin with her lip poked out. "It took your ass long enough to get here, Honore! And I can't believe you brought no baby out here at this time of night with you neither! You ain't even put a hat on his head!"

"Hell yeah I brought him out! What else was I supposed to do with him?" Honore snapped back as she struggled to get the baby strapped in. "Leave him up in that attic all by himself crying his head off? Forget his damn hat. You lucky I got my ass outta that house without getting caught! Or you really woulda been sitting around waiting for a ride!"

Honore finally settled in next to Cucci and the baby and she frowned at the look of pain on her cousin's pretty face. "You lookin real beat, Cucci. Are you sure you don't wanna go to the emergency room?" she asked.

"No!" Cucci said sharply. "Uh-uh. Them doctors see me looking all fucked up like this and they'll be asking a million questions. Don't worry. I'ma go to the free clinic later on and get myself checked out. I'll let 'em test me for STDs and check my shit out thoroughly. But right now all I wanna do is go home and get in the tub."

Honore tapped the Uber driver on the shoulder and he pulled away from the curb and took off toward the projects. Every little sway and bump of the car sent a shriek or a moan busting outta Cucci's mouth, and feeling guilty as fuck and sorry for her cousin, Honore tried to get her talking to distract her from the pain.

"So who do you think was behind this shit?" she probed like she was clueless. "The strippers, the white boys, or what?"

Cucci closed her eyes and shook her head wearily.

"It had to be one of the strippers because it damn sure wasn't the white boys. Like I said, I left one of them idiots with his thoughts leaking all over the rug."

"Damn! We gotta figure out how to get that money back!" Honore said as her brain worked overtime to come up with something slick. The chances of finding that Rasul nigga were real slim, but she damn sure wasn't about to tell Cucci that. Besides, how was she supposed to know they were gonna get licked! That lil babysitting job of hers didn't pay shit, and she had been looking forward to splitting all those racks with her cousin and getting caught up on all the shit she needed to do.

Honore bit down on her bottom lip real hard, straight-up disgusted with herself. *I can't tell her it was my stupid ass who fucked up the whole situation. I shouldn'ta been trying to be so greedy. I should have known the whole shit was too good to be true. How could a slickster like me be so careless?* Her dirty transgression was weighing on her heart. Cucci was her best fuckin' friend for life, and no matter how broke they got Honore never wanted to see her hurt. This was a real hard mistake to stomach. Only thing good about the situation was that Cucci was still breathing.

Honore ran her mouth and kept Cucci distracted until they pulled up in front of the building where they lived. To the casual observer the projects looked dark and deserted, but there was plenty of business being conducted and behind-the-scenes action going down if you knew where to look. Honore gazed toward the building's porch where a few winos and crackheads stumbled around in plain view.

"Can you make it upstairs by yourself?" she asked her cousin.

Cucci gave her the eye. "Girl, no! You see my knee is all jacked up! You don't wanna come upstairs with me?"

"Nope." Honore shook her head and nodded toward the sleeping infant. "Not if you can make it by yourself. *Sheeeit,* I ain't taking this white baby up in the building! Them niggas'll see me with him and they'll cut my throat then kidnap his lil ass and try to hold him for ransom." She shook her head again. "Bad enough he's gonna have colic from being out in all this night air without a hat. Nah, I need to get lil man home before his momma gets up to go to work and comes looking for him."

Honore waited while Cucci inched her sore ass outta the whip. She watched as her girl limped slowly up the walkway toward the towering project building, then she tapped the young Indian driver on his shoulder and gave him the address to a house out on Long Island.

"Listen here, Ahmed. I'm about to be in some big-ass trouble if I don't get this baby home real quick, so I'ma need you to take some shortcuts and run some red lights and do whatever you gotta do to get me back to Long Island before the sun comes up, you heard? So go 'head and push it, papi. Push this shit!"

CHAPTER 4

It was damn near five thirty in the morning when Honore finally made it back to the rich white people's house on Long Island. The only light that was shining from the property was the one over the front entrance, and Honore breathed a sigh of relief as she crept through the kitchen door and unbuckled the sleeping baby from his infant seat.

After all that hollering and fussing he had done earlier, the night air had Sal Junior knocked out and sleeping just like a baby, and he didn't make a peep as Honore crept up the stairs, passed the master suite, and headed farther upstairs toward the nursery.

Relieved as fuck that she had gotten the baby back in one piece and feeling pretty damn slick about herself, Honore twisted the doorknob and stepped inside the dark, spacious room. She was just laying the lil tyke down in his luxurious bassinet when a noise from the corner of the room scared the shit outta her.

"What the fuck!" Honore almost jumped outta her skin as a figure rose from the darkness and appeared before her. Her heart banged up in her throat when she saw that it was Sal Senior, the ugly-ass slimeball himself, who had been lurking in a rocking chair and waiting for her in the darkness.

"Hey, sir," Honore said as she finished settling the baby down and covered him up with a receiving blanket. "Ohhh, I'm sorry about my mouth, Mr. Silberman, but you scared the hell outta me. Is everything all right?"

"I don't know," Slimy Sal said quietly as he stepped over to the door and closed it firmly then turned the lock. "I came upstairs to check on my son, only to find that he wasn't here. And neither were you. You wanna tell me where you were, and what you were doing with my child in the middle of the night?"

"Oh, we didn't really go nowhere." Honore waved her hand and lied. She coulda kicked herself up the ass! This asshole probably had some footage of her sneaking out the door on video! The whole house was prolly wired and everything she did was probably recorded on camera for the world to see.

Honore almost panicked. She couldn't lose this cushy-ass night job. She just couldn't. The judge had been real clear when he sentenced her, and her jail time would only remain suspended as long as she kept her job. She had been so busy rushing out to get Cucci that she didn't even think about that shit.

"Seriously,"—she gave him a big, cheesy smile—"lil man was just being his normal fussy self so I walked him around the house for a little while until he calmed down. And see?" Honore nodded toward the crib like she had this shit covered. "It worked."

"Is that right?"

Honore peeped Slimy Sal's move on the door and the sinister tone in his voice. She nodded real quick as she tried to figure out what angle this muthafucka was tryna come from while hoping like hell he wasn't about to fire her.

"Yep, that's right. You know he likes to be walked around, so that's what I did. I walked him around."

Slimy Sal cracked a smile and Honore felt a chill go straight through her.

"I find that hard to believe because I went looking for you. I searched the entire house, and you were nowhere to be found. And neither was my son. So do you want to tell me where you took him, or do you want to tell your little lie again?"

Suddenly the baby started crying again and Honore quickly swooped him up in her arms. She plopped down on the bed and held him over her shoulder and jiggled him up and down.

"Look, Mister Silberman, I just walked the baby around, that's all. I mighta stepped outside for a second or two so he could get a little air, but I was just tryna make him comfortable, that's all."

Slimy Sal nodded as he went over and sat next to Honore on the bed. "Well I'm paying you good money for him to be comfortable. As a matter of fact, he looks pretty comfortable right now. Lay him down and rub his back."

"Okay, sir," Honore said as she laid the kid down. She wasn't used to this nerd-ass looking rich white man being all up in her grille like this but she didn't wanna believe what her hood instincts were telling her. She tried to scoot over a little bit but she was already on the edge of the bed so there was nowhere else to go.

"Lil man love him some Honore," she said, playing it off nervously as she gently patted the baby's back. "He's gonna be knocked out again in no time."

Instead of answering, to Honore's surprise Slimy Sam leaned over and stuck out his tongue and licked her neck like a dog.

Honore jumped up off the bed looking shocked as hell. No wonder they called this bastard slimy! She frowned in disgust as she wiped his spit off her neck and backed away from her boss.

"What the hell are you trying to do up in here, sir?" Honore barked. "I hope there wasn't any miscommunication going on between us because I don't get down like that!"

"Like what?" Slimy Sam said softly as he stood up and unbuckled his belt.

Honore peeked the stiff little woodpecker tryna poke outta his pants and she shook her head real fast.

"Uh-uh. I'm not with that shit sir, and I'm not trying to lose my job neither. What if your wife finds out what you tryna do with me?"

"My wife won't find out," Sal said. "Because you're not going to say a damn thing. If you don't get your beautiful ass over here and park it in my lap I'll fire you right now and then call the police and tell them how you kidnapped my son. You'll be arrested and sent to jail so fast it'll make your pretty little head spin. And you don't want that, do you?"

"Sir, you know I need this job," Honore pleaded. She was so damn mad that she was on the verge of crying. This slimy fucker had her hemmed up tight between a rock and hard spot, and what he wanted from her was the same damn thing every man wanted from her: some pussy!

"C'mon, now, chill with that, Mister Silberman! Don't be talking about calling no cops on nobody, son! You know I'm on probation and I can't get in no legal trouble. Don't do me like this sir. Please. I don't want any problems."

"Problems? You haven't seen problems! In fact, I think I'm going to just go ahead and call the police right now," Slimy Sal said as he cracked a big smile that indicated he was enjoying Honore's distress and her state of nervousness and desperation. "Unless you agree to cooperate and give me what I want when I want it, that is."

Honore was stuck like fuck. There was no way in hell she wanted to open her legs for this bony-ass creeper but she didn't really have a choice. His dirty white ass had her by the panties and there wasn't shit she could do except submit to it. Reluctantly she walked back across the room and went over to the bed and sat on his lap.

A few moments later her luscious tits had been ripped outta her bra and Slimy Sal was sucking the life out of her caramel-colored nipples.

"Act like you like it." Sal stopped sucking for a moment and glared up at her and demanded. "You can either go to jail, or you can make me feel good."

Honore knew when she was licked. This fucker had two handfuls of titties and a nipple between his lips, and she could feel his stiff woody stabbing her right in the ass.

Go to jail or make me feel good!

The choice was easy, and Honore sighed as she stood up and wriggled outta her jeans. Slimy Sam gasped at the sight of her bold honey-colored hump of an ass, and with the baby sleeping peacefully on the bed beside them, Honore pulled his slimy father down to the floor and got ready to put the best pussy on him that he ever had in his life.

"Lay back," she ordered him after yanking off his wrinkled khakis and polka dot drawers. Honore felt his bulging eyes crawling all over her in the darkness as she slowly stripped outta the rest of her clothes, and she knew this was gonna be a two minute job. It was obvious that Sal had never seen such a prime, naked body like hers before because he was watching her with tears of lust in his eyes.

Honore knew what her best look was, and as Sal lay stretched out on the floor she faced away from him and shook her massive ass cheeks like she was a race horse about to come outta the blocks. Slowly, she stepped backwards until she was straddling him with her ass right above his face. She did a real deep squat and wiped her pussy on his nose, then rubbed her clit all over his thin, puckered up lips. Duck-walking forward, she paused with her pussy hovering over the head of his stiff little dick.

Sal reached out and grabbed two handfuls of her glorious ass cheeks, and Honore paused while he lifted and lowered their weight in his palms and massaged her booty with glee. Lowering her knees to the floor, Honore guided the tip of his dick to her slit, then plopped down on it hard, impaling herself on his rigid meat.

She rode him backwards, and Sal gasped and moaned as he watched her naked ass bucking up and down. Honore put that shit on him wickedly, squeezing and milking his balls in her hands while she clenched down with her pussy muscles hard enough to make him yelp.

This sucka's about to cum, Honore told herself with a satisfied smile. She started fucking him even harder. Her booty cheeks clapped and quivered and he slapped her ass loudly on every downstroke. Honore was working up a sweat. For fifteen long minutes Sal took everything she threw at him, and still his dick remained brick-hard and lodged inside her slippery pussy.

"Hurry up and bust," she finally told him, glancing over her shoulder. "Let's get this shit over with." Sal didn't answer right away. Instead, he pushed her off of him and crawled up on his knees. Urging Honore down flat on her back, he looked down at her and grinned. He jammed two fingers straight inside her wet pussy then pulled them out and sopped up her juice.

"Hurry up, my ass," he said with a wicked laugh. "You get paid to work a ten hour shift, my dear, and I'm about to fuck you all night long!"

CHAPTER 5

As Cucci lay stretched out in the bed the next morning with a raggedy fan blowing cool air all over her aching body she couldn't help but replay the bullshit that had gone down the night before in her mind. She had soaked her aching ass in a hot bubble bath as soon as she stumbled inside the apartment that her and Honore shared with her mother, Frita, and right now she was holding some ice cubes wrapped in a washcloth against her swollen cheek.

Cucci was hood to the bone and she had given and taken her share of ass-kickings in her day, but none that had ever left her feeling this fucked up. She was planning to go to the free clinic as soon as they opened so she could get herself tested for any sexually transmitted diseases that might have gotten through those condoms. Thankfully, she had been knocked out during the worst of what was done to her in that hotel room, but it was the wounds to her pride and spirit that hurt even worse than those that had been inflicted on her body.

The truth was, it was very hard for a slick chick like Cucci to accept the fact that she had gotten booked, beat the hell up, and banged all in the same damn night. Her face and her body bore the evidence though, and she was trying to figure out what the hell kind of lie she was gonna tell her mother when she got home. She had a little time before she needed to worry about that though, because today was Sunday and right now Frita was out visiting a few of the sick and shut-in church members in her congregation. Cucci was alone in the apartment with Honore, who had just come home from her night job, and she was in the kitchen cooking up some bacon, eggs, and grits.

"Here," Honore said, handing Cucci a hot plate of food as she walked into the small room they shared.

"Ungh," Cucci grunted as she snatched the plate and got to grubbing.

"Um, how about a little thank you, damn!" Honore snapped as she pulled the sheets back and got into the bed next to Cucci and balanced her plate on her thighs.

"Yeah okay, *thanks* for coming to get me last night!" Cucci smirked and said sarcastically. "And *no damn thanks* for making me come upstairs by myself! You knew I didn't have no shoe and my damn knee was jacked up, Honore!"

"I had that little white baby with me, Cucci! Shit, coming to get you is what got me in trouble last night!"

"You think *you* had trouble last night? Bitch, please! Not only did I get mad burners pulled out and brandished in my face, I got robbed and beat the hell up and I also got *fucked* last night, just in case you forgot!"

"Well I hate to bust ya lil bubble, but I got *fucked* last night and fired *too!*" Honore snapped.

"Fucked by who?" Cucci demanded.

"By my boss," Honore admitted. "Slimy fuckin' Sam, the same savage who fired me. That old skinny doofus with the hot breath and the funny teeth pushed up on me last night. He found out that I left the house with the baby and he threatened to call the cops and report me for kidnapping if I didn't go along with the go-along. I put a real strong booty game down on him but as soon as he busted his nut he got up and fired my ass."

"That fuckin' asshole fired you?" Cucci shrieked. "Even after you let him smash it? That's madness! Wasn't nobody tryna snatch his old big-headed baby anyway! He was asleep the whole time! Did you tell him that?"

"Since when do the truth matter when a man is tryna get him some pussy?"

Cucci chewed on a slice of bacon and shook her head. "Dang, I'm sorry you lost your job, mami. I know what kinda jam that's gonna put you in with your probation officer. We gotta find you another job real quick, but I'm just so fucking tight with how that bullshit went down last night, yo! Them stick-up kids knocked me out and walked outta there with all our money so what we gonna do now?"

"That money . . ." Honore muttered under her breath as she tried to play it off and hide her look of shame. "I can't believe somebody got us like that."

"Me either," Cucci said, frowning. "But they did."

"A'ight, pick ya lips up," Honore said brightly trying to boost their mood. "Shit happens. The streets is crazy and niggas is out here playing for keeps these days. Losing that money was bad, but it coulda been much worse, you know. True, them hittas put they paws on you and stole a lil pussy outta ya box, but they bodied that white boy and left him all wet up for real! You better be lucky they ain't say fuck it and clip you in the forehead while you was knocked out too."

"Yeah, I can dig it," Cucci said as she dug back into her breakfast. "But I'm telling you the whole thing had to be an inside set-up because some kinda way they knew we were gonna be there holding that bank. I mean, they got a damn key and they walked up in that bitch going ham! I just wish I had a piece on me. I woulda *rocked* one of them niggas though!"

"Girl cut all that gangsta shit out," Honore said as she set her plate down and reached up on the dresser and took down a small bottle and rubbed some lotion on her feet. "You ain't no gunslinger, bitch. If you had'a been strapped last night it woulda turned out even worse."

Cucci twisted her lips. "How so?"

"Because you was out-manned and you never even saw it coming. We just gotta take the loss, Cucci Momma. It's all a part of the game. But I'm telling you, if Sly McFly wasn't in the joint that shit wouldn'ta went down like that. He woulda made sure none of those new niggas out there even thought about violating our hustle like that."

"Yeah," Cucci agreed. "Sly is definitely thorough like that. Don't nobody wanna fuck with a dumb-out killer like him. When he was out here going hard he had the drug game and the street game on lock."

"Sho' did," Honore said. "It's a damn shame that his connects won't fuck with us just because we females. They won't even let Chimp Charlie vouch for us. I guess I gotta wait till Sly calls so we can see what the next move is. He has to let his peoples know we good money so we can get the cash flow rolling again."

"You ain't never lied," Cucci said. "'Cause my lil paycheck from the jewelry joint don't be lasting but a hot minute these days. Matter fact, that shit be already spent up before I even cash it. Thank God I'm about to get me a promotion, though."

"Damn," Honore said, impressed. "Already?"

"Yep. I got the big boss so strung out he can't keep his nose outta my twat. His lookin'-ass stays all over me, and he's forever telling me how I could really rise up lovely through the ranks of the company if I keep my mouth closed and play my cards right. But you know what that shit really means, right? He wants me to keep my trap shut and don't tell nobody how he be slippin' and dippin' on them diamonds he be taking outta the vault."

"That's what's up, Cucci Momma. You really got yourself a

good-ass come-up at that spot," Honore said as her agile mind started racing. "You better hop on that promotion opportunity and work that damn program, girl."

"Oh you know I sure the hell am." Cucci giggled as she bent over and set her empty plate down on the floor. "Trust, baby. Joel Samuelson is taking damn good care of me and he's elevating my whole game in the jewelry biz. Like I said, he done already told me that the new floater job that just came open is mine, and that means he's gonna have me going from store to store selling small diamonds all over the city. I'ma *keep* my hands on all that pretty-ass ice," Cucci said as she grinned.

"Yo, you should try to snatch a couple of them shits up on the low when ain't nobody watching," Honore suggested as she chewed on a thick slice of slab bacon. "If you get you one, make sure you get me one too. You know diamonds are a girl's best friend."

"Bitch don't be stupid," Cucci snapped sharply. "I'ma pimp the situation to the max, but I ain't going to jail behind that shit! There's levels to this diamond business, Honore. You just can't walk up in there and stick a diamond in ya bra and think won't nobody notice it's gone. Nah, this game is way more sophisticated than that."

Honore shrugged. "I'm just saying it's stupid to be busting ya ass surrounded by big money and millions of jewels every day, and meanwhile you only bringing home minimum wage, Cucci! That's like being a bank teller and taking in all them hundreds of thousands of dollars for the white man all day long, and at the end of the week you only walk away with three hundred dollars for your own damn pockets. It just don't make no sense not to try to find a way to get some of them riches and rewards for yourself. That's all I'm saying."

"I know what the hell I'm doing," Cucci said, acting fake annoyed. "I already told you the boss is on my damn heels so hard he's giving me a promotion! Girl, please. I got that nigga's dick jumping like Jordan to salute me every time I walk in the room, and no matter how many times I put it on him he still can't get enough of this funky stuff! On the real, I hear what you saying though. Don't worry, cuzzo. Once I get that promotion shit is gonna be real grand for both of us. I'ma slow grind every inch of this diamond shit and milk it for all it's worth."

"Now that's what I'm talking about," Honore responded, and then she said quietly, "but why you ain't never asked your boss to hire me at that diamond joint, Cucci? Hell, you over there in Money-Making-Manhattan rubbing elbows with the big shots and getting benefits and shit. I want me some of that corporate action too. Why'ont you tell that nigga Joel to put ya fam on too?"

Cucci cut her eyes and gave her cousin a wary look. "I already asked him to look out for you one time already, damn, don't you remember? How the hell do you think you got that babysitting job with Sal and stayed your ass outta jail, Honore? Joel talked to Sal and gave you the hook-up like I asked him to. You think he's gonna go outta his way for you again just like that?"

Honore shrugged. "Hell, yeah. Why not? You fucking him real good, ain't you?"

Cucci Momma shook her head and twisted up her lips. Hell no. She wasn't feeling this shit at all. She liked the lil setup she had going at the New York Diamond and Jewelry Exchange. Finally, she was somebody important and had herself a real career. Joel Samuelson had seen how special she was, and he had taken her under his wing and was showing her the ropes in the black market diamond business. Honore didn't know it, but Joel had recently taken Cucci with him to make a drop at an old jewelry store in Brooklyn where he passed off a diamond he had stolen from the Jewelry Exchange's vault. An elderly Jewish dude who had been in the game forever took them into a back room and made a cloned copy of Joel's diamond and then gave him the fake diamond to slip back into the store's vault.

The next day, Joel had introduced her to some cat named Avi, who he said was an underground diamond trader on the black market in Belgium. Joel had given this dude Avi the real diamond that he had stolen, and Cucci had overheard Avi saying something about crushing it up into ice and talking some real big numbers that he was gonna get for it on the underground market.

Cucci knew Joel was grooming her for something really amazing, and when he told her there was a new job opening and asked her if she would be willing to help him bait and switch company diamonds for a small share of the profits, she had said hell yeah with a quickness. Cucci was scheduled to go out on a job with Joel real soon, but she was keeping all that secret shit under wraps. Nah, she thought as her eyes slid over to Honore. She had shared just about every damn thing in her whole life with her favorite cousin, but Cucci wasn't wit' none of that slide-in-on-her-shit kinda action that Honore was talking right now.

"Yeah, *I'm* the one fucking him," Cucci finally said with mad snap on her lips. "Remember that. Besides, they ain't hiring nobody down there who don't have jewelry store experience right now."

"Yeah, well whatever," Honore said, taking note of the shade, "we still gotta switch up our hustle then 'cause this escort shit gonna fuck around and get us killed or locked up. We gotta use our heads and lock in. We can't just roll over in the game and slip all the way off, Cucci! When you let them niggas roll up and take our money it put us all in a bind. We need to start thinking about our future and how we can come up on some more cash."

Cucci Momma hit her cousin with the side-eye as she nodded and took mental notes. Honore had one fucking thing right. It was time for Cucci to start thinking about the future all right. *Hers!*

CHAPTER 6

The visitor's area on Rikers Island was jam-packed and noisy. Some of New York City's most brutal criminals were awaiting trial behind those bars, and Sly McFly was one of them.

Honore had left home early so she could catch the bus and ride over the bridge, hoping to be one of the first visitors in line. She hated coming up to this bitch-ass jail. The correctional officers were just as crooked as the inmates that they were paid top dollars to keep locked up. Crime and treachery ran amok just like on the streets up in there, and the prisoners weren't the only ones who had drugs flowing through the joint like toilet water through shitty pipes neither. You could best believe that the guards were being paid to be mules too, and they were getting a real nice piece of all the action that went in and out of those doors.

For the visit today Honore had braided her long hair in two cornrows and she wore a dull baggy Polo sweatsuit so she would draw less attention to the wide hips and curvy ass she had on her. The last thing she needed was a bunch of corrupt ass COs eyeballing her shit and tryna holla like she was gonna take them in the bathroom and fuck them in a stall.

The visit was taking place in a high-security area, so first

Honore had to fill out all kinds of forms and submit to being questioned and thoroughly frisked, and then finally she was allowed to walk across the room to the cubicle and sit down so she could wait for the man himself to walk in and take a seat on the other side of the glass.

It had been a minute since she had seen him last, and as she sat waiting for her handsome godfather, the notorious OG Sly McFly, the anxiety she had been feeling inside for the past few months showed all over Honore's face.

A few moments later Sly McFly stepped in the room, cool as shit. Unlike the other prisoners he was swinging his arms with no handcuffs on as he joked around and talked easily with the veteran guards who escorted him in.

Honore grinned inside.

Her favorite old-head looked strong and confident up in that bitch. Life on Rikers Island had done nothing to diminish Sly's swagger or detract from his glow. He was a king-ass lion who looked real comfortable in the concrete jungle and he still had his roar. Sly sat down on a stool and smiled broadly at Honore through the glass before he picked up the phone.

"Damn! You looking happy as fuck to be in the worst place in New York City, nigga!" Honore said sarcastically with a smile on her face. "This must be some real easy time because you over there grinning just like a kid in a damn candy store."

"You know how I do baby girl," Sly said smoothly as he laughed at her sarcasm. "I'm just enjoying my lil vacation, ya know? They treat me pretty well in here, as you can see. I'm laid back in this bitch with my feet up not worried about a damn thing. I'm doing my time and not letting the time do me. Now what's going on that you had to come all the way out here and see me? All you had to do was wait for me to call."

"Forget waiting. Shit ain't moving right, Sly," Honore said, showing her irritation. "Those connects you told me to holla at won't even acknowledge me because I'm a chick. They won't let me collect on the debts they owe you so my cash flow is real funny. Plus, me and Cucci gotta step away from all that escort shit because niggas are starting to line us up. Cucci got caught in a bad one and almost got pushed messing around with some greedy-ass hittas the other night. We think somebody on the inside set us the fuck up!"

"Calm your ass down, baby girl," Sly said gently as his hawk eyes scanned the room. He was a tall, thin man with light skin and long, wavy hair that was pulled back in a ponytail. He was well into middle age, but due to his good genes and disciplined lifestyle, he was strong, fit, and trim. Sly was dressed in the same prison clothes as all the other inmates, but somehow his shit looked regal and boss on him. Like he was wearing royal robes or some shit.

"Is that all you got to say is calm down? You don't know what it's been like for us out there on them streets without you, Sly!"

"Don't worry, lil mama. Everythang is gonna be all right."

"But I'm telling you shit is getting real funky out there," Honore insisted. "Without you steering the ship the supply is drying up and all them businesses of yours are veering way off course."

Sly shrugged coolly. "I said don't worry about it, baby girl. The streets will always be the streets. Anything I got once, I can get it again. Just take care of yourself and help Cucci hold Frita down until I get out. My court date is gonna be here before you know it and I guarantee you I'm gonna walk outta that courthouse a free man."

Honore nodded. "I sure hope so because me and Cucci are both broke as hell."

"She still got her job at that diamond joint, don't she?"

Honore nodded again. "Yeah, but they don't hardly pay shit. And like I was saying, we had a lil situation the other night . . ." she started, then her voice trailed off.

"What kind of situation?" Sly leaned forward and probed.

Honore shrugged. "Just some stupidity. Some predator-type niggas got wind of a party we had set up at a hotel and they showed up to crash it. Cucci got fucked, we lost out on some bread, and a drunk white boy got his melon split. So now me and her are both broke again."

Sly shook his head in disgust. "I wish I could help you out more, baby girl, but you know them federal muthafuckas got my shit all tied up. They seized my houses, my whips, and they ran down on Frita for almost all my cash too."

"Damn, it's like that?" Honore was shocked. She had always thought Sly McFly was a legitimate bankroller who had endless dollas stashed away in secret underground vaults all over the big city. His name and "broke" just didn't even go in the same sentence as far as she was concerned, and to hear him say all his chess pieces had gotten wiped off the board was a real blow to her system.

"Damn, I didn't know we was doing that bad," Honore said, miffed and sounding close to tears. "I mean, yeah, Cucci's still working so she's holding shit down, and I get a couple of ends from Chimp Charlie ere'now and then . . . but I didn't know our shit was so crucial, Sly."

Sly waved his hand at her and grinned. "Don't even sweat that shit," he said in a cock-sure tone that always immediately calmed Honore's anxiety. "Niggas never pay you what they owe you when you locked up. I could get them niggas touched from right here if I wanted to, but I ain't living like that. I got shit clicking like clockwork in this joint, and as soon as I get out life's gonna be lovely for all of us again. Y'all just gotta find a way to survive for a little while longer, and then shit will be back to normal. I promise you. Anyway, now you done told me all the bad shit and we got that outta the way. You got some good news for me or what?"

"Not really," Honore said. "I got fired from my job, though."

"Fired?" Sly frowned. "Goddamn, baby girl. Seem like you ain't been working but two goddamn days!"

"Three," Honore corrected him. "I worked for three days. Nights, really. And then Cucci got caught up in that bullshit and I had to go get her. It was in the middle of the night and I was watching that hollering-ass baby. I couldn't bring myself to leave the lil guy all by himself, so I took him with me. My boss busted me when he saw me leaving the house on his security video, so he fired me."

"So whatchu gonna do now? Try to find yourself another gig? What about that jewelry joint where Cucci works? Just tell ya cousin to put you on so both of y'all can make some money."

Honore's eyes lit up. "You would think she would look out for a bitch, right? Man, I been tryna get Cucci to gimme the hook-up for a minute now but she be acting all funny-style whenever I bring that shit up! She keeps saying I don't have no job experience with that type of thang or some shit like that."

"Neither does Cucci!" Sly bucked, then stared deeply into her eyes. "Look, fuck Cucci. You can suck a dick just as good as she can, right?"

Honore nodded vigorously.

"Then cool. You been properly raised, Honore. When you see something you want don't you let Cucci or nobody else stand in ya way. Go get that fuckin' job, baby, and make sure you come out on top! Now, that's enough for today. I need to get back to running my game. Take heed to what the fuck I said and stay above water until I touch down."

CHAPTER 7

Joel Samuelson was a big-money roller and he executed whatever he pursued with style and class. His deep pockets showed in almost everything he did, which is why the dinner party he was holding tonight for his district managers and their families was nothing less than elegant and extravagant.

Joel was dressed to perfection in his smoke gray Armani suit, and he exuded supreme confidence as he sat at the large banquet table surrounded by people who adored him. Guest speakers from other major jewelry companies were in attendance, both to show their support and to soak up game from Joel and his team.

While it looked all good on the outside, on the low a lot of his co-workers and colleagues actually despised Joel for his bluntness and cut-throat business tactics. He could be outright snide sometimes and he was definitely cocky, but he was at the top of his game and he commanded their respect.

As a senior executive at the New York Diamond and Jewelry Exchange, Joel was responsible for bringing in nearly half of the company's revenue. His attitude was such that the haters could hate all the fuck they wanted to. As long as he was producing profits at a high level, there was not much that could be done to him. And while Joel was bringing in top dollars for the Diamond and Jewelry Exchange, you could best believe he was racking up some real pretty side dough for himself at the same time.

"Ladies and gentlemen," Joel stood up and announced with stern authority as he popped a bottle of Dom P. "I would like to thank you all for coming out tonight for our dinner celebration. The New York Diamond and Jewelry Exchange has been on a steep upward trajectory for the past two years and I would like to celebrate that success with each and every one of you. As you all know, I've been a major component of the company's success, and I've worked tirelessly to make this brand a major competitor in the most beautiful city in the world. I've also—"

"Yes, yes! Let's make a toast to the Diamond Kings of Fifth Avenue." Slimy Sal Silberman stood up from his seat and rudely interrupted his senior executive. Sal was a junior member of the executive board and a significant earner for the New York Diamond and Jewelry Exchange as well, and he hated Joel's guts. Although they were partners-in-crime together in a highly lucrative underground diamond scheme, Sal was as greedy as he was slimy, and he wanted Joel's job like he wanted his next breath. Joel was well aware of how his colleague felt about him, and the feeling was mutual. They took public jabs at each other and tried to show each other up at every opportunity, and tonight would be no exception.

"Hard work and dedication has always been our motto," Sal continued, ignoring Joel's bristling look, "and our stock is rising daily. And *that*, my dear friends and colleagues, is a testament to the drive and passion of not only Mr. Samuelson here, but to our entire staff and *all* of our associates. So, on behalf of the New York Diamond and Jewelry Exchange—and I'm talking about from the front desk clerks all the way up to the executives—we thank you all for your sacrifices and contributions."

The smiles were bright and the applause was thunderous, and judging from the hard line of Joel's jaw, it was obvious that he couldn't wait to regain the attention that had just been stolen from him.

"Thank you, and we appreciate your knack for the obvious, Sal," Joel said in a joking but dismissive tone. Joel knew Sal was secretly trying to get the lower-level employees to rally around him by interrupting his speech and highlighting their worth to the brand. It was an obvious slip-up, and Sal had taken advantage and exploited the opening, and now Joel was left steaming on the inside but standing at the podium he played it off like a boss.

"That concludes our remarks for this occasion," he said cheerfully. "I hope everyone enjoys the lovely meal that was prepared for us, and we'll have more festivities later in the evening. Dig in, people, dig in!"

With everyone dining and conversing with one another the mood at the banquet was festive and upbeat. Former co-workers, colleagues, and associates in the jewelry business were catching up with each other's lives, and promises to get together at future gatherings were being planned. Sipping a cocktail on the sidelines, Joel was secretly eyeing Sal like a hawk on a snake, waiting for his time to strike so he could sink his sharp talons in his colleague's bitch-ass neck. Minutes later he got his opportunity as he walked over to a table where Sal was engaged in conversation with two billionaire jewelers and their wives.

". . . and this is my son, Sal Junior," Sal said as he showed a picture of his baby boy to the sharply dressed gentleman, whose wife's finger bore a diamond so rare and exquisite its worth could feed a small country for years.

"He's a funny little guy," Sal said with a prideful smile. "He's always happy and pleasant. I can't get enough of him."

"Hey Sal," Joel said as he inserted himself in their midst.

"Let me get a look at baby Sal, the future up-and-coming executive of this company."

"Sure," Sal said as he passed him the picture.

"Wow, such a cute little guy," Joel remarked as he eyed the picture. "But his skin is a little dark, yes? In fact, he looks biracial. I don't know . . . your wife is very fair, Sal. Pale, actually. So what gives here? You have some African ancestors swinging from your family tree," Joel joked, "or is there something else going on? Something a little more . . . shall we say . . . illicit?"

"Excuse me!" Sal said jumping to his feet. His face flushed beet red with embarrassment and his jaw worked furiously as he tried to come up with a response. "What in the world did you just say?"

"I'm just saying, Sal," Joel said, loving the look of shame and rage on his business associate's face, "the kid looks like he has some Zulu in him. Some Shaka Zulu! Now, I'm not saying Mrs. Silberman ever caught herself a case of jungle fever or anything like that, I'm just saying your kid looks a little dark, that's all. I mean really, he's as handsome as can be. Just . . . dark."

The two high-society ladies at the table gasped and covered their mouths while their husbands tried to hide their laughter. Sal's face flamed red-hot with anger and embarrassment and he pushed his chair back and stood face-to-face with Joel with his fists clinched menacingly.

"You're taking things too far, buster," he fumed. "Children and wives are off-limits!"

"Relax, pal," Joel said, tamping down the heat as he patted Sal on the shoulder. "I apologize if you took my words seriously. I didn't mean to offend you or anything. I'm just busting your balls for old times' sake, that's all. Come on man, I know you can take a little joke. There's nothing dark about your baby. Your kid is fine. I mean, his nose is big as hell and he looks like he can nail a jump-shot from the concession stand, but he's nowhere near dark."

Sal sat back down trying to gather himself as Joel grinned and then confidently strolled away. The men at the table were still snickering at the major shade that had just been thrown on the junior executive, and Slimy Sal Silberman couldn't have been more humiliated. Rage bubbled up in his chest and threatened to burst from his mouth. Joel Samuelson had crossed the fucking line by insinuating that nigger shit about his wife and kid! Business partners or not, Samuelson was going to have to pay for that dirty stunt he had just pulled. Sal was too pissed off to even think about eating, and with his blood boiling under the other guests' snide looks of pity, he excused himself from the table and stormed out of the event altogether, vowing vengeance on Joel Samuelson with every step he took.

CHAPTER 8

Honore was shitting major bricks as she sat in the waiting room of the probation office. Her PO had called requesting a letter of employment to satisfy the terms of her probation, and now that she wasn't working, getting such a letter from Sal Silberman was outta the question.

Honore sat there mad as fuck and tryna look cute at the same time. She couldn't fucking believe that sucka-ass white man had fired her after she let him nibble all over her cookies and even lick up the crumbs! Stretched out on the floor of the attic nursery, she had put her wet juicy stuff down on Slimy Sam like a real pro; sucking his lil dick down to the bone until he sprayed her with his hot seed, and when he was finished she'd even licked all up under his saggy balls! She was the lip-lock queen, but he had *still* fired her!

Honore was dumb tight about the whole situation. As she sat down in the chair with her leg shaking from nervousness, all she could think about was her anorexic-ass PO violating her and sending her off to the Rock. Honore didn't like that bitch and the officer didn't like her ass neither. The only lever-age Honore had was the fact that she'd paid her fine on time, and up until the other day she had stayed fully employed. And now her freedom was in jeopardy over a series of unfortunate events that had ended in total fuckery.

"Forget all this shit," Honore muttered to herself as her eyes darted around the crowded room. A fine-ass nigga with long dreads and pretty teeth was checking people in at the desk, and they had given each other some real long looks on her way in. "I already know that bitch PO is gonna try and do me filthy since my job situation ain't A-one. Her ass is gonna straight lock me up. I might as well just dip on this appointment and buy myself some more time. Yeah, fuck it. I'm out. I'll call her later and make up some stupid shit just to reschedule."

Honore jumped up and jetted toward the exit, but just as she was nearing the door she heard her name called.

"Honore Morales? Is Honore Morales here?"

"Oh, shit!" she muttered under her breath as she ducked her head and switched her booty straight out the door. Honore knew if she went up in that office she would be coming back out in handcuffs, and there wasn't no way in hell she was marching back past fine-ass Mr. Dreadlocks with her hands behind her back wearing no goddamn metal bracelets!

Honore was beating feet down the steps and planning to duck into the subway when her phone rang. She snatched it outta her purse and glanced at it and saw that it was Slimy Sal's dickless ass.

"What the fuck do you want?" Honore spit with mad attitude. "Last time I checked you fucked me and fired me, you stank-breath clown! What the hell are you calling my phone for?"

"Honore, Honore," Sal said with a laugh. "Why all the hostility, sweetheart? I thought we grooved pretty good together the other night. I made you cum, didn't I?"

"Fuck you!" Honore shot back. She was embarrassed as hell by the way she had rode that asshole's face with her legs shaking and quivering like she was having a seizure. Sal's tongue job was way better than Chimp Charlie's was. Ten times better!

"Why the hell you calling me, Sal? I just left the probation office and I coulda messed around and went to jail today fucking with your grimy ass! I don't work for you no more so don't be calling me no more! Matter fact, you can kiss my ass!"

"Oh, I've already kissed it several times, and what a nice ass it was to kiss," Sal said as his creepy ass laughed in her ear. "But anyway, you're right. I did fire you. Sorry, but you're not the type of person I want taking care of my son. But you do have other qualities that I greatly admire, and another job just came open that I think you'd be perfect for."

"I took damn good care of your ugly-ass baby so I ain't trying to hear none of that noise. Besides, I ain't beat for you or nothing you gotta say," Honore said, still heated. "I don't trust lying-ass lil-dick creeps like you, Sal! Plus I ain't ya fucking puppet. If you ain't talking no real shit and ready to write me an employment letter for my PO, then I'm done rapping with you."

"Just meet me at the diner around the corner from my house," Sal said. "I promise it'll be worth your while. And you don't have to worry about your probation officer finding out that I fired you either. I'll have my secretary fax the letter of employment in right now, and I'll go along with everything just like normal, okay? Now you can cheer up and drop the attitude. Meet me there in a hour."

Honore hung up the phone feeling suspicious as fuck. She couldn't front like she wasn't relieved about that letter being faxed in, and now that she didn't have to explain shit and suck up to her probation officer, a huge weight was lifted off of her shoulders. Spotting a deli across the street where she knew some good kush was sold outta the back room, she decided to skip out on her appointment anyway now that her ass was covered. She was gonna go get her head right, slam down a turkey and cheese hero, and then go see what kind of bullshit job Sal had planned for her.

★ ★ ★

Dressed to impress, Honore strolled inside the crowded diner about twenty minutes late and saw Sal sitting in a booth alone. The joint was full of old white people, the kind of pot-bellied, red-nosed dudes who smoked cigars and wore those stupid little golf shirts. Honore swung her happy hips from left to right in her thigh-high Versace plaid skirt as she flounced by, knowing damn well that every old man in the joint was focused on the sweet honey-colored flesh she was hiding up under it.

"I knew you were going to be late," Sal said as he shoveled a plate of sausage, eggs, and pancakes into his face. "What do you people run on, nigger time, or something like that?" He laughed and then shrugged. "No worries. With that hot mouth of yours, you've already shown me that you're a meat lover, so I took the liberty of ordering you some steak and eggs."

"I ain't hungry so you can skip all the small talk, Sal," Honore riffed as she twisted her lips and gave him the stupid look. She slid into the booth across from him and said, "So what's the move? I came here to talk business, so what you got for me? Ga'head and spit it out because I got other shit to do."

"A straight-forward woman who knows exactly what she wants, huh? Yeah, I really like that about you Honore," Sal said as he wiped his mouth with a napkin. "That's why I picked you to do this particular favor for me. Because I need somebody who will just go in and do whatever has to be done."

"Oh yeah? And what type of shit you cooking up that's gotta be done?"

Sal shrugged as he chewed. "Just a little sneaking around. You know, the kind of sneaking in and sneaking out that you did at my house the night you kidnapped my son."

Forgetting where she was, Honore broke. "For the last fuckin' time I ain't *kidnap* your fuckin' son!"

"*Didn't*," Sal said quietly. You mean you *didn't* kidnap my son. We'll work on your grammar later, but right now I'm having a little issue that needs to be resolved. I'm going to be traveling out of the country in a couple of weeks, and while I'm gone I need to have a certain package dropped off in a certain person's house without him knowing about it."

Honore nodded as she smirked. "So you saying you need some shit planted on somebody and you wanna be outta town when it's done so nobody knows you were down with it, huh?"

"Right," Slimy Sal said, looking up from his plate. "You're smarter than you look, and that's a good thing. The person I want you to target is very rich, but he's also very ignorant. He's an arrogant prick and he's been a major thorn in my side for quite a while now. Plus, he insulted my wife in the presence of guests! I want you to sneak into his house and leave something there that will get him buried ten feet deep in a federal prison cell where he'll rot away for the rest of his life."

Right off the bat Honore bucked. "Uh-uh, my nigga." She shook her head back and forth making her soft curls bobble. "Hell no. I don't care what kinda shit you call the cops and tell 'em about me, I ain't playing mule-mama and carrying no drugs for you or nobody else, okay? Been there and already got busted for that shit. You want somebody to plant some meth or rock or lady on ya boy, you betta find somebody else, 'cause if shit goes left I ain't going to jail."

Sal shook his head and laughed. "I'm not involved in the drug trade, Honore, and nobody is going to jail. I'm a legitimate businessman in the diamond industry."

"Yeah, and you's a slimy asshole too, for fuckin' firing me!"

"Listen, the past is in the past, and this job is a fairly simple way to make a lot of money. You sneak in, leave the item where I tell you to leave it, and you sneak out. That's it. Either you're game to do it or you're not."

Honore thought about it for a second and then she nodded. "A'ight," she agreed, picking up a piece of sausage from Sal's plate and popping it in her mouth. "That sounds like something I might be able to pull off," she said, figuring what the hell. She had lined up plenty of niggas to take a fall in her time. This sounded like some easy-money shit that was right up her ally.

"So what's in it for me?"

"Well, first off, I'm offering you my word that I won't have your sweet ass prosecuted and thrown in jail," Sal said with authority. He watched her face turn red hot with anger before he spoke again. "And when the job has been completed I'm willing to give you a five-thousand-dollar cash payment to put in your pretty little pockets. That should buy you all the bubble gum you can chew and still be ample compensation until you find another job."

Honore played like she was considering his offer, but she knew she couldn't turn a five-rack lick down. Her and Cucci were down to eating Vienna sausages and crackers so she needed the damn money. Plus she had to keep Sal's big-ass mouth shut. He knew damn well she wasn't trying to kidnap his brat, but he had caught her on video so he had her by the nipples and she had to find a way to make him let go.

"Here," Sal said as he slid an envelope across the table toward her. "Take it. Here's half the money and all the instructions and background information you'll need on your mark. Study everything very carefully and when I give you the word I want you to move in and complete the job. I'll supply you with the object before I go out of town, and you make sure you leave it exactly where I tell you to. I don't care how you get inside of the mark's house. You can smash a window, break down the door, do whatever it takes, as long as the job gets done."

"Yeah, a'ight, Sal," Honore said with a shrug as she slid the envelope deep down in her designer purse. "Tell 'em to put that steak and eggs in a doggy bag for me and we got a deal. Hurry the hell up, too. I got shit to do."

"No problem, sexy." Sal laughed, eyeing her bulging cleavage. "Just be sure to answer your phone when I call you. In fact, I might need a little midnight snack before our mission gets set in motion. Come by after Leah goes to sleep tonight and I'll throw in an extra couple of hundred dollars just to help you out."

"Go fuck yourself," Honore said good-naturedly as she stood up to leave with half the cash secured in her purse. She paused with her hand on her hip knowing she looked like a sweet caramel Popsicle dream. "I ain't never sucking your lil bent-up dick again in life, baby, so don't hit my damn jack until it's time for me to do what I do. You want ya knob slobbed, you better call that flat-booty wife of yours and make a wish muthafucka. Make a wish!"

CHAPTER 9

Cucci was about to complete her first solo caper of selling crushed ice on the black market and she was hyped as hell. A couple of weeks earlier the big boss Joel Samuelson had picked her up in a limo and taken her to a sleazy-looking jewelry store down on Fulton Street in Brooklyn. There, Cucci had dropped off a mid-priced diamond that she had signed out of the vault at the New York Diamond and Jewelry Exchange based on a fake requisition request to showcase it at an area diamond conference. She had been shitting bricks when she handed the diamond over to Joel, but he had told her not to worry because both she and the diamond were in very capable and experienced hands.

"This is a very clandestine and methodical diamond ring I belong to, Rayven," he told Cucci. "I've been doing this for many years now, and there's practically no chance of being caught. Unless you're stupid enough to trust the wrong person, that is."

Cucci was bright-eyed and eager as they got shit moving. The elderly owner of the Fulton Street jewelry store had just called to tell Joel that the stolen diamond had been successfully sold on the underground black market, and that an exact cloned replica of the original diamond was ready to be picked up so it could replace the stolen diamond and be returned to the company's vault.

Cucci was so amped up on dollar signs that her mouth was watering as she and Joel stepped outta his shiny new whip and headed toward the side door of the jewelry store looking to make their score.

"Listen and learn," Joel instructed Cucci. They hurried down an alley adjacent to the bustling streets of the ballistic town of Brooklyn, and now as they waited for the ancient security guard to unlock the door and let them in, Joel warned her to keep her mouth closed and let him do all the talking.

"Remember, I'm the teacher and I want you to be a very good student, because one of these days you're going to play a much bigger part and have a much larger role in this operation. And of course that means you'll be making a lot more money too."

Cucci was so excited she damn near peed down her leg like a puppy. She didn't care if she had to buy Joel a juicy red apple and be the teacher's favorite pet as they entered the musty old jewelry store. All she knew is that she wanted that damn money!

They were led in the back by a real ugly white girl who looked like she mighta been the owner's daughter. The hit chick took one look at Cucci sporting her silky hair, artfully applied makeup, and a perfectly round ass that twitched back and forth under her skirt, and she turned up her lips in a jealous smirk.

Cucci gave not a damn about that gray bitch as she followed Joel into a back room where the owner was waiting for them.

"Hello my friend," said a tall white man who was standing next to the old jeweler. He was a handsome, well-dressed cat who looked to be in his late thirties or early forties, and he had one of those sexy French accents. He reached out and shook Joel's hand and the two men greeted each other warmly.

Immediately, Cucci remembered exactly who the hell dude was. He was the damn key to this whole operation because he was the one who smuggled the diamonds outta the country, crushed them up into smaller pieces that looked like crystal ice, and then sold them on the underground market in Belgium and other places in Europe. Cucci's nose was twitching and she was licking her chops like a bloodhound. She could practically smell all the cash that was stuffed in his pockets.

"Avi," Joel reintroduced them, "you remember Rayven, the young protégée that I told you about. Rayven was actually responsible for acquiring this particular jewel for us, and she's here to be rewarded for her hard work and exceptional efforts."

Cucci grinned as that French nigga took her hand and pressed his warm pink lips to the back of it.

"Pleased to meet you again, Rayven. You provided us with a marvelous jewel, and I think you'll be quite pleased with the proceeds."

With the small talk out of the way, the three men began having a back-and-forth conversation about some past work they'd done together, but Cucci wasn't hardly paying none of that shit no attention. She was too busy thinking about that moolah and wondering if she should hit Neiman Marcus first, or one of those quaint little shops on Fifth Avenue that always had the priciest shoes and the baddest gear.

Finally, Avi pulled an envelope out of his jacket pocket and passed it to Joel. Cucci's eyes locked on that thick shit as Joel opened it and reached inside. He tore off a stack of bills and handed them back to Avi, then he tore off a smaller but still nice-sized stack and passed it to the old-man jeweler, and then finally he slid off a smaller slice and passed it to Cucci.

"Here's ten grand," he told Cucci with a proud smile. "Not

bad for five minutes' worth of work, eh? Welcome to the team, Rayven. I have a feeling we're going to do some very good business together my dear."

Cucci floated outta that jewelry store on a money-green cloud, and she was still riding that shit hours later when she arrived back home weighed down with designer bags and boxes from the hottest stores in town.

She had shopped until the stores closed down, and she was like a junkie riding the waves of a high, already anticipating how she was gonna get the next one. But as eager and excited as she was, her cousin Honore had her beat.

"Ooooh, Cucci Momma!" Honore had growled when she saw the colorful boxes and bags representing some of her favorite shops. Cucci fell in the door carrying all her goodies and collapsed in the middle of the living room floor.

Sitting on her ass, she began digging in bags and pulling out designer shit and flinging it toward Honore as they both shrieked in happiness.

"Givenchy?" Honore screamed in disbelief as she held up a butter-yellow laced dress that she knew was gonna fit her ass like a second skin. "Bitch where you get this from? How you get the money? Who the fuck took you shopping???"

"I took my damn self shopping," Cucci said proudly as she continued reaching in the bag and pulling out sexy and expensive gear. "I worked my ass off for this money!"

"Damn!" Honore hissed as her greedy hands snatched at all the finery. Money made her world go around, and there was no way in fuck she was telling Cucci about the twenty-five hunnerd she was sitting on from Slimy Sal!

"That's the kind of work I wanna do!" Honore said eagerly. "Y'all got anymore jobs lined up at that jewelry joint? How the hell can you get some more work like this?"

"Oh, there's more work to be done," Cucci said mysteriously as she separated all the clothes out and split them into two equal piles, one for her and one for her cousin. "And don't worry, I didn't spend it all up, neither. I saved some money to pay the rent and to put some groceries in the fridge, and guess what else I saved some for?"

"What?" Honore said breathlessly with her eyes all lit up.

Cucci's eyes sparkled and a devilish grin spread across her face as she pulled out her purse and divided the remainder of her cash up and then handed Honore half. "Me and you 'bout to turn up a bottle of Krug, bitch! We toasting up and hitting the club tonight, boo!"

CHAPTER 10

Despite Cucci's good fortune and generous nature, Honore had a shitty look on her face a week later as she made the long-ass bus ride back to Rikers to visit her infamous godfather, Sly McFly. The last time she had crossed the bridge and traveled to the Rock to see him was because she was broke as all outdoors and she needed some cash. This time she had some yardage in her pockets and she was going to see Sly because she had a lick to hit and she needed his guidance and opinion before she stepped off into it.

Honore knew this was something she could never talk about over the phone. It was the kind of street shit that the authorities listened for on all inmate calls. She even had to watch her mouth when she and Sly were sitting face-to-face because everybody knew the walls in jail had ears.

"Hello, beautiful. I see you back up at this hell hole again, huh?" Sly grinned as he was led in by a guard, swinging his arms freely, and took a seat on a stool on the opposite side of the glass. Sly was cooler than the other side of the pillow, and as usual he was his normal upbeat self. With his wavy hair pulled back in a ponytail, his mustache and goatee neatly trimmed, and his prison jumpsuit pressed and starched with the edges sharp enough to cut a vein, he sat there looking like he ain't have a care in the damn world.

"Yeah," Honore said softly. She loved the shit outta this old man. Sly had been like a father to her for her whole life. He had looked out for her and taught her every damn thing she knew. "I just wanted to come see how you was doing, and plus I need to run something serious past you."

"Hey, I ain't complaining," Sly said, leaning back as he relaxed. "What's going down? Watch how you say shit outta ya mouth, though. The usual officers that I got a grip on ain't here today."

"Well, you know I hate seeing you locked up in here," Honore said as she shifted positions in the filthy chair. The dirt and grime all around her disgusted her and that shit was making her itch. "But I got a situation that can be real profitable if handled the right way. Of course, there's a few strings attached to the whole shit and I gotta be in major focus mode, but I think the reward really makes it worth my time. Bottom line, a power move is about to go down. Two big hittas in the diamond industry are having a long-dick pissing contest. One hitta wants me to knock the other one off his square."

Sly frowned and nodded. "A'ight. I see where you going with this." He rubbed his goatee as he thought about it. "So tell me this, baby girl. Which one of them muthafuckas are you in the bed with? The bigger fish or the smaller one? Who can you gain the most leverage from? Is this a dirt nap game or just a scandal?"

"I'm in the sheets grinding all over the smaller guy," Honore said, understanding the code and not speaking names. "We ain't taking no naps though. It's more of an insider scandal. The dude I'm boning wants me to plant a certain item on the big guy and line his ass up with the alphabet boys."

"Hmmm . . . I'm guessing it's one of those shiny rocks," Sly mused. "Am I right?"

"Exactly," Honore responded enthusiastically. "There's a

few grand in it for me and Cucci, but dude's got my hands tied because he caught me slipping with some shit I did to help Cucci out. I basically don't have a fucking choice. I need the money and I need him to keep his mouth shut or probation will violate me, and the next thing you know I'll be right across the way from here, chilling in a bunk in Rosie."

"You always have a choice baby girl," Sly said as he narrowed his eyes at her. "If that nigga has you by the balls then it's time to turn the tables. I'm sure the big boss wouldn't like the fact that his underling is attempting to get him jammed up. So what you gotta do is stall the little guy for a while until you get it all figured out, nah'm sayin'? Make up some shit about why you can't make ya moves for a couple of weeks. Then in the meantime, switch shit up and bring the plot to the bigger guy. Make him an offer he can't refuse. I guarantee he will be very appreciative of the information you provide and he'll compensate you properly. Bottom line, you gotta ass-fuck the little guy. That's what every successful businessman does."

"Damn Sly, you right!" Honore said as her eyes lit up. "Why the hell didn't I think of that? It's a risky move but it's well worth it. The little guy can't fucking stand the big boss and I'm pretty sure the feeling is mutual. So how do you think we should approach the head nigga in charge?"

"Whatever you do, don't go in on no soft shit," Sly responded with a warning in his eyes. "Make it clear that he don't have a fuckin' choice. Either he rocks with you and your demands, or he can be a victim and suffer the consequences. Remember, you ain't going in there asking him for no favors. Men of power respect power, whether it's in the pussy or in the pocket. So be cold and collected. Let that muthafucka know that he either gets down or he *lays* down. Plain and fucking simple. So get with Cucci and make sure y'all put ya heads together and come correct. You dig me?"

"Yes. Damn right," Honore said as she spoke into the jail phone. "Sly, I can't thank you enough. You always know the right shit to say. You're always on point old man, I'll give you that."

"They don't call me Sly for nothing, youngin," Sly said as he smiled at the beautiful young girl that he had practically raised.

"By the way," Honore said as she prepared to leave, "Cucci got a real good side-hustle going on at her jewelry-joint job. She just brought home some real nice ends last week and I'ma put some money on your books on the way out today, okay?"

Sly waved her off. "Don't worry about me, my darling. Just make sure you handle that business properly and then come back and see me when the shit is done. Matter of fact, I'm gonna put a few guys on stand-by just in case. You and Cucci stay on ya game and gimme a call before the shit gets real."

"Gotcha," Honore confirmed with a big grin. Getting closer to the nasty glass between them, she pursed her lips and blew a kiss, and after saying her goodbyes to Sly McFly, Honore walked outta the visiting room at Rikers Island reinvigorated and full of spunk and energy. Thanks to her criminal-minded godfather, she and Cucci had a solid plan. Now it was time for them to get their scheming asses out there and execute it!

CHAPTER 11

If there was one thing Cucci had on her that beat every damn thing else she had going for her, it was her eyeballs. Cucci Momma saw every damn thing all the damn time, and couldn't nothing go on under her nose without her greedy eyeballs picking up on it. So when her cousin Honore told her about the deal she'd made with Slimy Sal to ass-fuck Joel Samuelson, Cucci was down all the way to the ground, and she knew exactly how they could get inside Joel's house.

"Wake yo punk ass up!" Cucci barked as she flung a whole damn Kool-Aid pitcher full of cold water down into the white man's sleeping face. His mouth was gapped open and his thin pink lips were stretched tightly over his teeth. "C'mon! Get the fuck up. Sleepy time is over, boss man."

Joel Samuelson, a millionaire tycoon, senior executive at the New York Diamond and Jewelry Exchange, and the plug that Cucci was fucking, lunged up choking and spitting like a muthafucka as his eyes fluttered and he fought to breathe and get his bearings together. A look of shock and horror fell down over his sleepy face as he saw the two masked figures lurking over him in the privacy of his own bedroom.

"What the hell is going on?" the powerful executive

screamed. He yanked at the expensive bedspread and pulled it up over his head like it was gonna shield him from an assault. Then, like the big bitch that he really was, Joel pissed on himself and lay there in the darkness, quivering in horror. "Please don't hurt me," he begged. "I'll give you whatever you want, just please don't harm me."

"Shut up!" Cucci snapped as she took off her mask. "It's me, stupid ass!"

"Rayven?" he shrieked, surprised to find that the beautiful young employee he was fucking and plucking was standing over him.

"Uh-huh," Cucci said, tooting up her lips. "It's me. Damn right it's me."

"Oh my God! What's going on? Why are you doing this? I thought we had a good deal going between us! We were working so well together! I can't believe—"

"First of all,"—Cucci clicked on the light switch and cut him off with a raised hand—"ya think I didn't notice when I got the littlest slice of that lettuce pie you dished out the other day? *I'm* the one who took all the risks by signing that diamond outta the vault, and you and Avi got most of the bank! Second of all, stop all that damn yelling. Trust me, you woulda woke up dead and in hell if we had come here to hurt you, Joel! Me and my cousin are just here to put you up on some major game and to give you the opportunity to make some choices. The rest is up to you."

"R-r-rayven," Joel repeated like he hadn't heard a damn thing she said. He licked his lips nervously and squinted under the glaring light. "I-I-I just can't believe you broke into my house! Goodness! What the hell are you even doing here? How the hell did you get in?"

"I used your security code," Cucci said simply. "You know the one you texted me that time when you wanted me to deliver you some head on heels in the middle of the night, remember?"

Joel damn sure remembered that dick-licking Cucci had put on him, and now his voice rose in fear and anger. "You were supposed to delete that text dammit! What the hell do you want?"

"Relax, old man," Honore said as she took her mask off as well. "Cucci already told you. It don't matter how the hell we got up in here because we ain't the ones you need to be worrying about! Seems like you done made yourself an enemy who wants to see you take a real bad fall. I'm sure you know who I'm talking about. Your homeboy Slimy Sal. The dude you convinced to hire me to babysit his brat. Good looking out for that one, but Sal is a real scheming-ass prickster and apparently you done said something stupid to piss him off. He's all hot and heated behind that shit, and he offered me and Cucci ten thousand dollars each to set you up."

"What?" Joel shrieked.

Hearing that, Cucci cut her eyes at her cousin and smiled. She peeped Honore's trickery and she loved it! Her girl was lying her ass off. She had told Cucci they were gonna split twenty-five hunnerd from Sal, and here she was spitting Joel some shit about ten grand each. Cucci was impressed. It was a real smoove move on Honore's part, and it wasn't like Joel was gonna call that nigga Sal up and verify that shit.

"He wants to set me up? Set me up for what?" Joel demanded as he sat up in his wet bed. The thin spread fell down to his waist and his nasty taco meat chest hair was exposed.

"Jail time!" Honore said.

"You must be kidding me!" Joel exploded. "I don't believe it. That whining bastard Sal isn't stupid enough to cross me. Tell me what the hell is going on! Why the fuck would he try to take me down?"

Cucci shrugged. "Beats me. But whatever you did it must have upset him real bad." She sat down on the edge of the bed that she had fucked him in numerous times and tried to make him feel more comfortable as she explained, "Look, Sal wants to fry your ass until you're real crispy. He's willing to pay us a pretty penny just to plant some shit in here that could send you to prison for years and totally fuck up your good name and ruin your reputation."

Cucci reached down in her back pocket and pulled out a picture of a diamond. It was the rare Moussaieff Red Diamond, and that shit was worth *boo-coo* cash. According to what she'd read in a bulletin at work, the diamond was supposed to be auctioned off soon to the highest bidder, but right now it was the property of the New York Diamond and Jewelry Exchange, and the only two people who were authorized to sign a stone of that magnitude out of the store were Joel and Sal. They were the only two with access to that security level of the vault, and they were planning to yap that shit before it could be auctioned off and replace it with a clone.

Cucci saw the confusion in Joel's eyes turn into rage as the wheels started turning around and around in his head. A few moments later realization set in and he knew the girls were telling the truth.

"That dirty son of a bitch!" Joel bitched as anger replaced his earlier fear. A shock of thin gray hair fell over his forehead and flecks of spit were on his lips as they trembled in a crook's indignation. "Oh, so I'm supposed to help him steal the diamond, and then that slimy piece of shit is gonna try to get you to plant it on me so he can turn me in? After all the work we've done together and all the money we've made? I'm the one who brought him into the game in the first place! I introduced him to the key players and showed him the ropes!" Joel shook his head in disgust. "That's the kind of thanks I get for helping a fellow Jew get a toe up in this business. I should have known that spineless fucker would try to double-cross me some day!"

Honore shrugged as she chewed and popped on her spearmint gum. "Well, that's why we here yakking with you instead of jacking your ass up," she said. "We ain't feeling Sal's slimy ass either, and we figured since you're the head honcho you might wanna get some get-back on him and make us a counter-offer. So instead of helping Sal send you to jail and ruin your lil jet-setting life, me and Cucci are giving you a chance to turn the tables on him and up-up the stakes. So what do you think about that?"

"What exactly is it that you two want?" Joel snapped. His face was turning red with quiet rage. "You wanna shake me down, is that it? So what's to stop me from calling the police and letting them in on your whole little brainless plot? I can have you both arrested for breaking and entering on top of attempted blackmail at the snap of my fingers."

"Is that right?" Cucci said as her eyes flashed darkly and her ghetto blood started flowing hotly through her veins. "Now why in the hell would you wanna do some stupid shit like that? Even if you change your security code it won't be enough to stop two killer project bitches like us," she warned him evilly. "We'll just cut some wires and disable all your high-tech security bullshit and end up right back inside your house. We'll catch your ass laying up here raising the roof and snoring deep in your third dream, and you won't hear a damn thing until the devil calls out your name, ain't that right Honore? Trust me, what we just did can easily be done again, and the next time it won't be just me and my cousin standing over you while you sleeping, I can guarantee you that. Nah, next time we'll bring two big black niggas along for the ride. They'll be standing over your bed swinging baseball bats and they won't be willing to do no talking to you at all. Now, don't get me wrong, Mr. Samuelson. You're a real good boss and I appreciate you for putting me on with ya diamond hustle and for getting my cousin that babysitting job too. But I been sucking your dick for a minute now and you ain't never gave me no twenty grand payday for all the work I been putting in. So the way I see it, I did you a real good solid by coming over here peacefully to give you the heads-up, and to offer you a choice in this matter. Can't you see I'm giving you an opportunity to flip the script and turn the tables on that greedy sucker-ass Sal? Even if I don't get the job done for him that's not gonna stop him from sending somebody else after you. And the next person might not like the way your old wrinkled-up sweaty balls smell coming straight outta ya drawers. They might wanna bash your brains in without even waking you up. So, whatever you do is up to you, but now is the time to choose, buddy. If you like living you'll choose wisely."

Joel leaned back against his headboard and exhaled heavily. He was in a fucked-up situation and he couldn't deny it. The girl was right. If Sal Silberman was after his head, then he wouldn't stop here, even if he picked up the phone right now and had the two girls arrested. Besides, there was no way Joel could complain to the authorities about Sal trying to get a stolen diamond planted on him anyway. Hell, he was gonna be the one signing it out of the Diamond Exchange's vault so it could be fabricated by a crooked jeweler in Brooklyn and then handed off to be crushed and sold by an underground Belgian trader. No, calling the police and reporting Rayven and her cousin would be a very foolish move indeed. A foolish move that would likely expose all of his black market dealings and get him thrown in jail for life.

And right then life was what Joel wanted from Sal Silberman. He wanted that whining little fuck to pay for this transgression with his life.

Joel looked up at Rayven and nodded his head. He was a shrewd businessman and he knew when to pluck and when to hold. These two ghettofied scammers were obviously about their business, and the way they had caught him with his pants down told him he was lucky to even be getting a choice in the matter. They could have easily waited until he handed the diamond over to Sal, then planted it in his house and left it for the police to find, or worse, they could have rearranged his whole face while he was sleeping. But they didn't.

Rayven Jones, aka Cucci, was the best piece of ass he'd had in a very long time, and she blew cock like she was born with a silver dick in her mouth. But both of these girls could be very beneficial to him in the future. He already knew Rayven was smart and cunning, and her beautifully gorgeous cousin Honore seemed just as ambitious and crafty.

"Okay," Joel finally said. "I'll pay you double—no, triple what Sal is paying you. But I don't want you to plant anything on him. No, that's too simple-minded. What I want you to do is *plant* his treacherous ass in the ground. That's my offer. I'll give you thirty grand to put Slimy Sal Silberman down like a rabid *dog*."

"Thirty grand *each*, right?" Cucci clarified.

Joel nodded. "That's what I said. Thirty each."

Honore and Cucci quickly glanced at each other as dollar signs jumped in their eyes and the *cha-ching!* sound of a cash register sounded off in their brains. There was no doubt in their little scheming minds that they were thinking the absolute same thing. Hell yeah they would plant Sal's ass! Triple the cash was sweet music to their ears!

"A'ight, I guess triple sounds fine," Cucci said, sporting the poker face.

Joel nodded. "I'll give you half of the money in cash, and then you'll get the other half when I see word of that shithead's murder on the news and then sit shiva with his family at his funeral. Are we good?"

"Hell yeah, it's all good, boss," Cucci giggled as she thought about all that cream. "Now make sure you get up outta that wet bed and take care of yourself! If I was you I would forget about fuckin' with that Moussaieff diamond though, because if you ever get down with Sal again he's gonna have some FBI jokers and them Pinkerton boyz banging down your door. Now, I'ma take it that you ain't tryna get knocked and end up out on Rikers Island washing none of

Crazy Haz's dirty drawers, so ga'head and get our cash up and don't try nothing stupid."

Cucci grinned down at her boss and then she pushed her chest out so he could get a good look at her thick nipples and her puffed-up cleavage. "Hey, me and you was supposed to meet up and have us a lil play date this week. So what's up? You still wanna fuck?"

Joel's eyes roamed over those perfect tits with the inch-long nipples, and despite his anger his dick leaped a country mile and almost came up outta his pissed-up drawers.

"Yeah." His voice was gruff and he had a big-time attitude, but he had a serious boner going on too. He reached out and slapped Cucci on her thick, round ass. "But there'll be no more hooking up at my place anymore. From now on we'll get together at a hotel because I want you two bitches to stay the fuck away from my house!"

CHAPTER 12

It was hot and muggy in the tiny project apartment and Honore was stretched out on the couch watching a stupid reality show on television while her aunt Frita was in the kitchen putting a hurting on some homemade sweet potato pies. Frita was her mother's older sister, and judging by the old photos that Honore had seen, the two beautiful women looked just alike.

Honore's mother had been murdered by her father before she was old enough to remember her, and Frita had raised Honore right alongside of her daughter Cucci, just like they were sisters. Even though Frita had always loved on Honore and treated her the same way she treated Cucci, Honore had always been drawn to her godfather, Sly McFly, who had guided her and looked out for her for as long as she could re-member. While Cucci and Frita were closer than close, Sly McFly was much more than Honore's mentor and friend, and she was thankful that his court date was right around the cor-ner and it looked like he would soon be hitting the bricks and coming home.

But right now Frita had the small apartment stankin' like a mutha. The delicious-looking pans of heaven had been in the oven just long enough to send their delightful scents of cinnamon, nutmeg, butter, and vanilla wafting through the warm air, and Honore couldn't wait to get her a slice.

She had just grabbed the remote control to flip the channel when the telephone rang.

"I got it," she called out to her aunt, who was running water in the kitchen sink and probably washing dishes.

"Hello?"

Honore picked up the phone and waited while the familiar recording played, the one you got whenever you got a call from jail. She pressed the required numbers and then waited until she heard a click and Sly McFly's deep male voice slid into her ear.

"Ay, hit this jack real quick," he said and spit out ten digits at her real fast before hanging up the phone.

Honore knew what time it was. Somebody musta snuck a cell phone in to the jail and Sly wanted to talk to her without them nosey COs listening in on the line.

"What's good, baby girl?" he picked up the line and asked as soon as she called. Honore grinned. This nigga sounded like he was chilling on a yacht somewhere throwing back shots of Ciroc and cranberry juice. Jail didn't have shit on Sly McFly, because no matter where he was, he was always free in his mind.

"Ain't nothing much happening," Honore said, trying to amp up the tone in her voice so she didn't bust his good mood. If there was one thing Sly McFly couldn't stand it was no whining-ass bitch. He was the type of OG playa who believed in staying up at all times and making shit happen for yourself.

"I'm doing pretty good. I'm still tryna find a way to get a job in that diamond spot in Manhattan where Cucci works, though. I figure if I can just get my toe in the door and get access to a few pieces of that expensive jewelry, then maybe we can snatch up a few of those diamonds on the low and then hustle them off to some of these niggas around the way."

"Now I know I taught yo ass better than that," Sly said turning serious with his voice going low and deep. "You cut from my type of cloth Honore, so don't be thinking with no bird-type brain. I raised you to be a hustler and a go-getter, my princess. I purposely ain't send nobody to give you no money yet 'cause I wanted to see what the fuck you was gonna do if I wasn't around."

"I'm bustin' my ass out here," Honore said, getting aggravated. "I ain't sitting around waiting on no handouts. I'm tryna stay outta jail and make shit happen at the same time. Some of the plays I'm making ain't panning out how they should, but that don't mean I ain't thinking and scheming and putting in work. You know how it is out here, Sly. I'm a female so niggas be steady tryna yank me. Plus, I don't have all the resources and connects you have either, nigga. But that don't mean I'ma lay down and roll over. Hell no. I'ma get mine."

"Yeah. Now that's the type of fire I wanna see in you," Sly said smoothly into the phone. "Whatever kinda gigs you got going, you gotta make 'em work in your favor, darling. But you also gotta know when you're looking a gift horse dead in his mouth."

"Huh?" Honore said, confused as fuck and failing to follow him. "What you mean by that?"

"I mean *fuck* tryna get that damn job just so you can steal shit and sell it to some bum-ass low-level niggas on the corner! Don't fuck around and get fired before you get ya foot in the door! You gotta think bigger than that, baby doll! It's time for you to be your own fucking boss. If you lucky enough to get up on that job you better walk on eggshells and play every last one of your cards right! You gotta take that damn job and look to make it even bigger than what it already is!

"The first thing you wanna do is learn how them diamond niggas operate inside and out. Be a perfect employee and get them to trust you. Study the craft and identify all the major power players. Next, find out who can be corrupted. Throw some pussy juice at a few of them big boys and see who licks it up. You know how to play the game. Drop ya damn drawers and get on ya knees if you have to.

"Next, when you feel you got a handle on the whole hustle, go get yourself a team of chicks who think just like you and teach them the game. Put them in position to help you make money so you can build you an empire, baby. It's all a state of mind, Honore. An empire state of mind! Girl, if you just do what I say and follow my instructions you can be the fucking Queen of Diamonds one day. All you gotta do is elevate ya hustle and think bigger. This could be the ultimate power move if you can use your brain and put yourself in the right position. You betta act like I raised you, girl! Swing ya damn bat and go for the home run!"

"That's what I needed to hear on some real shit," Honore said as she soaked in the game that Sly had just dropped on her. "I was tryna tell Cucci the same type of shit. We gotta think bigger and go harder! I didn't know exactly how to organize all that shit in my head, but you just made it much clearer to me. And trust, I already know how you do," Honore said, catching the wave of Sly's excitement, which put her mind at ease for the first time all day and boosted up her confidence. "I promise I'm not gonna let you down. I'ma take your advice and make this shit shake. Plus, I like how 'the Queen of Diamonds' sounds. Sounds like a name that's fit for me."

"You damn right it is," Sly chuckled and agreed.

"Thank you so damn much, Sly," Honore gushed. You always come through for a bitch. I'ma take over this shit. Just watch me."

"That's what I'm here for," Sly said as he laughed at his young protégée. "But first you gotta get the damn job," he reminded her.

"True shit," she said with a frown. "I've been working on Cucci tryna get her to hook me up, but now I'ma really have to start leaning on her even harder."

"Do what you gotta do," Sly said. "Look, I gotta run. I'll see you in a minute, but in the meantime I want you to give Frita a message for me. Tell her I'ma send Charlie over with some scratch to put in y'all pockets just to hold you over until you get your plan mapped out. Now what *you* gotta do is handle your fucking business, 'cause I got my court date coming up and I'm getting the fuck outta here. Believe me, when I come home I'ma set them streets back on fire like I ain't never missed a fucking beat. Everybody in the quantum town of Queens better be fully prepared for the return of this here Sly nigga. Ya heard?"

As it turned out, Cucci Momma caught a case of the guilts and the next time she was riding Joel Samuelson's dick and whispering sweet nothings in his ear, she mentioned her cousin Honore.

"Remember, if me and Honore take Sal down for you then that means my cousin is gonna be out of a job."

"And?" Joel gripped her magnificent black ass and gasped in between moans.

"Well,"—Cucci humped down on him hard and licked his earlobe—"that means I'm gonna need another lil favor on top of the deal we already have."

Joel shuddered and wheezed as her tongue darted out from between her chocolate lips and licked his pink nipple. "What kind of favor?"

"A job type of favor. I need for my cousin Honore to get hired at the New York Diamond and Jewelry Exchange, and come to work right beside me and get the same benefits I get."

Cucci winded her hips in fast circles as she milked his stiff meat with her inner muscles. "All you gotta do is hand us off our cash, then put Honore on the payroll and get her set up with HR, and then you can just go back to work like nothing ever happened and everything will still be sweet in your life. How's that sound? Do we have us a deal or nah?"

"Yes!" Joel cried out as he felt the best damn orgasm he'd ever had struggling to bust outta the tip of his swollen dick. "It's a deal!" he shrieked as he slapped Cucci on her ass like a jockey on a slow horse. "It's a deal . . . oh, goddamn," Joel moaned as slobber slid outta the corner of his mouth and his eyes rolled back in his head. "It's a sweet, delicious motherfucking deal!"

CHAPTER 13

Dressed to impress, Honore was sitting outside of the court-house in a rented all-white Audi that still smelled brand-new. She'd spent most of the twenty-five hundred she'd stashed on the whip, some blow, some top-shelf champagne, and a brand new diamond earring for the only man who could ever get a dime outta her.

The sun was shining high in the sky and her heart was full of excitement. Today was the day her favorite old-head was going to court and getting released from the bing, and she couldn't wait to see him. In addition to the other gifts she'd bought him, she had a mix CD with all the oldies that he liked on deck, and a hot bag of some Shin's take-out Chinese food, which was his favorite. Honore had missed the main man in her life, and she couldn't wait to tell Sly McFly about all the good shit that was going on in her life, but she also had a re-quest to make of him because she needed his muscle.

"Hey baby girl," Sly said as he opened the car door and got in the ride. He leaned over and gave Honore a big hug and kiss on the cheek and grinned. He was dressed clean as fuck in his tailor-made Brioni suit, casual shirt, and premium alligator shoes, looking relaxed and easy, like he had never done one damn day in jail.

"Hi Sly!" Honore said, smiling brightly with excitement dancing in her hazel eyes. "I see you looking good as usual. How you feeling?"

Sly McFly hit a button to move his seat back as he stretched his long legs and shrugged. "It feels good to be a free man again I'll tell ya that. What's that smell?" he asked, looking over the backseat. "You got me some Chinese from Shin's joint? Damn, baby girl. You sure know how to treat a fly nigga like me."

"It's only right, Sly," Honore said as she smiled big enough to bust her whole damn face. She felt lifted up, up, up! Her security blanket was back on the scene, and she was feeling real confident about anything that might come up in her path.

"You know I got ya back. I made sure to get the food special-wrapped to keep it hot too, 'cause I know you ain't been eating shit but that commissary junk out there on the Rock. I knew you was feening for some General Tso's chicken and some shrimp fried rice, and I told them to throw a couple of chicken wings in the bag too."

"Damn right," Sly said as Honore handed him a cloth napkin and he tore through the wrapper and dug into his food. "Thanks for coming to pick me up love. They couldn't hold a real nigga down forever. All they did was give me an opportunity to meet some new connects for all types of future shit I'm planning. But now that I'm out I got a few rounds to make. There's a couple dumb-asses I gotta put in check for coming up slow with my money while I was locked up. Nothing new. What you got going on? How did that lil situation you had going on turn out?"

"The shit is lit, Sly," Honore said as she drove down the highway. "We pressed up on that big boss real hard just like you said. Me and Cucci got a nice-ass stack of greenbacks and guess what? I finally got me a real job! I ain't start yet, but I'ma be working right there with Cucci. Her boss ain't really have a choice once we let him know the low-down. You're a fucking genius, Mister McFly."

"I don't know what the hell 'lit' means," Sly said as he licked sauce from his fingers. "But I'm glad it all worked out. Don't nobody wanna get stabbed in the back, so anytime you're able to see the knife coming you gotta make sure a muthafucka pays for that shit. All that is fine and cool, but what's the catch with the situation now?"

"Murder," Honore said flatly. "Joel wants Slimy Sal put in a fucking wooden box. But Sal is expecting me to carry out the mission and plant the diamond on Joel real soon, so I don't have much time to flatline his ass before the whole thing falls apart. I'm worried that Sal might put a contract on my head before we can get to him if he finds out I switched up on his bitch ass."

"Well I can't say I would blame him for trying," Sly said as he wiped his mouth with a napkin. "I'd be tryna plant a turncoat six feet deep in somebody's graveyard too. Good thing the murder game is something I happen to specialize in. You just give me everything you've got on this Sal cat and his ass will be nothing but a memory real soon."

"I knew I could count on you old man," Honore said with a smile. "How much do you want in return? Joel gave me a nice down payment and I can break you off with some cash today. I already know ain't shit free out here. You the one who taught me that."

"You right, ain't shit free," Sly said as he leaned back in his seat. "But I don't need your money, my darling. You just get ready to go in and do some good work at that new job of yours. Remember to keep your eye on the goal. This shit is just the first step. All I need you to do for me right now is take me straight to your aunt Frita's house. I need me some *pussy* goddammit!"

"Yuck nigga," Honore said as she as she made the stink face at the thought of Sly fucking the shit outta her aunt. "I don't need to know about that shit. Too much information there, sir. But I got you. I know you need that good shot of leg before you get yourself back in the game. Don't you go hurting my auntie though, nigga. I'll have to cut ya."

"Sheeeit," Sly said, eyeing the city streets as they rolled. "You must not know your aunt the way I know her. You see them hips and all that solid ass that old lady got on her? She the one who's gonna put a hurting down on me!"

They both bust out laughing at that one. Sly and Honore felt real good riding together again. With their scheming minds, fine looks, and endless thirst for the good life, they were going to paint the town red and make some real good moves now that Sly was back on the scene.

CHAPTER 14

Just a few days after Sly McFly hit the bricks, Slimy Sal Silberman was loosening his paisley tie as he walked down the steps of the New York Diamond and Jewelry Exchange after a late night at work. It was hot and humid outside but he didn't mind. The hot-shot junior executive had just closed a major deal that would allow them to open up another store over in New Jersey, which was something none of his senior executives had been able to do.

Sal was in a great mood and enjoying the power plays he was making in his professional career. Not only was his arch-enemy Joel Samuelson about to be set up and incarcerated, Sal would probably take that bastard's job, get a raise and earn a big bonus, and continue his side-hustle of selling crushed ice on the underground market as well. With a lovely banker wife who washed their illicit earnings through offshore accounts, and a handsome and healthy baby boy at home, life was good as fuck for Sal, and tonight he was smiling inside and enjoying every moment of it. His face lit up even more when his cell phone started ringing and he recognized the number on the screen.

"Why, hello there," Sal said brightly. "Talk to me, lil lady. Tell me something good."

"W'sup, Sal," Honore said bluntly. "I'm just calling to let you know that you can go ahead and drop that rock off to me whenever you're ready. Do you have it yet?"

"No," Sal answered. "But I will in a few hours. Right before I head to the airport and leave for my vacation."

"Okay, whatever," Honore said coolly. "I just wanted you to know that everythang is everythang. I got the plan lined up and shit is in order just like you said you wanted it. It's going down first thing tomorrow morning, so be sure to send them blue boys in with the search dogs bright and early. By the time you wake up in Bermuda and shit, shower, and shave, Joel will be knocked and this scandalous shit will be all over the news."

"Great! That's the kind of news I like to hear," Sal said as he walked into the dimly lit indoor parking garage. "That son of a bitch Samuelson is going to get exactly what he deserves tomorrow. I can't wait to see the look on his face when he's carted away in handcuffs. This will be a working vacation for me so I'll be keeping a close eye on things from Bermuda. A crime of this magnitude is sure to make front-page headlines and once Samuelson is arrested he'll be fired immediately. Make sure you go over every little detail and execute this plan properly, Honore," Sal warned. "Your freedom and the other twenty-five hundred dollars of your deposit depends on it."

"Oh, trust and believe, I got it all covered on my side," Honore said with confidence. "You just make sure you have my money ready, you hear me? And don't try to play me out either, Sal. I know how your grimy ass gets down."

"This is serious business, Honore," Sal said sternly as he clicked his car key fob and opened the door. "If you do the job right and deliver like you say you will, I will definitely honor my half of the deal. Fair and square. No funny business. Just get it done."

"Yeah, you're right, Sal," Honore said as a small giggle escaped her lips. "No funny business. This whole game is just business. Nothing personal. Have a great night."

Sal slid behind the wheel of his Mercedes, then pulled the door shut and disconnected the call. He was about to crank his shit up and head to his mini-mansion, but right before he put his key in the ignition his head was snatched backward and something sharp pierced the skin of his neck.

"Hello there, Sal," Sly McFly greeted him with a chuckle as Sal struggled in his seat. "How was your day, buddy? Don't you make a slick fucking move or I'll detach your goddamn head from your shoulders."

"Please don't hurt me," Sal begged, scared half to death. All sorts of shit was running through his mind. Who was this nigger in his backseat with a knife blade to his neck, and what the hell did he want? "Sir, I don't know what's going on here, but I don't want any problems. I have about five hundred dollars in my wallet. Please take it."

"Relax, Sally boy," Sly said, toying with him. "Everything's gonna be all right in a minute. I didn't come here for your money, my brotha. See, your ass just got out-maneuvered and you don't even know it. You took a shit on somebody I love, Sal. Not only that, you underestimated her just because she's got a pussy. But she's a fast learner, Sal, and a fly nigga like me taught her everything she knows. She's hood and she's got a smart-ass mouth on her, but she got a lotta heart too, and she can be real vicious if you try to do her dirty. What got you fucked up tonight is the fact that she made a deal with a devil who's got a longer dick and even deeper pockets than you do! The gun game got turned right on you, my man, and now you sitting on the wrong end of the muzzle."

"Oh my God! That bitch screwed me!" Sal shrieked as he realized what the stranger was telling him. Honore! That bitch had double-crossed him. She'd suckered the shit out of him! Which meant that Joel was in on this. He had to be! The realization and the thrust of Sly's knife hit Sal like a ton of bricks and he lost control of his bowels. A long stream of warm piss flowed into his three-hundred-dollar gray slacks and soaked the leather seat of his Mercedes.

"What about my son and my wife?" he gurgled desperately. "Please don't hurt them! I'll do anything you want!"

"Fine time to think about them muthafuckas now!" Sly joked from the backseat as he dug the tip of his knife deeper into his victim's neck. "Ol' Joel Samuelson got himself a family too, my nigga. What about them muthafuckas, huh?"

Sal flailed his arms and Sly chuckled as he shook his head. "This is the kinda payback you brought on yourself so don't start complaining now! But hold up! What kinda bitch is you? Why the fuck do it smell like shit and piss up in here?"

Sal tried to break free and make a move to open his door, but he was way too slow. The sharp blade ripped across his throat in one swift motion and he fell over with his head plopping down in the passenger seat.

Sly opened the left rear door and watched as Sal violently twitched like a gutted fish. The mark gasped and gripped his neck as he tried to fight off the clutches of death. A few moments later Sal's body jerked one final time, then he lay still with his drawers full of shit, his pants soiled in piss, and the rest of him soaked in blood.

Sly McFly methodically hummed one of his favorite Bob Marley tunes as he lit up a Cuban cigar and walked away from the scene with the swagger of a true playa. He gave less than a fuck about the dead jewelry thief whose dead body was already cooling off in the car. The only things on his mind were the leftover ham hocks and butter beans that Frita had waiting for him on the stove, and getting him another shot of her good sweet pussy.

CHAPTER 15

It was Monday and Honore was styling her best curly hair-do and hot pink miniskirt ensemble, and she just knew she was looking gorgeous for her first day of work. Her cousin Cucci was modestly dressed in a sharp Alexander McQueen business suit with a white silk shift beneath it, and she smiled when she saw Honore walk in slaying the scene in true hood fashion.

The cousins were back in sync together and they grinned at each other knowing exactly what it had taken for both of them to get where they were right at this moment. Slimy Sal was now maggot food, thanks to Sly. And not only was Honore's bank account heavier than it had ever been before, she now had a real job at New York's top jewelry store too. Things were looking gooder than a mutha for the sexy home team.

"Hey cousin," Cucci said as she came out from behind the counter. "You looking like a million big ones today, girl! Welcome to the New York Diamond and Jewelry Exchange, bitch! They done fucked around and hired both of us and we 'bout to have this shit lit! I'm so souped that I get to work witcho ass now."

"Yeah girl, I'm hyped, too," Honore said as she smoothed out her clingy lil miniskirt nervously. "I'm just trying to get in where I fit in and get this mothafuckin' money, nah'mean? I'm so glad this shit worked out in our favor. I'm just amped that my fucking PO can get off my back now and I don't have to deal with them nosy bitches no time soon."

"I know that's right, cuz," Cucci said in a whisper as she waited for a customer to walk past and then stared at Honore's gangbuster booty and exposed thighs. "Look, I forgot to hip you to this, but these people up in here are real high-class, you know what I'm saying? I mean, the people who come through these doors are practically drowning in money, and the bosses like us to look a certain way for them and talk a certain way too."

Honore cut her eyes. "A certain way like how?"

"Like we got some damn class!" Cucci blurted out and smirked. "I mean, you can't just walk up in here in ya club clothes and cursing outta both sides of your mouth, Honore! You gotta put some finesse on ya shit, you know? Tame ya tongue and try to talk like a lady. Everybody don't have to know we from the projects just because we open our mouths, you feel me? We gotta talk proper and kinda white while we on the job, and once we bust outta here at the end of the day we can go back to talking how we really wanna talk."

Honore smirked. "Oh, so you saying if I wanna work up in here around all these rich-ass white people I gotta be somebody who I'm really not and fake-talk all damn day and pretend like I'm one of them, huh?"

"Damn right." Cucci nodded. "That's exactly what you gotta do! And if you fuck around and slip up, just watch and see what happens. The first time you open your mouth and all that trifling hood you got in you comes rolling out, you gonna be out the door! I can guarantee you that! My boss been working on me for months now tryna get me to sound like I got some sense, and I've learned how to speak white-girl talk real good if you ask me. Now Mister Samuelson just got in his office a few minutes ago. He left a message that he wants you to go back there and sign some orientation paperwork or some shit like that, so pull that lil-ass skirt down to ya knees and get your shit together before you knock on his door. Other than me, he doesn't ask for his front desk clerks to come back in his office that much, so I guess he wants to make sure your first day is gonna go real smooth. Just remember to keep it all about professional business. No matter what, talk white and don't get personal."

"A'ight girl, that's cool," Honore said as she yanked on the hem of her skirt and tried to pull it down over the hump of her ass. When she was done she checked her mug out in her little pocket mirror and then grinned. "Okay, wish me luck. I'll be right back."

Leaving Cucci at the receptionist desk, Honore headed toward the back of the large jewelry outlet where Joel's office was located. She banged on the door until she finally heard a voice tell her to come in.

"Hello, Honore, come on in and take a seat," Joel said as he sat chillin' behind his expensive desk in his huge corner office. "Nice to officially meet you," he said, dumbing out, "and I'm glad that you've chosen to seek legitimate employment at the New York Diamond and Jewelry Exchange."

"It's very nice to be here, sir," Honore said, practicing her white-girl talk with a nervous giggle. She had peeped Joel's sarcasm too, but she decided to just go with it. They both knew that her being there was a big part of the deal that mutually benefitted all three of them, and their business compromise was now complete. Honore and Cucci had held up their end of the bargain by taking Sal out, and Joel had gotten the ultimate revenge on his cut-throat rival.

"So," Honore said with a small smile, "I'm here now. What will you have me doing today, Mister Samuelson, sir?"

"Please, just call me Joel," Cucci's cocky sugar daddy said as he sexed Honore with his old-man eyes. Deep down inside Joel respected the power move that his lil fuck-bunny Cucci had pulled on him. Even though it was pretty grimy of her to use their relationship to break into his house, she had made a sound business decision that had also saved his ass from going to jail. And now he was about to make some sound decisions of his own.

"Don't worry," Joel told Honore as he examined the smooth, supple skin on her exposed thighs. "Your new job won't consist of anything that I don't think you can't easily handle. You won't even break a fingernail. In fact, to start out I'll have you doing some light clerical work. You know, filing papers and answering phones. I had to fire an intern to make room for you on the staff, so you'll be my personal assistant of sorts." His jungle fever–having ass eyeballed the delicious looking monkey sitting in front of him with all kinds of steamy thoughts running through his mind. "We'll be working very closely together, and I must say that I'm very happy to have you on board!"

Honore felt relieved that her schedule was going to be so light, and she had just pasted a big, cheesy grin on her face when Joel got up and walked around his desk and stood over her. Both of them were still smiling when he grabbed her by the hand.

"I appreciate you handling that little issue for me the other day," Joel said in a low voice, even though the office door was closed. "I knew the money I gave you and your cousin was well spent as soon as I saw the news broadcast about Sal's gruesome murder."

Joel placed Honore's hand on top of his swollen crotch and then said, "Of course I'll be attending his funeral, and I'll even give some type of bullshit speech about how we were the best of friends or some shit. It's all part of the game, you know? Just business. But there are a few other business games that I'd like to play with you."

Joel was squeezing Honore's hand and massaging it over his stiff prick when the office door flew open and Cucci strode in popping gum and holding the office mail.

"Do you think you can knock next time?" Joel barked as

he jumped a mile and dropped Honore's hand. "Have a little respect for my privacy, would you please!"

"Ay, sorry about that. My fault," Cucci said, looking confused as she poked her lip out. "Any other time you be dying for me to come in here with you. But I see what you're saying. Y'all go 'head with what y'all was doing. I didn't mean to disturb no grooves."

"Thank you," Joel said with deep sarcasm in his voice as he snatched the mail out of her hand. "Now do me a favor. I have a meeting coming up in ten minutes and I want you to take Honore to the outer office and get her familiarized with the front desk operations. I'll be unavailable for about an hour, and then I'll come and take her around to visit a few of the other store locations a little later so I can show her around."

Cucci bucked. "I thought *I* was the one going with you on the store visits!" she wailed. "You said you was gonna train me for that floater job so I could learn the ins and outs of every store location, remember?"

"Well, I changed my mind," Joel said stiffly. "I said the job was open, I never said it was definitely yours. I actually think Honore would be better suited for the position. She has the right looks and the right type of outgoing personality, and once I work on her diction and her wardrobe, she'll be the perfect decoy to distract and disarm while we do what needs to be done."

"That's some real fuck-shit right there," Cucci bitched, glaring at Joel before she turned on her cousin and hit her with the killer face. "Some real low-down fuck-shit, ya heard?"

"Cucci!" Honore hollered as her cousin stormed outta the office shaking her ass and clicking her dainty high heels on the floor.

"Don't you *Cucci* me!" Cucci hissed as the two cousins hauled ass down the hallway and headed back to the front desk.

"Girl why you trippin'!" Honore yapped.

"What the fuck was that all about?" Cucci demanded as

soon as she made sure nobody was near and could hear her. "I *seent* you, Honore! I seent yo crabbin' ass! That nigga was just pressing your hand down on his dick! I walked in there and you was looking like you was ready to start jacking that shit! Joel is *my* fuckin' mark, so don't forget that *I'm* the one making shit shake around here, Honore! This is *my* damn hustle!"

"I could give a fuck *less* about that corny white boy and his lil dick!" Honore shrugged and countered. "You already *know*. We both eating off of the same plate, Cucci Momma! I ain't come up in here tryna step on ya toes. You know how them white niggas be extra friendly with me all the time and shit. Get out your feelings 'cause we ain't here for all that, and whatever one of us eats, both of us is gonna get full off of it and shit it out! Hell, if he wanna give me that floater job, I'll take that shit! On the real, cuz, I'm just here to get up on some money and play my role, nahm'saying? All that other possessive-type shit is irrelevant to me."

"Yeah, a'ight," Cucci said as she gave her cousin the side-eye and kicked herself up the ass. She had felt some kinda way about getting Honore a job there from the gate. The last thing she had wanted was for her cousin's hazel-eyed ass to roll up in there and take over her situation. And now Cucci had a real funny feeling flowing from her head all the way down to her toes. She knew what kind of snake Honore was because they were both cold-blooded like that and they both wore the same scaly skin. But even still, she didn't want her cousin just coming up on the scene and tossing shit up and threatening her position. As far as Cucci was concerned, she was the head bitch in charge of Joel Samuelson's pockets, and she wasn't about to get pushed to the side for *nobody!* Not even her fam!

"Yeah, I guess you're right," Cucci said, fronting and biding her time. "Let's just stick to the script and let all this shit play out. It's your first day on the job and I'ma hold you down, cousin. Trust me."

CHAPTER 16

Honore loved working at the New York Diamond and Jewelry Exchange. She was born for that shit, and she had only been working there for a minute when Joel Samuelson texted her and told her to meet him outside the job at twelve noon sharp.

Honore was puzzled when Joel pulled up in front of the jewelry store in an all-white stretch limo. Looking business-sexy in her pale yellow skirt suit and contrasting camisole, she opened the door and got into the luxury vehicle slowly so she wouldn't break one of her brand-new Balenciaga heels.

"What's going on, Joel," Honore said as the limo pulled off. "I wasn't expecting to go anywhere today. I have a lot of paper-work that needs to be handled in the office."

"Forget that paperwork," Joel said as he lit up an expensive Italian cigar. "This is about some big bucks. It's time that you see where the real cash is made. The fact of the matter is my job puts me in position to get money all kinds of ways. On and off the books. I'm a capitalist, and I'm going to get it either way. Me and Sal were working deals and sharing some good paydays until he tried to cross me."

"I can dig it," Honore said as she crossed her legs. She

knew what was coming and she had been waiting for this day ever since she started at the New York Diamond and Jewelry Exchange. She was a hard worker and a quick learner, and everything Joel told her to do she did it to perfection. Already he had introduced her to all of the big movers and shakers in the city that were involved in the business. Honore charmed them all and made a lasting impression. "What about my cousin though? I thought she was rocking with you when it came to the backdoor shit."

"Rayven is loyal," Joel said as he poured himself a glass of Merlot wine from the whip's minibar. "But she lacks the class and the instincts that I need to see in my new partner. Rayven will be obedient and do whatever I tell her to do, but you're a little more free-thinking and decisive. You have your own mind and you're not afraid to tell me what you're thinking, even if I don't agree with it."

"Can't say I don't agree with that," Honore said as she shook her head and declined his offer of alcohol. There would be no drank-drank for her today. She needed to be fully on point because this was the big break she had been waiting for. "So where are we headed?"

"To a drop and pickup," Joel responded. "My partner Avi has some money for me and I have some goods for him. He's my underground connection to foreign buyers and individuals with deep pockets."

"I get it," Honore said as she reached inside her purse and discreetly turned on her phone's GPS tracker just in case Joel was trying to line her up. "So how do you know you can trust him?"

"Oh, I don't trust him," Joel said bluntly. "I don't trust you either, but we all have our secrets, now don't we? In fact, money and secrets is what binds us all together. Avi and I do good business together and we enjoy the fruits that we reap from it. Nothing more and nothing less."

A few minutes later the limo pulled into some nondescript abandoned parking lot where another vehicle was already waiting. A clean-cut white man in a dapper black Italian suit slipped into the limo with Honore and Joel.

"Nice seeing you again, Avi," Joel said with a smile. "I know you don't like meeting on short notice but I have the package that you asked for, and I need to get the ball rolling immediately."

"Who is she?" Avi blurted suspiciously. "You know I don't like meeting new people, Joel. I respect you and consider you an ally, but you know how I like to handle my business and this isn't it."

"Avi, this is Honore," Joel said dryly. "Trust me, I wouldn't bring anybody around who wasn't playing a role in what's going on. So just relax. Everything I do is calculated. Now do you have the funds from the last transaction?"

"Of course I do," Avi said, still staring at Honore with suspicious eyes as he passed Joel a briefcase. "But we have a situation with the upcoming deal. The buyers from England want the product to be shipped on their own boat with their own personnel. I don't trust them to pay up front, and I have a pressing matter I have to attend to so I can't oversee it."

"I'll go," Honore blurted out with confidence. "I mean I'll go make sure things run smoothly. A female face might ease some of the nerves for all parties involved. Plus, we can put a tracker on the shipment that's rigged with some type of explosives, so if they try some funny shit we can blow their asses away. I know it isn't the ideal way to handle things, but if you get robbed and they get away with no repercussions, then word will get around that you're soft and you'll get stuck up every day. I mean, there's no guarantees in this shit so the only thing you can do is cover your ass the best way possible. The only thing mothafuckas respect is money and violence. You need to be known for delivering both."

"You see why I brought her here?" Joel said laughing hysterically as he slapped his hand on his thigh. "What she just said makes a lot of sense to me, my friend. In fact, I think it's a damn good idea. What do you think, Avi? What's your paranoid mind telling you?"

"Being paranoid is what keeps me alive and well paid," Avi said as he loosened his tie. "But I honestly think it's a good idea. We don't want to get violent if we don't have to, but it's always good to have an insurance policy just in case. As long as your friend here can execute our plans, then I have no objections with it."

"Well then it's settled," Joel said as he sipped his second glass of wine, clearly geeked up. "Send me all the information so I can get Honore prepped. We'll take it from there. As always it's been a pleasure seeing you my guy."

Avi just nodded and looked at Honore and Joel with cold eyes before stepping out of the limo and slamming the door.

"Is he always such a tight ass?" Honore turned and asked Joel. "What the hell is his problem?"

"Avi is a very smart guy," Joel assured her. "He is a true professional and I can't blame him for being cautious. He's a great asset to have on our team because he sees and hears everything, and he's never been wrong. By the way, that was a very bold move that you just made, not that I'm surprised. I know firsthand what you're capable of. Now you have to deliver on your word and earn Avi's respect. If you don't fuck this up I'll make sure you get a nice cut out of this deal. I mean that. Just *don't* fuck it up because this is your moment to prove your worth."

Prove her worth? Honore smiled and nodded. Joel just didn't know. She wasn't really tryna be Joel and Avi's little errand girl, no damn way. Sheeeit, she was trying to build a strong coalition and go into business for her damn self!

CHAPTER 17

The next week or so was a whirlwind of activity for Honore. In addition to working out the details of the new come up business that she had conceived in her mind, she was also working very hard on her new job at the Diamond and Jewelry Exchange.

Joel had her chauffeured around some of everywhere in all five boroughs of New York City so she could showcase the company's modest, but still valuable diamonds. Each day a private car would arrive to pick her up bright and early, and Honore would go to the company vault and sign out a certain number of diamonds, mostly women's rings, and then mount them onto a custom-made display board that she carried all over the five boroughs.

Once she was on location, Honore would prance into several member and affiliate stores in each borough and present her used diamonds for sale, but while she was there she would also be steady scoping shit out and keeping her eyes open for the type of chicks that she was gonna need in order to build her secret coalition.

She found a real pretty chick named India working in a store in Brooklyn. The girl was so sweet and had such a beautiful body and a bright smile that Honore ran her get-money game down on her and snatched her up right away. She recruited two other chicks at the jewelry store in the boogie down Bronx. One was named Kellie, and she was an educated chick who also had a quick mind on her, and the other one went by the name Breezy, and she was pretty and eager, but also kinda hood. The last two chicks Honore picked were diamonds in the rough. One was a beautiful half-Asian chick named Mai with long, jet-black hair, a big ass, and lil bitty nubby titties; and the other one was a cute stud chick who was so damn masculine about herself that Honore just called her Man-Man.

This was going to be an all-female operation and she was gonna call her posse the Crushed Ice Clique. There would be just the seven of them to start, and they would all basically do the same things for the Clique that Honore and Cucci did for Joel: steal diamonds. But Honore didn't want no trouble outta Cucci Momma, and she knew the only way her plans were gonna work is if Cucci believed she had some say-so in the command and control of the operation, so Honore made sure to present each girl to Cucci as just a "possibility" who was waiting on Cucci's "approval." Her approach seemed to work too, because instead of being salty over losing her top spot with Joel, Cucci's nose was open on all the money that the Crushed Ice Clique was gonna be bringing in as they stole diamonds from their individual stores and had them replaced with worthless but convincing copies.

For the most part things were going exactly the way Honore had envisioned it, but of course Cucci had to get her last bit of attitude out and let her cousin know how she really felt deep inside.

"I don't care how much money we make," Cucci bitched one night as they were splitting up the dough they had made from one of India's stolen diamonds that Honore had gone behind Joel's back and paid Avi to crush into ice. "That was some dirty shit you pulled on me, cousin, for real. Joel was minez, and you made some violating moves on me that you ain't never made before. I ain't gonna forget about that shit neither."

Honore had looked up as her cousin was rolling her eyes and grilling her like she wanted to jump up and bite her and said quietly, "Tell me something, Cucci Momma. Did you really *like* fuckin' that old scraggly, gray-haired, fish-belly looking mothafucka?"

Cucci had smirked. "Girl hell no! The only reason I fucked with him was for the money. So I could get them extra ends and make these little side deals like we making right now. Joel ain't nothing but a plug, stupid. You should already know."

"Well all right then!" Honore said, full of exasperation. "I don't know what the hell you so damn salty about! So *what* if that nigga thinks I'm better suited for the damn job than you? If you wasn't catching feelings for him or busting a million-dollar nut every time he fucked you, then you shouldn't be complaining! You still gonna get paid the same amount you was getting paid before. Maybe more. The only thing changing is that now you ain't gotta fuck him no more. *I* do."

"Still!" Cucci complained. "I was supposed to get that fuckin' promotion, Honore! I been working there way longer than you and Joel was my sugar daddy first! Some shit just ain't legitimate and all this moving in on my hustle type shit you tryna do is a flagrant foul!"

"But look!" Honore pointed at the pile of cash as she pleaded with her cousin to understand. "You still *making money*, Cucci! We've got our own clique now and pretty soon we're gonna be expanding our operation big time! Together! Listen," Honore pleaded, trying to get the real deal shit through Cucci's thick head. "All our lives we've split every fuckin' thing between us fifty-fifty and that ain't gonna never change! Me and you sleep in the same bed and we eat outta the same pot. If I hustle me up a dollar, you know you got fifty cents. If you scramble up a egg sandwich, we slice that shit right in half. Whatever one of us gets, both of us have always prospered from, and I don't see why this shit gotta be any different now."

Cucci thought about it for a long minute, and then she shrugged and nodded her head. Honore was right, and she had to admit it. They were a tag team. Twins born from separate uteruses. If you cut Honore, Cucci's DNA would come squirting out. If you shot Cucci, Honore would fall over dead to the ground. They were bonded to each other in all the ways that mattered, and their shit was just that tight.

"A'ight," Cucci finally relented. "Ga'head and take the reins on the clique and let's build this shit into an empire! Plus, you can go 'head and fuck Joel all you want to, but don't blame me if that thirsty mothafucka gets on your last nerve! His balls stank, and I ain't never liked that stupid wheezing noise he makes when he busts a nut anyway. You ga'head and hop right on that shit, cuzzo. As long as we still making money, ere'thang is all good."

"That's what I'm talking about," Honore said as she grinned and beamed. "Don't you worry about a damn thang, cousin. Especially Joel. You just hold that old nasty white dog down and let me fuck him."

CHAPTER 18

The ladies of the Crushed Ice Clique had been working very hard to pull off their individual capers, and tonight they were enjoying their first night out on the town together as a team.

"Really, bitch?" Cucci said as she looked at an over-the-hill stripper who was onstage directly in front of them, dancing and shaking her flabby, outta-shape booty right in their faces. "You got a ass full of bullet holes and you got the nerve to be twerking on the pole!"

Honore and the rest of the girls busted out laughing hard as fuck as they chilled in their VIP seats. Club Starlets in Queens was all the way up! 50 Cent was in the spot throwing an EFFEN vodka promo event and all the pimps, ballers, and gangstas were in the club going hard. Dolla bills were flying everywhere, and DJ Envy kept spinning hit after hit to keep the vibe going. Strippers were giving lap dances and bussin' it open for the crowd. Honore and the girls sat back drinking and cracking jokes as they watched the movie being made. But soon it was time to conduct business.

"I'd like to thank y'all for coming out," Honore said as she stood up at the table and poured some vodka for her girls. "I wanted us all to get together and have a laid-back business meeting tonight. I handpicked every last one of y'all to be a member of my team, and by the way y'all been rolling I can tell I picked myself a handful of winners!

"What I know for sure is that each and every one of us are smart, sexy as fuck, and skilled at many different things. We all love money and ain't none of us afraid to go get it. With the amount of beauty and brains we're packing as a team, we can be bigger than these so-called hustlers who are busy throwing their money around in here tonight."

"Goddamn right," Breezy said. "I rock with you and Cucci real tough, Honore. I like your style and together we can rack up and stunt on everybody who ever tried to play us out. I don't know about the rest of y'all but I'm tired of pulling nickel-and-dime licks. I'm ready to step my game up."

"And that's exactly what we are here for," Cucci said with authority in her tone. "To take our shit to the next level. Fuck pushing drugs and taking charges for niggas. No more selling our bodies just to make pimps rich. Them days are over, do you hear me? We were all fortunate enough to land a gig at a branch of the New York Diamond and Jewelry Exchange, and this gig could be very lucrative for us all. So what I'ma do is have y'all put in job applications at different high-end jewelry shops all around the city. We're gonna infiltrate those businesses and see what other connections can be made. All them rich white executives we work for are just as crooked as the corner boys. We're gonna learn everything we can learn from them, then find their weaknesses and turn them into our profits."

"And believe me," Honore took over, "we ain't in this for the short change, neither. We need y'all to hook up with the very top bosses and executives. Pussy runs the world, ladies. So whatever you gotta do to solidify your position, then do it. We will have meetings once a week and we'll pool together all of our resources. Let's start making our skills work for us! If we do shit right on the lower level, then the next thing you know we'll be making some good connections on the black market and we'll really start getting this paper."

"But everybody gotta play their role," Cucci reminded the clique. "We don't discuss none of our business with anybody outside this crew, y'all understand? No gossip, no fucking pillow talk, no none of that shit! If y'all not willing to be professionals about this hustle then get up from this table and step the fuck off right now. This is how the big girls play, and if you ain't all in, then haul ass."

Cucci and Honore locked eyes with the other girls to let them know they were dead-ass serious. Both of them knew it was important to establish power and strength in order to earn respect and demand results.

"Good," Honore said as she waved off a stripper that was making her way over to them. "Now that we're all on the same page let's toast up. We are no longer hood rats looking for a come-up, ladies. We are bad bitches who get out there and take what we want. We plan and we execute. We are thinkers before doers. We don't get dick-matized and manipulated. We put the team above our own personal shit. When one falls we pick each other up. We are the Crushed Ice Clique, and we're gonna take this diamond game to a whole 'nother level out here in these streets!"

Joel Samuelson was sunning on the top deck of his glamorous and expensive yacht and enjoying a beautiful view of the ocean. As he lay back in his lounge chair sipping on a chilled margarita, he looked toward the dock and noticed that Cucci and Honore had just arrived on time, as he had requested.

"Hello ladies," Joel said with excitement dancing in his eyes. "I hope you brought your bathing suits. It's a great day to go for a swim, don't you think?"

"Hell to the nah," Cucci said with the stink face. "I mean I'll sit out here and catch me some sunshine on this beautiful brown body, but I'll be damned if I'm getting my fresh-ass hairstyle wet."

"I'm with Cucci on this one playa." Honore chuckled as she sat down next to Joel and put her slender hand on his pale thigh. "Pour me up one of those good looking drinks so I can relax. This is a nice-ass yacht, man. I need to get me one of these right here. I would throw a mean-ass party on this joint."

"This is nothing," Joel said as he got up to fix the girls some margaritas. "This is just one of the many toys that I like to show off from time to time. Work hard and put your time in and you can have plenty of these, designed specifically to your liking. Believe me, I work hard and I play even harder."

"Thanks for the motivation, boss man," Cucci said as she swatted an imaginary bug away from her. "We ain't got it like that yet, but I'm trying to get big like you sooner rather than later. Now, I know you like our company and all that, but there's gotta be another reason you called us out here, so pass them dranks and let's cut to the chase."

Joel laughed. "You ladies don't like to waste time, huh?" He took a deep breath as he handed them their drinks. "Well all right, let's cut to the chase then. I have an urgent issue that needs to be handled very discreetly. It's involving a former partner of mine by the name of Davie Shiloh. Davie is a very powerful underworld figure who is also a major player in the international diamond world. He's got his hands in everything that moves overseas, and he runs a crew of guys who are downright scary."

"So what the hell do you want us to do?" Honore bucked. "If your friend is such a big boy in the diamond game then how could me and Cucci possibly handle him? We don't have the kinda muscle or the kinda money to go at somebody like that."

"He has a weakness for pretty women," Joel said as he stared at Honore's perfect tits. "Specifically, he's very fond of pretty Asian women. I know neither one of you fits that description, but I was wondering if you knew anyone who did. Shiloh is extorting one of my friends and pressuring him to deliver a precious Black Stone diamond that just came into the country. If we can rob Shiloh and get our hands on that jewel, then my friend is willing to split the profits down the middle."

Honore shook her head. "Nah, I don't think—"

"So what's the cut?" Cucci interrupted as she raised her eyebrows. "I know you don't know the exact amount but just gimme a ballpark figure."

Joel shrugged. "Somewhere between sixty and seventy apiece," he said without blinking. "And that's a tax-free hunk of change that can be ours if we can come up with the right somebody who can help us get close enough to Davie to steal that diamond. Plus, I'd rather it be someone else who does it, and not you two. Honestly, I wouldn't be comfortable putting either of you directly in harm's way. So what do you think? Do you know anyone who can fill that role and who's also trust-worthy enough to get it done?"

Honore and Cucci looked at each other as they both pic-tured Mai from the Crushed Ice Clique doing the job.

"I think we might have somebody in mind," Honore said slowly. "I know a half-Asian chick who is so bad she can charm a fucking snake right out of his skin. But after she gets up on this Davie Shiloh cat, what happens next? What's the Plan B? What if she runs into some trouble and gets caught up with this dude? How do we cover her ass if the shit ends up going sideways?"

"Well that's part of the risk you'll be paid to take," Joel said as he shrugged his shoulders. "We don't have the firepower or the men to come at Davie forcefully. He's the type of man who has to be finessed, so whoever the girl is, she'd better be a pro because she would essentially be on her own. Look." He shrugged again. "I'm not trying to sugar coat it, this is going to be a risky task but then again, in our line of work, what isn't risky? We take crazy chances every day in this business. It's part of the lifestyle that we live because we want the big rewards. So can you make this happen or do I have to find someone else?"

"For that amount of fucking cash?" Cucci said as she downed her drink. "You goddamn right we gonna make this shit shake! Davie, Shavie, or whatever the fuck his name is won't be getting his hands on a damn thing. Let me and Honore work our magic. Just make sure your friend has the moolah ready when it's time to roll."

Honore sat back and didn't say anything but her gut was telling her that this might not be such a good idea. Joel was right about one thing though. This was a no-risk, no-reward type of business. If you were playing the money game scary then you would never make a real profit.

Still, Honore just couldn't shake off the feeling that this shit was gonna be way too dangerous. She was the one who had recruited Mai for the Clique, and this type of thing wasn't part of the program. But hell. The last thing she wanted was to hear Cucci bitching all day about a missed opportunity, and of course if they passed on this offer then Cucci would have every right to be upset, because that type of money was way too tempting to turn down.

Honore threw back her drink and shook off her misgivings. This diamond stealing shit was like Lotto. You had to be in it to win it, and a paper chaser like her was always down to play.

CHAPTER 19

Mai Taylor pulled up to one of New York's most exclusive clubs in style. Joel Samuelson had rented her a blue Porsche Panamera and provided her with a pocket full of cash so she could look and feel like money. Mai was the only Asian-looking member of the Crushed Ice Clique, so naturally Honore and Cucci had chosen her for the special mission that they needed to execute.

In reality, Mai was a half-black, half Korean bombshell. Her mother was a very light-skinned black woman, and her father was a Korean computer programmer. Mai's slanted eyes and her wide cheekbones combined with her black girl's hips and ass was a sexy sight to behold. She was a walking thirst trap as she glided through the rowdy crowd and made her way over to the VIP area of the high-priced club. Just as planned, she spotted her mark Davie Shiloh, who was relaxing on a Versace couch and watching two half-naked white girls passionately kiss each other beside him.

Bodyguards were posted up and turning chicks away left and right as they fought to get next to the rich underground trader. Mai downed her glass of Belvedere vodka and straightened out her sky-blue hip-hugging Dolce & Gabbana dress, knowing for a fact that she wouldn't be denied.

Slowly and confidently, she switched her slender body and curvy ass over to the bodyguards, making sure they got a full look at her.

"Hey, teddy bear," Mai said to one of the guards, smiling brightly and ensuring that her sex appeal was on fleek. "I'm looking for a good time tonight. I heard this is where the ballers hang out. Do you think I qualify to party with the big boys?"

"Well damn, sexy," the taller guard said. "Maybe you do qualify, but Mr. Shiloh doesn't go for ass implants or fake tits. If you want to get across these ropes I'm gonna have to make sure your shit is legit. Do mind turning around?"

"No problem." Mai winked. She turned around slowly and let them get a good look at her buns. She felt the guard's big hands rub her left cheek and then smack it. She heard him gasp as he watched it bounce.

"Yo," he said to his boy, covering his crotch with his hand. "This one right here is a hundred percent grade A *beef*. No additives or preservatives, sir."

Mai giggled. "So w'sup, big boy. Am I good or nah?"

"Yeah, you good baby because I can tell *all* of that is real," the guard said as his hungry eyes roamed over her sweet hips. "Go 'head in, lovely," he told her as he held the velvet rope aside, "and make sure you treat the boss man right. If there's any left when he's done with you, then maybe you can let me get seconds on summa that gushy shit."

"I might be able to save you some, big boy," Mai said as she reached out and caressed the guard's crotch, loosening him up and making him drop his defenses. "Just wait. I'm gonna take real good care of you later."

Mai stepped into the dimly lit private area and she immediately caught Davie Shiloh's attention. After just one glance at her his eyes bulged in his head and his dick got stiff as he pushed the two tongue-slobbering girls away from him.

"Well hello there," Davie said as he gestured at Mai to sit down. "You might be the most attractive chick in this entire club tonight. Please, come on over here and have a seat."

"Well thank you, daddy," Mai said softly as she walked over and sat her juicy ass right down on Davie's lap. "I was told that you're the man with all the power and I like that, but I also see you have company already. It's a little crowded over here, don't you think?"

"These two hood rats don't have shit on you," Davie said, sliding his tongue in Mai's ear as he caressed her thigh. "How about we cut the bullshit, all right? I'm a rich man and I would like to take you home with me. I'll make sure you're well paid for the night, and we'll have a lot of fun as long as you give me everything you've got. Does that sound like a good deal?"

Mai giggled. "Sounds perfect to me," she said. "And trust me, I'll make it worth your while. Just try not to fall in love because I'll be out the door first thing in the morning."

Shiloh grinned.

"We'll see about that. Let's get out of here."

Forty-five minutes later Mai and Davie were wrestling around in a king-size bed at his mini-mansion. She was riding his dick like a champion jockey and driving him crazy with her petite Asian body, long black hair, and curved hips.

Davie was giving her a run for her money though, because he had a fetish for tying women up and being very aggressive when he fucked. He was spreading her legs open way wider than they should naturally go, flipping her over roughly and jamming his dick up in her brutally, and pinching her nipples and squeezing her booty with a killer-grip. Mai took the pain as best she could, trying to ignore her aching body and keep her mind on the dough she was gonna get after lining this nigga up.

When Davie was all sexed out and had acted out all of his nasty, twisted fantasies, he collapsed beside her and fell into a deep sleep. Mai waited for thirty minutes until she heard him snoring deeply and was sure he was in his second dream, and then she made her move. She gently slid out of bed and rifled her nimble fingers through his pants pocket, searching for his keys.

Davie was still snoring when Mai crept her sore ass outta the room and tiptoed downstairs. She had no clue which room she was looking for but she started in his spacious office. It didn't take long for her to see a small safe in the corner of the room. She skimmed through his key ring as she headed toward it, but as soon as she reached out her hand to touch it the light clicked on and scared the shit outta her.

"Are you looking for something, Miss Sexy?" Davie asked as he stood behind her in his checkered boxers with a slick smirk on his face. "Did you lose something in my safe, lil mama?"

"Hey, Davie," Mai said as she whirled around and dropped the keys near her feet. She smoothly walked over to Shiloh and wrapped her arms around his muscular waist. "I couldn't sleep, my love, so I just figured I would take a little tour. I didn't think you would mind. I'm sorry if I offended you. Your house is just so amazing. I love it."

"That's okay, love," Davie said as he leaned forward and gave her a juicy kiss. Then in one swift motion he gripped Mai by her neck and lifted her straight up in the air until her feet dangled over the floor. He still had the slick smirk on his face as he watched Mai thrash around and struggle to get a scream out.

"Go ahead and yell. Nobody's gonna come help you. You're gonna have to wake up way earlier in the morning if you wanna scheme on me, you slant-eyed bitch! Fuck was you doing in my shit? Huh? You're gonna tell me why you came here and who the fuck sent you. Believe me, since you love my house so much you might never fucking leave here. At least not alive."

CHAPTER 20

"Ladies, we have a problem," Joel said to Honore and Cucci as they plopped down on the couch in his living room. He had called an emergency meeting and urged them to come over to his crib as fast as they could.

"What the heck is going on?" Cucci said nervously with her eyes bucked open wide. "What the hell is the problem?"

"The problem is that the goddamn plan fell through," Joel admitted. "It's all bad."

"Exactly what in the fuck are you saying, Joel?" Honore demanded as her lower lip quivered. "How bad is it? Is Mai okay? I didn't hear nothing back from her yet. She was supposed to check in, but I figured she was still sexing Shiloh up and working him over. Where the hell is she? Do you know?"

Joel grimaced as he grabbed his cell phone and pushed play on a video.

"Oh my fucking God," Cucci said in a chilling voice as she stared down at the screen. "No . . . this shit can't be happening."

A horrible picture of Mai filled the screen. She was beaten and bruised and in someone's bathroom. A naked light-skinned dude with a swinging dick and a brolic frame was standing over her, dunking her swollen, busted-up face in a bathtub full of water. Mai thrashed wildly and kicked her feet and clawed out as the man laughed deeply and kept right on submerging her under the water. Over and over again he held her down until her body twitched and spasmed, and then just before she passed out and drowned, he lifted her up and allowed her to take in a deep, sucking breath. The panic and fear in Mai's eyes as she coughed and choked was bone-chilling, and the torturous scream she let out before he dunked her under again was something that would haunt Cucci and Honore for the rest of their lives.

Standing there trembling beside her cousin, Honore couldn't believe what she was seeing. Her fuckin' protégée was being tortured. Waterboarded! Tears of rage filled Honore's eyes as she witnessed the terrifying cruelty being put down on her fellow Crushed Ice Clique chick.

"Turn that shit off!" Cucci yelled in disgust. "Turn it the hell off! I don't wanna see that shit! I wanna go find her!"

"That's not all," Joel said as he clicked off the video. "I got a text message along with the video. Your friend Mai must have broken down and told Davie Shiloh that it was me who hired her. And she told him why, too. The text message said Davie wants half a million dollars in three days or he'll cut off Mai's head and drop her body in the Hudson River."

"You have *got* to be fucking kidding me!" Honore shrieked and then covered her mouth in shock. "Half a million dollars? Is that nigga crazy? How in the entire fuck are we supposed to come up with that type of paper in three days? This Davie fool must be outta his mind!"

"Nah, fuck the dumb shit," Cucci said with her eyes blazing with anger. She liked Mai, she really did, and she felt responsible for talking her into what was turning out to be a suicide mission. "Tell us the damn plan, Joel!" she snapped. "C'mon, now. You better tell us the new fucking plan!"

"There was only one plan, and that was for your friend to

be careful!" Joel ran his fingers through his mop of hair. "Look, Mai knew the risks going in, and she was willing to accept those risks for the right amount of money, isn't that right?"

"Unh-unh, Joel," Cucci said in a pleading voice. "We ain't even tryna hear that stupid bullshit! You gotta do something, goddammit. You better get with all your criminal contacts and pull some strings and help our girl out! We can work the money off some kinda way Joel, but something gotta give so we can fix this shit. Just spot us the cash so we can get Mai back."

"Are you crazy?" Joel said with a confused and angry look. "The girl is probably dead already! I warned you that Davie was a monster! He's just toying with us, trying to see what else he can get out of us! Like I said, your friend went in there knowing that something like this could happen. Hell, we all knew it! I'm sorry, but one girl isn't worth the risk of me losing half a million dollars. There are always casualties in combat, ladies. Always."

"So let me get this shit straight, Joel," Honore growled. Her tears had dried up and now the flames of hell were shooting outta her hazel eyes. "You're willing to let that insane creep-ass nigga just dead my friend because you scared to lose some money? Cucci already told you we would work the shit off somehow! We just don't have the scratch to put up the ransom on our own right now or we would do it in a heartbeat. C'mon, now. We're talking about a *life* here. Don't tell me you're that petty and heartless, Joel!"

"I'm sorry ladies," Joel said as he shook his head. "This is a high-risk and high-reward business. There's no need to dig ourselves into an even deeper hole here. We gambled and took a long shot at this thing, and we lost, that's all. Shit happens. I know you care for your friend, and I really feel bad for her too. Let's just regroup and try to find another way around this situation. In the meantime, what you might want to start thinking about is whether or not Mai gave Davie Shiloh your names and whereabouts too. Because if she did, it could be bad for you. He could send some very bad people your way. You two might want to lay low for a while."

"Nigga fuck all that," Cucci said as she wiped her eyes on her sleeve. "You might be from the 'burbs, but we from the hood, Joel! That tucking your tail between your legs and hauling ass shit ain't how we were raised, and we damn sure ain't running away and leaving Mai behind. Please! Ain't nobody shook behind that goofy-ass Looney-Toons muthafucka! Davie Shiloh don't put no fear in my heart! He bleeds the same way the next nigga do. Besides, loyalty is everything and there ain't no price too high for that. We're gonna find Mai. You can turn your back on her if you want to, but this shit won't be on my conscience haunting me forever knowing I didn't try to get my girl back."

"You got that shit right," Honore chimed in. "Joel you's a real piece of shit, you know that? How can you just be cool with leaving Mai to get mauled out there by the wolves? I mean you're really not gonna lend us a hand, are you? Look at what we did to Sal over your ass! Me and Cucci saved your nuts when Sal tried to pull that fuck-boy move on you, now didn't we?"

"Yes you did, and you were paid very well for that, too," Joel argued as he raised his voice. "Look, you two aren't going to make me out to be the bad guy. I'm a businessman and I make sound business decisions. This situation with Mai isn't personal and there are no hard feelings involved. Mai received a very generous down payment up front for this job. I got her a nice clean ride and put some good clothes on her back. The outcome is unfortunate, but this is what she signed up for."

"So that's how it is, huh?" Honore said quietly. "This shit is just business as usual with you, huh, Joel? It's all gravy as long as you get to cash out on our hustle, right? I get it, and like I said, one day you're gonna get yours. With God as my witness mothafucka, you're gonna get yours."

"Don't you fucking threaten me!" Joel roared. "I picked both of your grimy ghetto asses up off the streets and brought you into my world! I taught you everything you know about diamonds and wealth when I introduced you to this fucking life! Don't blame me because your friend got caught with her panties down. You're the ones who sent her in there when she obviously didn't have the proper training. We're swimming in the deep end of the ocean goddammit, and it's eat or get eaten down here! So whatever the fuck you want to do, go ahead and do it, but I've said my piece. Now if you're still on my team, then put your big girl panties on and let's get back to business, because there's a lot of work that still needs to be done!"

Joel stormed out of the living room leaving Cucci Momma and Honore standing there feeling totally helpless. They were also mad as hell, and like Joel had said, feeling guilty as fuck for sending Mai into a hungry lion's den in the first damn place.

"What the hell are we gonna do, Honore?" Cucci whispered as she tried to swallow the lump that was forming in her throat. "That nigga Joel really ain't gonna fuckin' help us."

"*Fuck* Joel!" Honore spit in a low voice full of anger. "Grab your purse and let's get the hell up outta here. Don't nobody need Joel's fuckin' help! Call up the Crushed Ice Clique and get my ladies on the phone because us fly bitches are about to help our goddamn selves!"

CHAPTER 21

Using one of Sly McFly's special tools, Honore picked the back door lock on the large blue house and slowly twisted the knob. She moved into the foyer with the silence of a church mouse, and Cucci, Man-Man, India, Kellie, and Breezy followed right behind her dressed in all-black cat suits. All the girls had on ski masks and gloves, and they were strapped with Glock nines that were locked, cocked, and on the ready.

Sly McFly was sitting in a car across the street with Chimp Charlie as they scanned the area for any signs of trouble. He had a small team of shooters waiting in a nearby backyard ready to blast on the house and fire that shit up, but he wanted the girls to put in their own work first and earn their own stripes.

Despite all that shit he had talked about not helping them, Joel had pulled some strings and used his connections to find out where Davie Shiloh's mother lived. Honore wasn't above cracking an old bitch in the head or knocking her on her ass, because getting Mai back was the only thing on her mind and she would use any type of leverage she could get.

As the girls crept slowly down the hall, all kinds of delicious smells greeted their noses. They saw a light shining in the kitchen and heard someone humming a song. Honore was walking with her gun pointed straight out in front of her when she turned the corner and came upon an elderly white lady who was standing at the stove basting a turkey and tapping her foot on the floor at the same time.

"Drop the fucking baster, bitch!" Honore barked with mad venom in her voice. "Step away from that bird, and if you even think about screaming I'll split your old gray melon wide the fuck open. Now who else is up in this joint with you?"

"Nobody," the old lady said as she looked up at the crew of masked women and gave them a slight shrug. "I live here alone," she told them as she placed the baster on the counter and reached for a dishcloth to wipe her hands.

The old white lady looked like somebody's grandmama busy cooking a Thanksgiving dinner. There were pots full of delicious-smelling food simmering on the stove, and a big smoked ham glazed with pineapples and maraschino cherries was cooling on a metal rack.

The old woman looked shocked to see the clique standing in her kitchen, but she definitely wasn't scared. "You all could have just knocked on the door, you know. I'm sure your moth-ers raised you right, so I'm sure you're here for a good reason. Whatever it is, put those guns down before you hurt your-selves. Anybody hungry? I got turkey, ham, collard greens, baked macaroni and cheese, candied yams, and yellow rice. Homemade pound cake is on the table, sweet potato pies are just about ready to come out of the oven, and ice cream is in the freezer."

What the fuck?

Honore and Cucci looked at each other dumbfounded as shit, confused by the old woman's surprising tranquility and her complete lack of fear or alarm. Honore had to look down at her hand to make sure she still had a burner aimed at the el-derly chick because there wasn't a drop of fear in her old ass.

"Y'all go upstairs and check shit out," Honore directed

Cucci and Breezy with a head nod so they could go make sure they were alone. Cucci's greedy eyeballs lingered on the pretty-ass ham sitting on the rack before she ran upstairs to peep the scene.

"Where's your grime-ball son at?" Honore demanded as her and Man-Man walked up close on the old woman.

"I have no idea."

"Don't play no games with me, lady," Honore said as she kept her gun aimed high. "Do it look like we came here to fuck around with you, granny? If you wanna keep the rest of your teeth in your mouth then what I need you to do is pick up your damn phone and call that bitch-ass son of yours!"

"First of all, my name is Grace," the woman said with quiet dignity as she turned back to the stove and picked up a large spoon. "Mrs. Grace to you." She lifted a pot lid and the mouth-watering aroma of collard greens rose in the air. "You're my guest, you know, and I don't appreciate you coming into my house and using that kind of foul language," she said as she stirred the pot. "I'm pretty sure you were taught to respect your elders, so please act like it. Now," she said, putting the spoon down and covering the pot, "what in the world has my boy done now? He's hardheaded just like his daddy was, and he always has been. Did he do something to offend you in some way?"

Cucci came running down the steps and gave Honore a nod.

"It's all clear," she said, slightly out of breath. "There's no-body here but us. Now has this old bird started squawking yet? Where's her bitch-ass son, and where the hell is Mai?"

"You'd better watch your mouth in my house, young lady," Grace chastised Cucci as she put her hand on her stout hip and frowned. "Don't make me send you out in the backyard to get a switch, you hear?"

Cucci sucked her teeth. "Did this old hoe lose all of her marbles?" she whispered outta the side of her mouth at Honore. "Who she talking about whipping? Don't she know we here to hold her ass for ransom?"

"I'm talking about whipping *you*, with your fresh mouth self," the old woman said loudly. "And those guns don't scare me at all, and neither do those silly masks you girls have on. Now, I've been standing on my feet cooking all day long and I'm hungry. I'm going to cut myself a slice of pound cake and get something cool to drink. Y'all can have a seat and get comfortable and I'll fix y'all a plate of whatever y'all want. And then we can talk."

Thirty minutes later there were several dirty dishes stacked up in the sink. Empty glasses of cold milk and crystal saucers holding grubbed-up traces of pound cake and sweet potato pie were all over the table.

"My husband was from Alabama and I learned how to cook soul food right after we got married," Mrs. Grace explained to the deadly crew of hood chicks who were sitting around her kitchen table with their full stomachs hanging out. "Of course, he was African-American, as you can tell by my son's looks, and he was a big man who loved to eat. Seeing as how I loved to cook, and I still do, we got along just fine."

Honore and Cucci were floored. They had come up outta their hot ski masks a long time ago, and when Sly McFly texted Honore to see if everything was straight, she was too ashamed to tell him that her and Cucci were busy picking food outta their teeth, Kellie was wiping off the table, and Breezy and India were at the sink busting suds and washing dishes.

None of them could believe that a white woman had burnt up that good-ass soul food that she had served them! Cucci had greased down on so much turkey, greens, and macaroni and cheese that her stomach was poking out and her ass was about to bust outta her cat suit.

Man-Man and India had gone to town on that glazed ham, and Honore had tore shit up too. She'd greased back two huge slices of sweet potato pie that was so good it almost made her cry.

And now that the grubbing and the greasing was over, it was time to get down to business.

"I'm glad you girls finally settled down," Mrs. Grace said as she poured herself a cup of black coffee. "Now what has my Davie got you girls all riled up about?"

"Well listen, Mrs. Grace," Honore said as she took a deep breath. "No disrespect, but I'm just gonna tell you like it is. Your foul-behind son messed around and kidnapped a friend of ours. He sent us a video showing him beating her and dunking her head under water like he was drowning her. He said he was gonna cut her head off and throw her body in the river."

"That's exactly what he said," Cucci butted in. "Now, I don't know if you understand what type of craziness your boy be perpetrating out on them streets, but I can tell you he's a shot caller and a he's a maniac too! Like my cousin said, your son snatched our friend and beat the shit outta her, and now he's planning to kill her. Our only chance of getting her back is to use you as our bait. And since you're his momma and his only weakness, you're gonna pick up that phone and call him and let him know we got you and we ain't letting you go. Matter fact, you gonna tell ya lil pyscho-ass fuck-boy that Cucci Momma said she's gonna blow a hole straight in your goddamn throat unless he brings my friend here alive and breathing and gives up that Black Stone diamond too! Tell his ass he's got an hour," Cucci said, taking her gun off her waist and aiming it straight at the old lady's head. "Nah, fuck that. Tell him *your ass* got an hour!"

About a half an hour later a dark van came screeching down the street. Honore and Cucci were staring outta the window with their masks on and guns out, while Breezy and India were posted up on the door and Man-Man and Kellie were in the kitchen standing guard on the old lady.

The tires had barely stopped turning when the back door to the van flew open and four big niggas jumped out. One of them was half-carrying a woman who looked like she was wrapped in a blanket.

"Okay, it's game time," Honore called out loudly as she rushed back in the kitchen. She jetted over to Mrs. Grace and slapped a long piece of duct tape over her mouth. "Sorry Meemaw, but I don't trust your serial killer son! If this shit goes bad then we're all going out blazing. If you love your life then you better make sure his ass comes correct."

The front door burst open and suddenly Davie Shiloh stood there in the foyer looking totally enraged. All eyes were locked in on him as Cucci, Honore, and Davie all silently sized each other up, with all their guns up.

"Get that fucking barrel away from my mother's head," Davie spit, breaking the silence. "I don't know who y'all raggedy bitches are," he threatened passionately, "but one day I'm gonna roll up behind you and slit both ya fuckin throats. Believe that!"

"Man, *fuck* you, Davie!" Honore snapped as she cocked her gun and aimed the barrel dead at him. "I got this shit sur-rounded so you should watch ya mouth when you talking about what you gonna do to somebody! How about what the fuck we gonna do to *your momma?* Now tell them scrawny niggas to back away from Mai and slide that Black Stone dia-mond in her hand. Then all of y'all turn around and beat feet the fuck up outta here!"

"And don't forget to take your lovely mother with you, you bitch-ass nigga!" Cucci barked. "You lucky I didn't beat her half to death like you did to my girl! It's your turn to take a loss now, Davie boy! See ya on the next go round, pussy!"

Davie nodded. "Y'all got the win this time, but tell that pussy nigga Joel I'm coming for him," he threatened as he nodded to his men to follow Honore's orders. "This shit ain't over. When I see you again, I'm gonna *see* you. You won't never in life catch me off of my game again! I can promise you that."

In a matter of moments, Mai was set free and given the diamond. She hobbled across the room, crying and trembling as she huddled behind Honore with her haunted eyes wide from shock and trauma.

Cucci checked everything out thoroughly before she gave Man-Man the signal to let Grace Shiloh get up and walk over to her son.

"I don't care if this is your momma's house," Cucci said, glaring at Davie with her lip turned down. "You better take yo momma and step the fuck off! And if you wanna act aggy, there's four carloads of shooters just waiting outside for you to get cute. Trust me, you don't want your momma to catch no hot lead in her ass tonight, so don't fuck around and get fucked around!"

Davie gritted hard on Cucci and Honore as he grabbed a hold of his mother and backed out of the house. Cucci ran over to the door as soon as it slammed closed, but Honore ran to the window and watched Shiloh and his crew head toward the porch steps.

Suddenly the door flew open again and Cucci ran out on the porch. She took a flying leap and cracked Davie Shiloh clean in the back of his head with her gun as hard as she could.

"Your momma's sweet potato pie ain't better than my momma's!" she hollered as blood shot outta Davie's busted skull and she ran back inside the house and slammed the door.

Honore busted out laughing as Cucci joined her at the window and they watched Davie and his posse get in the van and drive away. She had lied like a rug about how many shooters were waiting outside, but with his mother all up in the mix Shiloh knew not to take any chances.

Man-Man and India were fussing over Mai and trying to calm her down. The rest of the clique joined them and they gave each other a bunch of warm, grateful hugs.

"Yo, Sly is out there waiting for us," Honore finally said. "Let's get the fuck outta here before them fools come back and get stupid."

"Yeah," Cucci Momma agreed as she took one of Mai's arms and Breezy took the other one. "Let's go my beautiful bitches. I'ma call this a job well done."

CHAPTER 22

Joel's yacht party was in full swing when Honore and Cucci arrived on the scene. Expensive champagne flowed freely and the techno music blared on extra-loud. It was an employee party for all the major jewelers in the tri-state area and tons of people had turned out. Joel's official reason for the shindig was to keep spirits high and to make camaraderie tighter for the company's hard workers. But Honore and Cucci knew the real deal.

"Nice to see you ladies finally made it," Joel said as he greeted the two cousins at the mini-bar. His eyes were wide and the bridge of his nose was extra pink, like he had just sniffed a line or ten. "You two look beautiful tonight. Please grab a few drinks because everything is all on the house."

"Thanks for the compliment, Joel," Honore said as she looked around at all the food, drinks, and finery. "Looks like you spent a pretty penny on this party. How could we even think about missing a chance to hang out and rub elbows with all ya rich white friends? I mean we all work hard to make this business thrive as much as possible, right? Some of us just go above and beyond to make sure that we stay on top of the game. Ain't that right, Joel?"

"You're damn right," Joel responded as he sipped out of a bottle of Chardonnay. He gave a few head nods to various partygoers and shook the hands of a few men who came over to thank him for hosting the event.

"You know, Honore," Joel said, "I'm calling this a company party, but this is really my way of throwing a celebration for you and Rayven. The two of you have proven yourselves to be very valuable assets to my team. Not only did you knock off Slimy Sam, you've somehow managed to get the Black Stone diamond and your friend Mai back safely too."

"Yeah, and with no thanks to you," Cucci said with an attitude as she smoothed out a wrinkle on her tight red hip-hugging dress. "When the pressure is on, me and Honore are the ones out there shoveling shit in the trenches! We do the dirty work and get shit corrected out here for you, Joel. Remember that. I wanna make sure you understand that fact and that it's respected at all times."

"And who is it that pays you so handsomely?" Joel snapped as he squinted through his coke-high eyes. "Who makes sure you're compensated for your good services? I'm the boss, and you'd better remember that! I'm the bank, bitches! I make the connections, I line up the work, and all you girls have to do is execute my commands. That's how a thriving and cohesive team works. It's not about individuals. Everybody has to use their talents to achieve the team's long-term goals."

"Yeah, you right, Joel," Honore said, giving him a fake smile. "Just like shit and piss, we're all together floating around in this big-ass toilet bowl. There's a lot of money out there to get and me and Cucci are damn sure not complaining about it. As long as we keep everything on the up-and-up and the lines of communication stay open between us, I'm good. For real, me and my cousin ain't about to slow down now. We're hooked on the cash so we just getting started."

"That's the type of spirit and hunger I need from you two," Joel said as he reached out and gave Honore a big hug. "I'm going to make you girls rich and powerful. Together we can take over the Empire State. I want to apologize for not stepping up and helping you get your friend Mai out of trouble when you asked me to. You have to understand that I must protect myself and my livelihood at all costs. I promise you it was nothing personal. I hope all is forgiven."

"Oh, no hard feelings at all, Joel," Cucci responded with a cheesy grin. "It's all good and everything worked out. No need to cry over spilled milk, right? Besides, hard times build strong minds. We not trippin' over that petty shit no more. We're tryna get rich just like you said, and boss up on the whole damn city of New York! There's always gonna be a few bumps in the road here and there, but as long as we can trust each other to stay focused we're good. I ain't the type to hold grudges anyway."

Cucci was skinning and grinning her ass off in Joel's face when a short blond woman in a gray Vera Wang split dress and high heels walked up and said, "Hello, Mr. Samuelson, I'm Laura. Don sent me over to meet you."

Laura was dripping sex appeal and was clearly an executive groupie.

"I'm sorry to interrupt you, sir, but this is my first time ever being on a yacht, and Don said you'd be happy to give me a personal tour of this huge vessel of yours if you aren't too busy."

"Yes, Laura, I was just finishing up here," Joel said as he eyeballed the blonde's huge fake breasts without even trying to play it off. Prying his eyes off her nipples, he then turned his attention back to Honore and Cucci for a quick second. "If you'll excuse me ladies, we can finish this conversation at a later time. Enough about business. Today I want you both to kick back, relax, and celebrate the moment at hand. I'll be back for an official toast once I finish escorting my new friend Laura around."

"Oh, no problem," Honore said with a smirk. "Take your

time. We'll be right here when you get back. Me and Cucci are just gonna grab a couple of bottles and turn up some drank while we wait."

Ignoring Honore and Cucci, Joel hooked his arm under Laura's and walked away. He was going to give her a tour all right: a tour of his sweaty nutsack while she gave him some quick head below the deck of his yacht. Joel turned around and caught one last look at Honore and Cucci as he made his way across the deck. They were staring at his back like a pair of hungry piranhas eyeballing a fresh piece of bloody meat.

Yeah, Joel thought to himself smugly. Those monkey-ass bitches were just too smart and devious for their own good. Later on down the line he was going to have to get rid of them both. But the smart one, Honore, was definitely going to go down first.

Sitting at the bar, Honore and Cucci watched Joel stroll off with his new bitch for the night.

"That was a nice little speech you gave him," Honore told Cucci as they eyeballed their boss, "but that mothafucka ain't getting off that easy."

"I know damn well he ain't," Cucci said with an evil glint in her eyes.

"Trust me," Honore said as she ordered a glass of Ciroc from the waitress. "That nigga is plotting and scheming. Just a-waiting for the right time to get us clipped. But I can promise you this, I'ma beat his ass to the finish line and take home his trophy. But he was right about one thing though. We got spirit and we're hungry as hell! We're gonna run the Empire State one day, Cucci. This whole shit is gonna be an empire state of *minez!* Just watch and see. By that time Joel Samuelson's ass won't even be in the equation. It's gonna be all about *us,* baby. All about you, me, and the Crushed Ice Clique! And I'm telling you right now cousin, the whole damn world better get outta our way and watch us *work!*"

DON'T MISS

Saundra's tale of revenge, Detroit-style, in
HER SWEETEST REVENGE 2

A master thief's ultimate payday delivers the deadliest
game of all in Kiki Swinson's
THE MARK

CHAPTER 1

*P*op. *Pop. Pop.*

"Agh!" I screamed as the hot bullet that left Luscious's gun pierced my left shoulder. Grabbing my shoulder, I instantly felt the hot blood start dripping down my sleeve. But the thud of Luscious's body hitting the ground had my attention. Then Luscious disappeared and on the ground in his spot Monica lay covered in blood. "MONICA, MONICA!!" I yelled over and over.

"Mya!" I heard someone yelling my name, but my body was frozen in one spot. Panic set in as I tried to force myself toward Monica. "Mya," I heard my name again. I felt myself blacking out.

"Mya." I finally opened my eyes and realized it was Hood shaking me, calling my name. "Babe, it's only a dream again. You at home and safe. So is Monica." I looked around the room as I realized I was home in my bed. "Shit, I hate these dreams." I sat up then slightly, pushed my Donna Karan stitched quilt off me, and climbed out of the bed. Realizing I had interrupted Hood's sleep again, I apologized. "And I'm really sorry for waking you up with this shit again." I went into our master bathroom to wipe all the perspiration off my forehead that had built up while I was panicking in my dreaming.

"It's a'ight, you know I got you. Besides I'm 'bout to get up anyway. Gotta handle business." As usual, I could always count on Hood to be supportive. No matter what. But I was sick of having these dreams. It had been well over a year since Luscious had tried to sneak up on me at Stylz by Design to take me out. He thought he had me too, but his plan had failed when Monica came out of nowhere and shot him in the back of the head, killing him instantly. I was lucky, because had it not been for my sister Monica, I would be dead. Luscious did end up shooting me in the shoulder, but I recovered so fast it was like a pat on the back. To be honest, the dreams were worse than getting shot.

The only regret I had about the whole incident was Monica getting caught up in the middle. I hated that she now had murder on her hands. Even worse, it was her daughter Imani's father that she had killed. It was only a coincidence that she had even showed up at the shop that morning. On her way to school she remembered she needed money. She later said that she had attempted to call my cell but got no answer so she came because she knew that was where I would be. As she pulled in, she happened to see Luscious, who she thought was dead, slip into my shop. Monica said she knew he was up to something and without a second thought she grabbed the .22 pistol that Hood had given her for protection out of the glove compartment of her all-white 2012 Dodge Charger. Just as she entered the back of the shop, she saw me running toward Luscious as he fired shots at me. So even though I regret her having to kill Imani's dad, I thank God that she did.

As I came out of the bathroom, Hood headed into our triple-sized walk-in closet. "Well, since I'm up, would you like me to make you some breakfast? A little eggs, bacon, maybe some hash browns," I offered. There was no way I was going back to sleep. I refused to close my eyes only to get a glimpse of Luscious. Hell no. I would stay woke.

I had told Rochelle I was coming in late today since I stayed over the night before, but what the heck, I might as well drag my ass in. I could get an early start on inventory since I didn't have any appointments scheduled. Even though I owned the shop, I still had a few special clients. And for my services they paid top dollar.

"Nah, babe, I'm good. I'ma meet up with my people early this morning so I'll just grab some on the way." Hood walked into the bathroom as I plopped back down on the bed and quietly contemplated my next move. I decided a latte would do me good so I made the kitchen a part of my mission for the morning. Not soon after Hood left the house I jumped in the shower. An hour later I had searched through my closet and fished out a pair of white Vince tennis shorts with a black Helmut Lang tank. I completed the outfit with Alexander Wang ankle-strap sandals. I had to admit my new style was classic. I had put the Brewster Projects dressing behind me. At least a little bit—I still would represent from time to time. With not as much as one glance in the mirror, I concluded I was ready to head out.

From *The Mark* by Kiki Swinson

CHAPTER 1

I MESSED WITH THE WRONG GUY

I can't believe I finally got the life I've always wanted. It seemed like it was yesterday when I left Virginia from a life of crime. Even though I was on the run, I met and married the man I love and finally have a baby. No one would've ever told me that I was going to leave Matt, the hustler I'd been with since forever, after all he and I had been through. But him screwing around on me with Yancy changed everything. Taking all the money that he, Yancy, and I stole was the best revenge plot I could've ever mustered up. It felt good to be the last woman standing. It also helped me that after I ran off with the money, Matt and Yancy both got arrested. But Matt wasn't away for long.

Now here I was in my hospital room, looking at a man I'd hoped to never see again. I'd just delivered my baby boy and everything was supposed to be right in my world. But here he is, turning my dreams for the future into a nightmare. After Matt told me he had a couple of people on the outside pay off a couple COs on the inside to help break him out of jail in exchange for some of the $3 million payout, I watched as he walked out of the hospital room with my baby in tow. My entire body cringed at the sight of him holding my infant baby. There was nothing I could do that would calm me down and quell the alarming fear that flitted through my stomach right then. "Matt," I sobbed, barely able to speak. "Please . . . don't do this."

"Do what? Take your son like you took my motherfucking money?" he chuckled wickedly. I crinkled my eyebrows in response. He stopped laughing abruptly and started talking in a very serious tone. "Bitch, I want back every fucking dime you took from me. And just know that if you don't come off it, you will be making funeral arrangements for this little motherfucker right here," he barked. His words sunk in on me and I felt hopeless. I didn't know what the fuck I was going to do, but I knew I had to come up with his money or else.

The thought of him mishandling or mistreating my baby made me sick to my stomach. Thankfully, he grabbed a few Pampers and bottles of formula to carry along with him. I cried silently, avoiding any unwanted attention. But I knew that if I stayed around here much longer, either the doctors or nurses would know something was wrong after they found out my baby was nowhere around.

Still somewhat medicated, I got up on shaky legs, but I couldn't let that deter me from getting out of there. I got dressed pretty fast and managed to walk out of the hospital without being detected by the staff who were assigned to treat me.

When I arrived downstairs on the main floor, my body felt hot all over. I felt like I could just faint. But I pressed on and got into the first taxi I saw. I gave him my home address, sat back in the seat, and tried to pull myself together. I couldn't help but wonder whether Matt really had Derek like he insinuated, so I called his cell phone and prayed that he'd answer it. My call was picked up on the second ring. "Hello," I rushed to say.

All I got was laughter on the other end. The laughter came

from Matt's voice. "Matt, where is Derek?" I asked. I was completely irritated by his insensitive behavior.

"I already told you where he was. Didn't you believe me?" he replied.

"I wanna speak to him now. I need to know if he's all right," I demanded.

"Hold on. Let me see if he's available." Matt continued his laughter.

The cell phone went silent for five long seconds. Then I heard my husband's voice. "Hello, Lauren, is this you?" Derek asked.

"Yes, baby, it's me. Are you all right?" I whined desperately. I needed answers and I needed them now.

"Yes, I'm fine."

"What about the baby? Is he all right? Has he been crying?"

"He's fine. He's drinking his bottle now," Derek replied, his voice sounding weary.

"Baby, don't worry. I'm gonna get you and our baby out of this okay," I tried to assure him.

"Now that's the spirit I like! Save your man and your baby!" Matt interjected. When I heard his voice, I knew that he had taken the phone from Derek.

"If you put your fucking hands on any one of them, I promise you'll fucking regret it!" I roared. I knew I couldn't actually speak of the money in front of the taxi driver nor the gun I was going to bring along with me when I finally met up with Matt to make the switch, so I said the next best thing. Matt knew what I meant.

"You only have twenty-four hours! So call me as soon as you pick up the money," he demanded, and then the call went dead.

Hearing Matt's usual warning play in my ears now made a huge lump in the back of my throat. Tears sprang up to my eyes, but I fought to keep them from falling. I couldn't let anyone know what was going on with me concerning Matt and my family. Letting someone know would be too risky. And I couldn't let anything happen to my family.

I swallowed hard and closed my eyes because I knew he wasn't going to let this go. I had to think quickly. This thing had gone from complicated to nightmarish. I was now responsible for two lives. Lives of two people I loved dearly.

I swear I blanked out after Matt disconnected our call. I had no idea I had arrived at my apartment building until the taxi driver announced it to me for the second time. "Ma'am, we are here at your destination," the taxi driver said.

I looked at the cabdriver and then I looked out the back-door window and realized that he was absolutely right. I was home, so I needed to pay him and continue on with my mission. I reached into my purse, grabbed thirty dollars, and paid him. Before he could give me my five dollars in change, I had already gotten out of the car and closed the door.

My family's life meant more to me than fucking five dollars. I walked into my apartment building as fast as I could, considering the amount of drugs I had in my system. The building doorman spoke to me upon opening the door. I spoke back without giving him eye contact. He knew I had been in the hospital to have the baby, so he made mention of it. "Ms. Kelly, where's the bundle of joy?" he asked cheerfully.

"He's still in the hospital with his dad," I yelled back without turning around. But the questions didn't stop there. He must've noticed the pain I was in when I walked by him because he asked me if I needed any help. "No, I'm good," I continued. I couldn't get on the elevator and away from that meddlesome doorman soon enough. As badly as I needed help to deal with getting my family back, I knew the doorman wouldn't be cut out for the job.

Thankfully, the elevator was empty when I got on it. When the elevator doors dinged open, the reality that Matt had resurfaced in my life had become a permanent fixture in my mind. I rushed through the elevator doors and sped down the long, carpeted hallway that led to my apartment. The hallway was pin-drop quiet as usual. In a ritzy building like that it was the norm. Although it was quiet and empty, I was looking around like a burglar about to rob someone's house; that is how nervous I felt. I don't know if I was nervous about going in my apartment or nervous about someone being there after I opened up the door.

My heart jerked in my chest as I reached down to unlock my door. Before I pushed the door open, I looked around again, paranoid that someone was watching me. But why? That damn hallway was empty as hell. So I pushed the door open and walked inside. Immediately after I closed the door and locked it, my mind was racing at an unbelievable speed. Trying to hatch a plan to get the money and get my baby and my man back was becoming a little more than I could bear. Deep down in my heart I knew I couldn't fuck this up. The depth of hatred that Matt had for me was indescribable. Not only had I robbed him of the heist he and I crafted together, I'd also left him and started another family. At this very moment, I needed to focus solely on giving Matt what he wanted. And if I didn't deliver the goods to him within twenty-four hours, I knew my family would die.

"Come on, Lauren, you can do this, baby girl," I started telling myself. I needed as much pep talk as I could get. "Get yourself together and go down to this bank and get that money so you can get your man and your baby back. They're all you have in this world. Fuck that money! Let that sorry-ass nigga have it. He needs it more than you."

I looked over at the clock on the DVR and noticed that I didn't have a lot of time before the bank closed. With my bank being ten blocks away from my apartment, I knew I had to hurry up, change clothes, and hop in the first taxi I saw. My family's lives depended on me.

On my way to my bedroom I had to walk past my baby's nursery. Derek and I designed this room ourselves. It was

Derek's idea to paint the room blue, white, and yellow. But I picked out the thin-blue-striped wallpaper. His room was simply gorgeous. So when I entered it, my heart dropped at the sight of his empty, white, laced bassinette. Seconds later, tears formed and started falling from my eyes. Next thing I knew, I had broken down and started crying. All of the emotions I was feeling from the kidnapping consumed me. My baby wasn't supposed to be with Matt. He was supposed to be here with Derek and me. "God, please help me get my baby back!" I cried out after I fell down to my knees. "Lord, please don't let anything happen to my baby. He needs me, God! So please let me get him back safely. And I promise I will surrender my life totally to you, Lord!" I ended my prayer.

I think I wallowed in my sorrows for another ten minutes before I snapped out of it. Remembering I now had less than fifty minutes to dress and get the money got me back on my feet and focused. I wanted to take a shower but I couldn't. I didn't have enough time. Nor did I have the energy, so I took off everything I had on and slipped on a pair of dark brown cargo pants with pockets along the leg. Then I slipped on an old brown flannel shirt, two pairs of socks, a pair of tan Timberland boots, and a camouflage-designed cargo jacket. I looked like I was ready for war, but my body felt otherwise.

I looked back at the clock on the DVR and saw that another ten minutes had gone by. Panic-stricken, I grabbed an old backpack Derek owned that was on the floor of the hall closet. And then I grabbed his gun from the lockbox that was hidden in the back of the closet but on the top shelf. I wasn't going anywhere without it.

After I placed the pistol inside the backpack, I grabbed my house keys and two forms of ID from my purse and shoved all three items down inside the right front pocket of my pants. I was ready to get back what belonged to me and I was willing to risk my life to do it.